Sargon came to an abrupt halt, staring, as a gray-haired old woman with a basket came wandering down the lower hall, in spite of security, in spite of guards, in spite of every precaution against invasion.

A man felt the fool reaching for a sword against an old lady—even one who advanced, tapping her stick, as if she were both blind and slightly daft.

"Who are you?" Sargon demanded. The hair stood up on his nape. Not a reaction to the rasp of a drawn sword. Deaf, daft, and blind, then—or one of Hell's more sinister entities, which feared no bronze blade and no iron either. The soft scuff of the granny's sandals, the tap of the stick in the terrazzo hall, maintained a sinister rhythm as if she meant to walk right through him—indeed, as if she might *do* that; and while the Lion of Akkad had no wish to run, he had no wish to be touched by some Power, either, so he flinched aside and pressed his shoulders against the marble of the corner. She had the smell of mildew and dry rot.

"Stop there!" he yelled, and finding the anomaly of the basket the out of place thing, the perhaps significant thing in this apparition—"What do you have in that basket?"

The granny turned, slowly—she was veiled in cloth that might have begun as gray; or maybe it was black. The movements of her head were slow and deliberate as a snake's; and the small, jerky movements of her yellow-nailed hand as it peeled back gray gauze or cobweb, unveiling the contents of the basket, sent a chill down Sargon's back that very little in Hell had ever put there.

"Bookssss," she h

PROPHETS IN HELL

Created by
JANET MORRIS
with
David Drake • Robert Sheckley
George Alec Effinger • C.J. Cherryh and more!

BAEN

CONTENTS

Eye of a Needle, Chris Morris   1

Exile, David Drake   19

The Garden of Blood Narcissus, Brad Miner   50

Death Freaks, Robert Sheckley   95

Profits in Hell, Bill Kerby   148

Terminal, George Alec Effinger   160

I, Hermes Trismegistus, Richard Groller   191

Fast Food, Nancy Asire   193

The Sibylline Affair, C.J. Cherryh   221

Moving Day, Janet Morris   251

EYE OF A NEEDLE
Chris Morris

The bent and canted street sign said Temptation Alley in rusted white letters on a red background.

Hughes consulted the note he'd scribbled in his address book when the angel had told him where to go. Number 7 Temptation Alley. This was it, all right.

He brushed back shoulder-length hair with a long and twisted fingernail. The angel wouldn't have steered him wrong. The angel couldn't lie, everybody in Hell knew that.

Hughes' sandals scraped on ancient cobbles as he left the thoroughfare for the alley. The first number he saw was 87, Tzu's Opium Emporium; opposite it was 86, Zia's Chiropractic and X-rays While U Wait, Sa'ib.

A long way to go, down that twisted alley of cobble and low-hanging mist and overhanging buildings, semi-detached and settling audibly as Hughes moved among them. Number 7 had to be at the far and dead end of the alleyway.

Hughes didn't like dead ends. He looked furtively over his shoulder every time a building groaned or a shingle flapped. Hell was a dead end, wasn't it—New Hell and every place else he'd been among the reaches of the damned?

Still, meeting with the angel had brought him a ray of hope. That was what he'd paid for—hope. And paid dearly: used up the entire proceeds of the retrofit of the Devil's personal suite in the Tower of Injustice, paid it to mercenaries and spies and lawyers, just to be able to sit with the angel for a few minutes.

Some said the angel was a supporter of the Dissidents. Hughes didn't give a fig about that. The angel had been everything Hughes had dreamed an angel should be: he'd been tall and blond and blessed with remarkably aerodynamic and pristinely white feathered wings. He'd had the white robe to match, the golden aura around his person, the beatific smile and the smell of springtime about him.

In the dockside slum bar where Hughes' lawyer had brought him for the meeting, the smell of cleanliness (like freshly ironed linen) was like the smell of godliness. It banished the body odor of garlic and onion-eating mercenaries and the stench of centuries of spilled beer as if they'd never existed—for a full three feet around the Angel from On High, the air was as clean as air could be.

In that den of iniquity, no more proof of the angel's identity had been necessary. The angel was introduced to him by Hughes' lawyer, whose slimy tail had left a trail that not even one of the Oasis' mercenaries would cross, and the lawyer waddled away, belching.

Hughes had been unsure as to the etiquette. Could a damned soul such as himself shake hands with God's representative in New Hell? His fingernails were a little long for it, a protection of sorts against the germ-ridden populace.

Nonetheless, he stuck out his hand and said, "Lord Altos, I'm Howard Hu—"

"I know who you are," said the angel in a voice that could have made him president of the United States in

Hughes' day. "Why did you employ a lawyer to find me when all you needed to do was look deep in your heart and uncover a glimmer of repentance, and I would have found you?"

Hughes felt his neck grow hot. So they didn't like lawyers in this part of Hell. The stink of them, the drooling jaws, the tyrannosaurus-rex tails . . . The reaction of the patrons had been understandable; the reaction of the angel . . . wasn't.

The angel called Altos was God's emissary, wasn't he? The promise of forgiveness, the hope of salvation. And then it struck Hughes that God had many faces, and that some faces were sterner than others.

All of this passed through Hughes' mind in an eyeblink, while the angel's question remained unanswered. Eyes so blue that they caused Hughes physical distress awaited a response.

And all Hughes could think of to say was, "Why do they use lawyers instead of rats in Hell's laboratory experiments?"

"I'm sure I don't know," said the angel, knitting his perfect brows.

"Because there're some things even rats won't do," said Hughes heartily, and laughed to show the angel that he'd made a joke.

The angel looked confused, and then distressed. Hughes stopped laughing. No one else in the bar was laughing—or even talking. Everyone was watching them.

The Beirut marines were watching them; so were their compatriots, the boys who'd died at Desert One in helicopters that choked on sand and burned like kindling. American boys. Boys who'd never grow old and never forget. Boys who'd trained on Hughes equipment and depended on Hughes technology and gotten here in part because of it.

The Oasis was a dockworkers' nightspot, a nightmare place of revetted machine guns and sawdust red with the blood it had soaked up. In a silence that told Hughes that those boys knew who he was, and they

weren't happy about it, he could hear his own breathing and the beat of his heart.

He could hear the blood coursing his veins. He'd
read somewhere that the sound of your blood rushing
through you could drive you mad. But that was when
you were alive. He didn't understand the afterlife. But
then, he hadn't understood life. Life had continually
disappointed him.

The afterlife was worse. The Beirut marines knew
who he was. The Desert One Delta commandos knew
who he was. He'd never have gotten out of there alive—if
he'd been alive.

But he was dead. They were all dead. All except the
angel, Altos of the white robes and sea-blue eyes, who
looked at him pityingly and didn't understand jokes,
especially jokes about lawyers.

"What is it you want of me?" asked the angel when
the silence became so unbearable that Hughes was
beginning to sweat.

The eyes of the Desert One boys were burning holes
in his back. He almost said, "I want to get out of here
in one piece," but it could be that the money he'd paid
his lawyer had actually secured him an answered prayer,
a grant of three wishes, or more. He couldn't chance
wasting his advantage.

He leaned forward and as he did, some raucous men
came reeling through the outer door, arguing about
giving up their weapons to the bouncer.

In the sudden commotion, which took the eyes of the
Desert One boys from his back, Hughes leaned forward
and whispered, "I want a second chance. I want a
hearing with God. I want to be forgiven for my sins. I
want out of here . . . before the prophesied End of All
Things comes to pass. And I want your help. I'll give
you anything you desire—wealth, power, whatever. I
have it all, here. I can help your damned souls. I've got
contacts with Authority, in the Pentagram, in the Dev-

il's own Tower of Injustice. I'm an insider, you must realize. I can—"

"*Stop!*" The angel's volume brought everyone in the bar up short.

Or was it more than that?

Hughes turned in his chair. The bouncer was frozen in mid-ouster, two collars in his meaty fists. The barkeep was as still as a statue, interrupted as he slid two drafts down the bar. The slosh of the foam heads of those beers was stilled also, so that foam hung in midair.

The Beirut marines were half out of their seats, on the way to help the bouncer disarm the remaining Hussars. Behind the weapons cage, the guncheck girl was half-way through rotating the cocking lever on her Ingram. Ganga swirls were eddies of blue that might never make their way to the spider-webbed ceiling. In a far corner, Zulu warriors with zebra-hide shields were caught as if in a photograph, heads together, pointing black fingers at a uniformed British officer who sat with some Assyrians in full trappings, pouring over a lambskin map.

Nothing in the bar moved but the angel and Howard Hughes. No one else even so much as breathed.

In that discrete moment of frozen time, the angel leaned forward and said through unsmiling lips, "Do you presume to bribe an emissary from Heaven? Have you never heard the one about the rich man and the eye of the needle?"

Finally, Hughes believed that the angel really and truly was . . . an angel. He said, "Look here, I didn't mean any harm. You've got to realize that, when I was coming up in the world, you did things a certain way."

"This is not the world. I *have* to realize nothing, where you are concerned. But I do realize why you are here. If you are repentant, then how am I to know it?"

"I just told you I was sorry. I want to redeem myself. I want to go to heaven, where everything is beautiful and clean, where there are no germs and no evil little people scheming to destroy me and no projects in cost overrun . . ."

"And how do you propose to do that?" asked the angel.

"They call you Just Al, I'm told." Hughes looked around, behind him. The patrons were still unmoving, still suspended in time. "You champion the Dissident cause. The rebels. I can help the rebels. I'll do anything you want, just help me to find a way to get out of here, to find the Pearly Gates—"

"To find the Pearly Gates?" echoed the angel. "That's what you want?"

"It is," said Hughes, sensing the incipient possibility of a deal to be made.

"You must do what you want, Howard Hughes. Not what I want. God will judge you on your merits, when the time comes. The rebels are those who believe that Hell is what they make it, and want to make it better. You do not need the rebels to find the Pearly Gates."

Hughes was excited now. "What do I need, then?"

"An address. Courage. The proper frame of reference."

"Give me the address and I'll give you anything you ask."

The angel sighed a deep and somehow despondent sigh. "God is not so easily fooled," he said. "I shall give you the address. You will do with it as you will."

"This is a dream come true," said Hughes, getting out his checkbook and pulling forth a blank check drawn on the Hells Forego Bank and Distrust.

"But it is your dream, Mister Hughes—remember that."

"Take the check," Hughes said, forcing it into the angel's white and handsome hand. "Tell me what I have to do to get to the Pearly Gates."

"Believe. Make your heart pure. Let go this worship of Mammon. Repent. And speak the truth."

"Sure thing," Hughes promised. "But more specifically, what?"

"Go to this address. Do what will then become obvious to one of your sensibilities," said the angel, with a wave of the hand into which Hughes had just pressed his own blank check.

The bar exploded into violence. The bouncer wrestled with his two Hussars. The Zulus arose and began bearing down on the British officer. The Beirut marines near the door called for order and the sound of their weapons clearing leather hissed through the place like the warnings of a family of cobras disturbed in its cave.

"I must be going," Hughes said, and the angel didn't argue. A short man was calling to the angel from a back room full of smoke and shadow.

Altos rose in a rustle of wings and said, "God be with you, Hughes." Then he floated away, leaving a small square of parchment behind on the tabletop.

The tabletop was wet and the writing on the parchment was beginning to blur. Hughes had snatched it up and scribbled the address in his book even as it faded, blurring away like a bad dream as he made his way toward the door.

He looked back only once, hoping to see the levitating angel. But all he saw was the brawl that had broken out among the Assyrians, the Zulus, the Hussars and the American marines who protected the bar.

And the eyes of the Desert One commandos, all of whom watched him from their seats, only their heads moving to track his progress, grim and cold and full of promise.

He had to get out of Hell, now. Now that the Delta rangers had found him. The boys of Blue Lightning had a score to settle with him that made Satan's ire pale by comparison.

He had to get out of Hell. That's why he was here, on this cobbled street in a backwater byway, hoping to find a curio shop, Number Seven Temptation Alley.

There were dogs on the street here. He couldn't fathom where they'd come from. Big dogs with glowing red eyes. Little dogs with three legs. Dogs with wolf in them, whose jaws dripped green slather. Mangy dogs and poke-ribbed dogs and copulating dogs and fighting dogs who chased each other in circles, biting and spewing blood as they savaged each other.

Then he saw the sign above the doorway opposite: Hounds of the Baskervilles Kennel and Boarding—Hellhounds a Specialty. And below the sign was the number: 9.

Almost there, then. He hadn't been paying attention to where he'd been walking.

He looked back the way he'd come and paused, startled. When he'd begun his stroll down the alley, it had seemed short, dark, full of mist below one of Hell's inconclusive skies that proved neither day nor night, but only loomed with gloom, low over one's head.

From this vantage, the alley stretched back for what seemed like miles, bright as a carnival, cheap as the Vegas Strip. Casino marquees abounded. Strippers were limned in pink neon, a hundred feet high above the street. Giant flamingos seemed to flap their light-bulb wings and movie theatres promised sneak previews of *From Here To Infernity* and *As You Don't Like It*.

Hotels offered 'Hell Nights': fiend-sized beds, doomymoon suites, divorce chapels, free condoms.

Hughes blinked and rubbed his eyes. When he took his fists away, all the neon and chasing lightbulbs were gone. Temptation Alley was dark as a grave once more. Even the dogs were gone.

And right before him, where he hadn't seen it because of all the light, was Number 7—down a half flight, a basement store front.

There was a sign in its flyspecked window, hand-lettered, that said, "Today's special: Lost Souls Two for a Quarter/ Broken Dreams Repaired to Order." And, below that, an older placard, whose glitter had fallen away to reveal white lumps of glue beneath, promised: "Fortune Telling & Palm Reading by Circe."

Hughes was overwhelmed by a sense of foreboding. He told himself that the angel, Hell's only volunteer angel, who'd come straight from God, couldn't have steered him to an evil fate. The angel wasn't capable of that.

Or was he?

Hell was a place for evil; Hughes was here because of the evil he'd done, through action and inaction. Evil by the lowest bidder. Evil for the best of reasons. The evil that men do is the evil that makes them men. Who'd said that?

He wasn't sure. He wasn't sure of anything, looking down those crumbling concrete steps, past the wrought iron gate that was rusting and intermittently festooned with gargoyle faces. The below-street level shop looked more like a cave or a tomb or a crypt, with its gargantuan stone blocks all blackened with soot or worse.

He wasn't superstitious. He was cautious. He wasn't cowardly. He was conservative. He'd owned the world, as far as a man could own anything. He'd done it all. But he'd never lost the fear. The fear had grown. There'd been the Spruce Goose. There'd been . . . the germs. The disappointments. The traitors. The fools.

Who knew better than he the folly of mankind? Who knew better than he that God and the Devil were one, that the Almighty had set man an impossible task when he'd sent the Ten Commandments down from the Mount?

Waking in Hell, Hughes had realized that what Moses had brought to mankind weren't the Ten Suggestions, but by then it had been too late. And afterlife, even in Hell, was better than no afterlife.

Now there were these awful rumors that even afterlife wasn't eternal; that Hell in all its profound misery could not last; that time itself was drawing to a close.

One thing Hughes had always known was when to cut his losses. When to get out. Thus, here he was. But

suddenly he didn't want the answers to any of the
questions he'd thought he needed answered.

And down those stairs was a fortuneteller recommended by Altos Himself. A conduit to God's ear. A
mystic who held the key to his salvation, or so the angel
had promised. Or almost promised. Sort of promised.
Not exactly said.

But intimated, certainly. Hughes looked back once
more at the desolate street called Temptation Alley,
and up at the sky ruder than his most unsettling dreams.
In that sky was Paradise, visible sometimes, though not
today. In that sky was day, sometimes, but not today.
In that sky was night, sometimes, but not today. Today
Hell's very vault was noncommittal, cold and unwelcoming,
niggardly of even a hint of the rate of time's passage.

Nostradamus was on the streets of New Hell, spewing vilifications of everyone and verifications of his prophesies. The Antichrist had come in nineteen hundred and
seventy three, anno Domeni, and he was Gadaffi, wasn't
he?

For that and other prophesies come true, Hughes
would have had to take Nostradamus' word. And Hughes
took no man's word. But the prophets and the doom-criers
were too loud and too many not to give a man uneasy
nights.

Thus the search for the angel, and all that had come
to pass. You couldn't ask around in Admin, since Hell's
bureaucracy was undergoing the paralytic aftereffects of
a complex-wide purge. Thus Hughes' determination to
get out of Hell while he still could, no matter what it
cost.

You could buy your way out of anything, that was one
thing that both life and afterlife had taught him. He
checked his wallet and, throwing his shoulders back
sharply, descended the stairs until the wrought-iron
gate barred further progress.

There he looked for a knocker; he found a doorbell
set into a nipple of rusting iron. He pressed it. Nothing

seemed to happen. He looked about and saw, on the back wall where the low doorway canted up, a plaque that verified the owner: Circe.

She was somebody from mythology, he vaguely remembered. Well, stranger things in Hell than on earth, he'd known that since the day he'd hired his first law firm here, because the Devil's tower windows were falling out.

Waiting for the door to open beyond the iron gate, or a buzzer to sound so that he could push the gate inward, or someone to come or instructions to be shouted through the barred window beside the brass plate, he felt the weight of all his years settle on him. All his lonely, frightened years. All his disappointments and all his defeats. Sometimes it seemed to him, both in life and in well-deserved damnation, that winning was only what was required in order not to fail.

He was never happy, only relieved when things went right because they hadn't gone wrong. He couldn't enjoy success, because it was a requisite defense against failure, nothing more. He'd become so lost in protecting himself, he'd never felt safe.

So waking on the Undertaker's table in the Mortuary had been no surprise, just one more bad dream come true.

The sign had said, up there in Circe's window, Broken Dreams Repaired to Order. If that could be done, everyone in Hell would be lined up to consult this sibyl. Hughes would have been waiting in a Soviet-style queue that would have taken a millenia to bring him to this door.

So there was something less than truth in the lady's advertising. Expect nothing, he cautioned himself. Remember, this is Hell, he reminded himself. And Temptation Alley to boot, he thought just before the buzzer buzzed and the barred gate gave inward to his anxious shove.

It clanged shut behind him with such finality that he

turned back and tried it: it was locked tight. He was trapped in a four foot space, between the gate and the inner door.

He tried the inner door and it was locked too. Dizziness rose in him. He hated the feeling of being trapped. He went back to the barred gate and shook it, peering up at the spikes on its top. He couldn't climb over it. He shouldn't have taken the angel at face value. Everything in Hell was a trick, a trap. It was probably not Altos at all, but Tartarouches or one of Hell's vengeful fallen angels who'd set a trap for him. . . .

When he got out of here—if he got out of here—his lawyers were going to hear from him. . . .

"State your business," said a sibilant voice through a speaker grille set beside the inner door.

"I . . . I'm Hughes. I was referred to you by one calling himself Altos. I want to secure your services."

Click. And a staticy sound. "What services?" said the voice.

"I . . . was told you could help me find the Pearly Gates."

A laugh that chilled him, metallic and full of spume, filled the little space in which he was trapped.

"And broken dreams," he rushed on, afraid he'd said the wrong thing. "I've got plenty. And money. I can pay anything you ask—"

"Anything?" said the voice, and even through the metallic-sounding speaker, it was a changed voice. "Then enter and we shall see what we shall see."

Click. Clack. Creak.

The door swung open. By itself.

The interior he glimpsed through the partly open door was not inviting. It was dark and it smelled musty, like a woman past her prime.

But there was no going back. He knew it with the instinct that had guided him through the worst of times.

So he went forward. Hughes was no coward, had

never been. Only cautious. And a pragmatist. And a lover of life doomed to lose it.

Now he was afraid he'd lose his afterlife, this shadowlife he'd made in a place where nothing was but memory and nothing worked but badly and nothing meant anything but trouble.

Who could blame him for wanting to find his way to heaven?

The angel had been appalled by his demeanor, he knew. So he wasn't a saint. Saints murdered and burned and pillaged and warred and left legacies of prejudice and intolerance in the name of God—and went to heaven.

Perhaps, Hughes thought as he stepped across Circe's portal, ducking his head under the stone arch of her doorway, he simply hadn't been *bad* enough in life. Perhaps Hell was for the uncommitted, the dull and the uninspired.

There hadn't been a real saint in the whole of the twentieth century, just political appointees, he told himself. Hell was a political place, as he'd always known. Therefore, the angel was just busting his butt, with all that talk of rich men and needles.

He knew how politics went: they went the way of the shekel. Everybody who'd ever lived had learned that.

So into his pocket he reached, and as he made his way toward the light at the end of a long hallway of dressed stone, he got his money ready.

That was the way of the world, even the underworld: Speak Clearly and Have Your Money Ready.

He began ordering his thoughts. He began to rehearse his presentation. He began to look forward to meeting this woman Circe and dazzling her with his power and his moolah, with his generosity. He could get her into the movies; he was backing a Hellywood production right now. He'd give her whatever she wanted.

He'd give her . . . everything. He wouldn't need all that he'd accrued in Hell, not where he was going.

He'd step right up to Saint Peter and he'd say—

At the end of the hallway, there was a curtain. He swept it aside, anxious and bold, his step vigorous.

And he stopped, shocked.

The woman revealed lay on a couch surrounded by hogs, or maybe they were boars. They were big and they were mean. They looked up at him and lowered their heads. Their tusks gleamed. They snorted and they squealed. One, the closest, pawed the floor with a cloven hoof. Sparks flew.

"Oh, boys," she said from her couch and waved a round white arm. The boars (or pigs or whatever they were) sat on their haunches.

Every one of them sat. Exactly where it was. Sat like school boys or soldiers.

The woman said, "Come closer, Hughes. Let me see you."

He approached, threading his way among the boars with their hairy backs, and low tables bearing crystals and huge silver punch bowls at a level that a boar or a pig could drink from them, resting on Down Jones monitors running constant tallies across their screens.

She was beautiful, but he'd expected nothing less. She was . . . arousing. That, he hadn't expected. She had on less clothing than he, but more than a stripper—a veil upon a veil upon a veil that came down to her neat ankles but veiled nothing.

Her couch was of fine sueded pigskin, and Hughes remembered that pigskin and human skin had the same approximate number of hair follicles, so maybe it wasn't pigskin after all.

Her face seemed to dance before him as she spoke, as if it had left her body and come up to within inches of his.

The disembodied face said through luscious, moist lips: "The Pearly Gates, is it? Broken dreams, have you? Speak up, soul, and say what you will pay."

"Everything," he blurted. "I'll give you everything."

"And just what does 'everything' comprise?" the disembodied face of Circe wanted to know.

"My holdings in Hell. My political base. My companies. My bank accounts. My stocks. My bonds. My homes. My aircraft. My art collection. My—"

"Your soul, perhaps? Would you give your soul?"

"My soul? How can I give that, if what I want is to reach the Pearly Gates?"

"You don't need your soul for that, silly boy. You'll lose it anyway, when Judgment comes—which it will, soon. SOooo soon. Too soon for a wheeler-dealer like you."

"I won't give my soul. It's what I want to save."

The face of Circe dwindled. It returned to her neck and head. She sat up on her couch and Hughes' fingernails broke as he clenched his fists at her beauty.

No woman in Hell had stirred his manhood in eternity. No woman in Hell had been able to arouse so much as a thought of lust in him. No woman in Hell— but Circe, he was increasingly sure, was no woman.

"Broken dreams of success, of happiness, of . . . love . . ." He didn't even hear himself say it. The words slipped out.

They slipped out the way he slipped into her arms, as if he were in a dream.

Which he was: a remade dream; a dream repaired to the order of his subconscious mind.

In his dream, he was a hero. In his dream, Circe was a virgin. In his dream, all the pigs and boars were heroes too. In his dream, the cave was on an island and the island was paradisical.

In his dream, he lay with the woman who was a witch who was a sibyl who was his mistress. For a year he lay with her and it was good with them.

At the end of the year, after he and his heroic friends had parted company, she woke one morning and said to him: "Give me all that you have, my love."

"I have given you everything," he said.

"Give me your heart," she said to him.

"It is yours," he told her.

"Give me your soul," she said to him.

"It is yours," he told her.

"Give me your life," she said to him.

"It is yours," he told her.

And at that moment, she disappeared. Her cave disappeared. The island disappeared. The world disappeared.

And in its place was a great golden gate, pearlescent and taller than the sky. It went up forever and down forever and it was gleaming, forever.

There was no end to it and no beginning to it. It stretched far and it stretched wide, and through its bars he could see Paradise.

He knew it was Paradise. Everyone was laughing and everyone was playing and everyone was beautiful and healthy and strong.

Trees flowered and the hillsides bloomed with heather; there was a blue sky with fluffy clouds and there were white marble temples on every hilltop. The air was as clean as the breath of God and fruit fell into the waiting mouths of children riding tigers who purred and women wove silken robes from the grasses that grew by bubbling brooks.

He put his hands upon the bars of the gate and suddenly the golden, pearly shine diminished all about him. The sky above receded. The clouds grew dark. The forever below him became finite and a man in a painfully bright robe walked up to him from the gate's far side.

With the bars between them, the man frowned. He held a clay tablet in the crook of his left arm and a stylus in his right hand.

"Yes?" said the man, who peered first at him, then up at the darkening sky, then back at him.

"Yes, I'm Howard Hughes, and if these are the Pearly Gates, you must be Saint—"

"It doesn't matter to you who I am, sinner." The man

with the stylus pointed to the sky. "Look at the mess you're making. What do you think you're doing here?"

"I've come to be admitted. I gave up everything to get here."

"It says here," said the man, pointing to his tablet with the stylus, "that you tried to buy your way into heaven. That you sold your soul as a last resort, to a witch named Circe, for a trip to the Pearly Gates. Well, here you are. Here are the Gates. 'To' isn't 'through.' Take a good look and get out of here. You're ruining the weather."

"But there must be some mistake! The angel Altos—surely you've heard of him—sent me to the shop where I met Circe. He told me—"

"He told you you're a camel, and the eye of the needle's too small for men who got to Hell doing graft and corruption. Get out of here, rich boy. Go back where you belong."

"But I'm not rich," Hughes shouted to the man with the stylus and the tablet, who was now retreating, now turning his back. "I gave up everything. I gave all my money to Circe—"

"Even your soul," called the man with the stylus from over his shoulder. "You probably had a shot at it, or the angel wouldn't have sent you to the witch. But then, you still had a soul. Now you don't. And without a soul, you're nothing to us. Go back to Hell where you belong."

Hughes flung himself against the gates, and they dissolved, or the ground he was standing on did.

He kept holding on to the gatepost he'd grabbed, which was like a firehouse pole now, a firehouse pole down which he was sliding, forever, into infernity, far below.

When he got back to New Hell, he was going to hire a battery of lawyers and sue that bitch Circe for breach of contract—get back everything he'd lost, he told himself.

Everything he could. He knew he could never forget that single sight of Paradise, with its vast expanse of beauty and its bright, white light—or what it had cost him to glimpse the unattainable.

It had cost him his soul, which he hadn't really thought he could lose, or even thought he'd had. But if he could lose his soul—if souls could be sold—then souls could be bought.

He wasn't Howard Hughes for nothing. He'd rebuild his fortune, recoup his losses, and find himself a new soul. Whatever it cost, he'd find one. He'd get himself a soul that was the best around, one that would assure him admission into Paradise. He'd get a better soul than the one he'd sold to Circe—he'd get the best.

One thing he'd learned in life, and now in afterlife, was that money could get you whatever you wanted.

He knew he could find himself a new soul. That wasn't what was worrying him. He was even reasonably sure he could find the angel again—that was what connections were for. Arranging the demonstration wasn't going to be difficult.

It was finding the miniature camel and the giant needle that was going to be the hard part.

EXILE

David Drake

I tell the tale that I was told:
Mithridates, he died old.

—HOUSMAN

But he had died; and his status here in Hell—

"You fool!" Mithridates cried to the soldier, an Egyptian with a Garand rifle and a cheetah-skin helmet. "Do you know who you're pushing?"

The soldier answered with a vertical butt-stroke.

It was a clumsy blow, because the rifle was almost as long as the soldier using it was tall. Still, the Egyptian had thick wrists, broad shoulders, and a real enthusiasm for his task. The steel butt-cap raked up Mithridates' ribs and struck the left side of his face like a bomb going off.

Mithridates—King of Pontus; Conqueror of Asia; Liberator of Greece; Deputy Ruler of Hell itself—bounced back into the tailgate of the truck toward which he'd been herded. He could see—from his right eye—and his body could certainly still feel pain, but he was

19

barely aware of soldiers' hands gripping him and tossing him into the back of the crowded vehicle as if he were one more sack of rice.

Bodies shifted beneath him. Voices cursed without enthusiasm, the voices of men who knew that having a body flung on top of them was the least of the torments they could expect in the near future.

They were the losers, men the Romans had rounded up from the palace on suspicion of involvement in the failed coup. . . .

Involvement in Mithridates' coup, which had failed.

The interior of the truck stank. The canvas covering was moldy; gasoline had spilled or was leaking back from the tanks in the cab; and the human cargo sweated fear. The tailgate slammed. Chains rattled as the safety hooks were forced into place.

Didn't want prisoners to fall out if the tailgate bounced open, after all.

"Sit the Hell up!" somebody growled as he shoved at Mithridates with a cleated boot. Most of the prisoners were as apathetic as fish in a net, wide-eyed and gasping and hopeless.

"Here, steady," said a calmer voice, female, and a hand began to dab a wet cloth against his injured cheek. The truck lurched forward, throwing Mithridates against the tailgate again—but from the inside.

He must have closed his good eye when he hit the floor of the truck, on his back. He opened it now and stared at the ruins of his hopes.

They were pulling out, last of the line of trucks laden with prisoners. An armored car followed them. It ran on three large, cleated tires and a fourth tire meant for a much smaller vehicle—but it ran, and the bronze-helmeted Roman glaring from the turret was obviously spoiling for an excuse to use his twin machine guns on a would-be escapee.

The guns might jam; this was Hell, after all.

But there was no real escape from Hell either.

Men, most of them soldiers of one sort or another,

milled on the lawn of Augustus' palace. The building beyond looked immaculate, despite the black smoke trailing from several of the upstairs windows to merge with Hell's universally-sullen sky.

Someone ran out the front door of the palace, between the pillars which looked imposing unless you were close enough to see that the contractor had made them of stuccoed wood—and hadn't used a good grade of stucco. The man shouted at the departing convoy, but the truck rumbled too loudly for Mithridates to even guess at his words. He was a Roman soldier, a centurion from the fact that his helmet had a transverse crest and he wore his sword-sheath on his right side—

But he was waving the blade in the air, and Mithridates was sure that he recognized the man's face. It was the man who'd run beside him at the battle of Cabira, Mithridates' last chance of defeating the Romans and saving his kingdom from the systematic looting that would otherwise last as long as Rome ruled Pontus.

One of his bodyguards, armed in Roman fashion, he'd thought as he spurred his horse toward the routed enemy. But he'd looked down as the centurion looked up at him—

And plunged his sword a hand's breadth deep in the royal thigh.

The real guards had finished the fellow instantly, but it was too late by then. He'd felt red-shot darkness squeeze the consciousness out of his skull, barely aware that he was slipping from his horse—and that the battle was slipping away when his men saw their leader fall.

Serpent magic had cured the wound in a matter of days, but flight and exile were all that remained in life for the monarch who'd frightened the Romans as no one before in their history.

Mithridates screamed over the muttered curses of his fellow exiles as the truck jounced them toward whatever doom Hell and the Romans had in store.

"Careful," said the female voice; but the truck lurched sideways into a hole that threw it like an axle breaking.

Mithridates' head bounced into one of the stanchions

over which the canvas cover was stretched. Red light and darkness closed over his mind.

But through it glared the face of the centurion who'd failed—again—to finish off the enemy he'd died to stop.

* * *

Mithridates was dreaming of thunder as the sea crashed onto the coast during a winter storm. He opened his eyes, expecting to smell salt. He smelled sulphur instead.

Of course.

The convoy was driving down a gorge so narrow that the truck beds ticked the rocks, adding a sharper note to the echoing rumble of wheels and exhausts. There were streaks of dull red light on the walls, more like blotches of fungus than the irruptions of lava they probably were.

There was no other illumination. If the armored car still followed the convoy, it was blacked-out or hidden by the frequent angles of the zig-zag descent.

Nothing about the present surroundings encouraged thoughts of escape, even if escape in Hell were possible.

Mithridates leaned over the tailgate and looked up, ignoring the warning of the woman who seemed to have attached herself to him. He could see out of both eyes, though clotted blood cracked in tendrils of fire along the nerves of his left cheek when he moved.

There was nothing to see, no matter how high he looked, except more patches of gummy rock breaking sullenly through the walls of the gorge.

He sat back, shocked despite himself.

The woman's arm encircled his shoulders and pulled him firmly away from the stanchion that had knocked him silly once already.

"That won't be necessary," Mithridates said in a calm voice. He'd been King of Kings—and very nearly King of Hell. But now . . .

"You took a bad knock," the woman said. "A couple

of them." Though her grip loosened, he could feel the contact still when the truck lurched severely.

Mithridates squinted at her, though it was too dark to make out the woman's features beyond the fact her hair was shorter than his own. Her arm was slender, though strong.

"I expected to be held under house arrest until things were sorted out," he said. "Given in charge to Romulus, perhaps, in one of the outlying fortresses."

He heard the greater bitterness in his voice as he went on, "Or even to Pompey. Caesar knows *he'd* keep me close in the hope that if he did a good job, they'd let him crawl back into the power structure. But this . . ."

He stared into the darkness. The pain of failure was so overwhelming that he didn't attempt to massage the mere physical agony out of his face and battered ribs.

"You know where we're being taken, then?" the woman asked. For the first time, she spoke to him with something other than solicitude.

Mithridates didn't recognize her voice. He was certain that he'd never heard it before. So what was she doing in a truck loaded with supporters of his failed coup?

"Who are you, woman?" he demanded sharply.

He felt her shrug. "My name's Earhart," she explained without apparent rancor at his tone, "but call me AE. The Emperor of Xipangu sent me with a message for one of the big-wigs here, Mithridates. I'd just landed—"

"Landed?"

AE snorted. "If I can call it that," she said. "It was an autogyro, and when the wheels touched down on the back lawn of the palace, they fell off. Par for the course, here, I suppose. Better than par."

He'd sent couriers to Xipangu, asking for a troop of samurai to act as his personal bodyguard. He'd wanted men he could trust because they owed nothing to anyone else involved in the Mediterranean squabbles that had been Mithridates' life while he lived—and seemed destined to be his eternity, now that he was dead.

"What did the Emperor say, AE?" he asked, trying to keep from sounding too eager. If the samurai arrived unexpectedly, there was still a chance. A chance to get out of this immediate predicament, at any rate.

Her long leather coat rustled as she shrugged. "No idea," she said. "I was given a sealed dispatch case to deliver. Never been in this place—that place, I mean, the palace. So I walked in and asked somebody who was giving orders where I could find Mithridates."

She snorted, much as she'd done before describing her landing. "Not the right question, I'm afraid. They took the dispatches and hustled me into this truck just before they threw you in."

AE leaned forward, trying to get a look at his injuries. "Are you feeling better?" she asked. "I used to be a nurse. Not that there's much I could do for you, even if we could see. Not here."

"I'm Mithridates," he said. "I'm sorry that you've been dragged into this. And no, I don't know where we are, but I'm afraid I can guess."

Her body made another rustling shrug. "I'll listen," she said simply. The remainder of the truck's cargo seemed to have been jarred to sleep or their own personal nightmares by the journey thus far.

"The Pentagram has certain secret holding facilities," Mithridates explained. He enunciated precisely, so that he could claim that the words didn't frighten him. "I was aware of this, of course . . . but even I wasn't certain of all the locations. That's because nobody comes back from them."

He paused, swallowing back the bile rising in his throat and threatening to choke him. Caesar couldn't have arranged this; wouldn't *want* to have arranged this. Perhaps the humiliation of being dragged in a formal triumph, followed by decapitation and the hideous agony of the Undertaker's slab . . . but not this. This was forever.

Asmodaeus must have been very angry indeed.

Or Satan himself was.

Mithridates leaned out of the truck and screamed, "You're not done with me yet!" into the eternal night.

"Shut him the hell up, won't somebody?" a voice muttered in apathetic despair.

Mithridates sagged back.

AE touched his arm. "It's not your fault," she said. "Me being here, I mean. I just wanted to fly. I'd have done the same thing, even if I'd known what would happen when I landed."

Mithridates shook his head, too lost in the depths of his personal disaster to take in the details of what his companion was saying.

"I'd been trying to fly again ever since I got here," AE went on. "It never worked. . . . None of them ever got airborne for me. And then a man would say, 'Step aside, little lady . . .' and he'd get in the cockpit—"

"They *need* me in the Administration! Do they think Ramses is even *aware* of half the ongoing projects, much less on top of them? Without me . . ."

"—and go roaring off like a bird, his scarf flapping, and he'd turn and wave. Every time."

The tremor in her voice, the sudden rigidity of her hand on his arm, called Mithridates out of himself. "Pardon?" he said. "I'm sorry, I didn't catch—"

AE's muscles relaxed slightly. Her fingers squeezed his arm in a needless apology for the anger she'd allowed herself to show. "I was just saying," she explained, "that I'd never been able to get a plane airborne since I got here. Until the Emperor gave me the message to take to you. That little autogyro purred, simply purred, as we lifted off."

"You should have known when it worked for a change that something like this would happen on the other end," Mithridates said bitterly. He was going over and over again in his mind the way his coup had failed at the last instant, after he'd planned everything so carefully. . . .

"You don't understand," said AE. "It doesn't matter how things ended. I got to fly again, when I thought I never would."

She and the man who'd been King of Kings—but an exiled failure when he died—looked out at the starless, hopeless, night.

And thought of how long "never" could be in the eternity of Hell.

* * *

There was light again when the truck grunted to a halt.

Paradise, pitiless and pure, glared down on a cosmos in which everything was foul and pitiable. The convoy was so deep below what passed for Hell's surface that the illumination was only a line as jagged as lightning between walls of black despair.

The truck's human cargo was too numb from the ride's hammering to look out, even when the tailgate screeched down.

"Off and on, you dog turds!" shouted a man in field-gray coveralls and the cropped helmet of a Nazi para-trooper. He didn't expect a response, because even as he spoke his calloused hands were reaching for the ankles of the two exiles closest to the tailgate.

Mithridates and AE skidded out, onto a surface of basalt broken into chunks large enough to feel like all sharp angles. They staggered to their feet, hunched over from stiffness, and tried to stagger out of the way before the next pair landed on them.

The paratrooper was faster. Two Assyrian soldiers hurtled into the king and the woman, knocking them onto the jagged gravel again before they could get clear.

AE swore like a mule-driver, though under her breath.

"*Move* it, dog turd!" said an American wearing the

Smokey-Bear hat of an American drill instructor. He kicked her feet out from under her.

The DI's boots and other leatherwork were a mildewed gray. He scowled to notice them when he glanced at AE. His left thumb rubbed his Sam Browne belt fiercely. The mildew flaked off, but the leather refused to take even a vague polish.

Mithridates helped his companion up. A scarred man wearing a white shirt with lace cuffs and throat gestured them languidly with his sword toward exiles gathered at the mouth of a cave, under the watchful eyes of more armed men. They stumbled in that direction.

Only three of the trucks in the convoy had come this far. Mithridates glanced at the men still being pushed and dragged out of the earlier-arrived vehicles. He only vaguely recognized most of them. They'd been involved in the coup—most of them, at any rate—but calling them plotters would have been to over-dignify them.

They were nothing but spear-carriers: Assyrian and Anatolian peasants whose job had been to guard a door or a cross-corridor. Men who were to keep their mouths shut and do exactly as they were told, while their betters accomplished the delicate business of changing a government by force.

Mithridates wasn't their superior any longer.

There were about a dozen guards—cadres—emptying the trucks. That meant the prisoners outnumbered them by at least ten to one, but there was no real risk of a riot now. The men being hauled from the trucks were beaten to jelly by the long ride, mentally as much as physically, and the guards had absolute moral ascendancy over them.

Mithridates looked around and drew himself straighter. His mouth twisted itself into a sneer of contempt.

A man in high boots and a soft gray uniform with STATE POLICE on his shoulder patches sauntered over to Mithridates and Earhart. He was slapping a cattle prod—the side, not the electrified tip—into the palm of his left hand.

It would jab out like a striking snake, Mithridates knew. He held himself very still, a king in soul if not in fact, and waited for the pain.

The state trooper reached out with his left hand and took AE's chin between his thumb and forefinger. "What's this we hev hyar?" he demanded of nobody in particular. "There hain't supposed to be any wimmen hyar."

"We've got what they send us, Dauphin," called the paratrooper as he tossed the last prisoner from the third truck. "Let's get them in the hole and be done with it."

"Wimmen hain't good fer anything but fuckin' en fuckin' up," said the state trooper. "And there hain't no fuckin' here."

"Not a lot left to fuck up, either, Dauphin," said the paratrooper. "Let's—"

AE spat in Dauphin's eye.

The trooper swung his cattle prod at the woman, but Mithridates caught him by the wrist.

"Watch it!" cried a soldier in spatter-camouflage fatigues near the mouth of the cave. He leveled the nozzle of his back-pack flamethrower at Mithridates and began squeezing the two-stage trigger.

The mouth of the cave was about twelve feet high. The blue-furred demon who strode out had to duck to keep from brushing the rock.

"Dauphin, what's going on here?" the demon boomed. The claws of his hands and feet, and the spiked collar around his dangling penis, sparked when they brushed the rocks. The man with the flamethrower jumped aside, obviously afraid that the demon would trample him into the gravel if he didn't move.

"Nothing, suh," said the trooper, jumping back and bracing instinctively to attention. "We-uh jist bringin in the nixt draft, is all."

"Then bring them in!" said the demon, turning back

into the cave. A tail from which mange had stripped
half the bristles waggled behind him.

"You heard the man!" ordered the paratrooper. "Let's
move it, dog turds! Double-time!"

Mithridates, Earhart and the other prisoners shuffled
into the cave. They weren't capable of double-timing,
but neither did the cadre have to prod them along.

Nobody wanted to see what would happen if the
demon stepped out again.

There were three branchings immediately within the
cave-mouth. The sound of tools on rock echoing down
the central corridor was sharp enough to ring through
the human screams.

"This way, this way," called a centurion at the branch-
ing, waving his vine-wood swagger stick down the middle way. "Move it up, dog turds. There's a lot of rock to
shift before *you* next see daylight!"

He was a Roman. At this juncture, his nationality
didn't make him especially hateful to Mithridates; and
he *wasn't* the man from Cabira.

"This place doesn't look natural," commented AE.
She raised her voice with each syllable as she found the
background noise was much louder than it had seemed.
It filled everything. . . .

The corridor dropped into a ramp, down into a huge
excavation. The fitful lighting came from human bodies,
writhing in cages as they burned.

"Come on, get your tools," said a naval petty officer
wearing a striped shirt and his hair in a tarred pig-tail.
He stood behind a wooden counter; the alcove behind
him, carved out of the basalt, was filled with rock-
breaking tools and wicker baskets.

The Assyrian prisoner at the head of the line, just in
front of Mithridates, grunted without comprehension as
the sailor thrust the handle of a pick toward him. The
sailor's lips pursed and he rammed the shaft into the
Assyrian's stomach.

The load of prisoners had been out of the trucks and

mobile long enough to have regained some of their spirit. The Assyrian reached over the counter and grabbed the petty officer by the throat.

What he might have done next was interrupted by the demon, who stepped past Mithridates and plucked the Assyrian from the ground with the thumb and forefinger of his right hand. The demon's claws crossed in front of the prisoner's Adam's apple, but the grip wasn't lethal.

Yet.

The demon leaned into the excavation. "Liszt!" he shouted. "Do you need a—" he slacked his grip on the Assyrian's throat. The man began to bleat in terror. "—C below middle C?" the demon concluded.

The screaming paused. "Whatever your magnificence wishes, noble sir. I wouldn't dream of making suggestions to one of your supernal genius."

The demon stepped forward, carrying his prisoner with one hand and picking his pointed teeth with his left. The petty officer rubbed his own neck as he watched in fascination at what was about to happen.

Mithridates felt himself jostled from behind. He looked around and found that the whole draft of prisoners was pressing closer to get a good look at the fate of their fellow. The cadre watched with twisted smiles, making no attempt to push the prisoners back.

There were already a hundred or more workers in the excavation, hunched over their tools or weighted down by the baskets of rubble they carried toward an opening on the far side. They watched also; but their arms continued to move in almost a pantomine of working. Their eyes followed the demon to a keyboard in a niche near the entrance.

The man seated at the keyboard had white hair, wild eyes, and a cringing expression. He rubbed his hands in fear as the demon approached him.

A dozen naked men lay on their backs behind the keyboard, strapped to the bottom of a frame. Loops of their intestines were drawn up and over the top of the frame.

The demon held his prisoner up, choosing the location with care, and inserted the tip of a claw just beneath the man's sternum. He jerked his finger down sharply, opening the Assyrian like a trout on a flat stone.

"Oh," AE said, burying her head against Mithridates' shoulder. "Oh."

"One learns to expect these things here," he murmured to her in surprise.

She raised her eyes. "I spent the War," she said, "as a nurse's aide in a military hospital. I've seen horrors that bad and worse."

She paused. "I'm used to seeing pain. But I'll never get used to cruelty. God help me if I do."

The demon spread a place on the frame for the Assyrian; clamped the man's limbs; and drew out coils of intestine, yellow and purplish and slimed with blood.

The man began to scream as soon as the demon released his throat, but the victims already on the frame lay in panting silence beside him.

"Maestro," said the demon with a coy arch of his wrist. "The Mephisto Waltz, please."

Liszt bowed from his stool, turned to the keyboard, and began to play with exaggerated motions of his fingers. The loops of intestine quivered as hammers struck them. The men strapped to the instrument screamed in a ghastly parody of music—

And Liszt screamed also, for a coil of his own guts formed the upper register of his instrument.

The demon laughed, puffing out flashes of blue-white flame. He walked back up the ramp and past the prisoners who gulped as they squeezed aside.

"Take your tools, humans," the demon called over the screams in a bass trill. "Be good little workmen for your master."

Mithridates took the pick the Assyrian had refused.

AE snatched a mattock from the grinning petty officer. When she looked around her hesitantly, the state trooper gestured toward the excavation with his cattle prod and ordered, "Git down they-uh en dig, bitch. Thet's all they-uh is fer you fum now on."

The pick helve burned Mithridates' hands. He tried to put it down, but he couldn't get free of it. It stuck to him like tar, and it seared like burning sulphur.

At the bottom of the ramp, a man wearing the embroidered blue robe of a Chinese mandarin gestured with the hand that didn't hold a basket of broken rock. "Down here, noble sir," he called. "I'll show you what to do."

Mithridates and AE, at the head of a straggling line, walked down the ramp to the floor of the excavation. The cadre threatened and shoved, but for the most part the men behind the one-time king followed because they were used to following.

In the alcove above them, Liszt played and screamed with exultant enthusiasm.

"Good sir," said the Mandarin, bowing as they reached him. "I can see that you're a person of quality. And *madam*," he added, bowing again. "This is truly a surprise."

"My hands hurt," AE said. "This . . ." She twisted the mattock handle to which she stuck as Mithridates did the pick.

"Yes, one of the unpleasantnesses of this situation," the Mandarin said easily. "Just use them, please, madam. Dig. We can still talk."

Both of his listeners swung their tools at the rock beneath them. The blows were half-hearted—Mithridates chipped a handful of gravel from the refractory basalt while the mattock's broader blade accomplished even less—but the pain in their hands lessened measurably. They looked up at the Mandarin in surprise.

"Yes," he said, shifting his own basket. "The same with me, I'm afraid. But one learns."

His slanted eyes narrowed. "But you're Mithridates, are you not, good sir? Late King of Kings?"

"I was," Mithridates agreed. He swung his pick again, because the pain returned with redoubled force when he stood idle. "My companion is AE, a person who flies. And you?"

The Mandarin shrugged gracefully.

"A dabbler in hidden knowledge at one time," he said. "More of the knowledge was hidden than I realized until too late. Since then, various other matters, until some . . . of my superiors decided I might be better out of their way. Here."

Mithridates looked around him. The group of prisoners who'd arrived with him—because of him—milled in confusion and growing pain. They were trying vainly to drop the tools that hurt them, but it hadn't occurred to any of them that work was the way out of their pain.

They were soldiers, after all.

"All of you, listen!" Mithridates called. His own palms were beginning to ache with the strain of not swinging his pick. "Dig!"

He suited his action to his words, bringing the tool around and down with a clang and another slight spit of gravel. AE set her mattock blade in a crack and levered at it experimentally.

"This is the way to stop the pain!" Mithridates went on, raising his pick again. "Dig!"

A few, then more, of the new draft began digging at the rock. They were obeying Mithridates rather than hopeful of the result—but it did work, well enough for Hell, and their fellows joined in. The sound of tools redoubled, and more dust filled the air.

"They would have figured it out in time, you know," said the Mandarin. "That sort aren't worth your concern."

He bent at the waist and began gingerly to toss bits of rock into his basket. He'd had long fingernails at one time. The nails were broken now, and the skin of his fingers was raw.

Mithridates drew his head back. "What do you mean, 'not worth my concern'? They're my retainers."

"*Why* are we digging here?" said AE in an obvious attempt to prevent trouble. "Is it just, you know, make-work because we're being punished?"

"Madam," said the Mandarin as he straightened, "I would answer you if I knew. It is said that everything here proceeds according to Satan's intent—"

"That's nonsense," interjected Mithridates, finding that he could lean for a moment on his pick helve without unbearable pain. "Nothing happens here according to *anyone's* intent. Not even his."

"Of course, noble sir," said the Mandarin, bowing in false obsequiousness. "But the intent remains nonetheless . . . and it is certain from what I have heard the guards say among themselves that there are other groups nearby, digging as we are . . . for Satan knows what reason."

"Or God," AE murmured.

"I suspect, madam," said the Mandarin, "that Satan hopes his adversary does *not* know what he's doing down here."

Mithridates struck at the rock. There was an art to it. You had to choose the angle where the point would strike as carefully as you aimed an arrow. The pick, though heavy and awkward, was capable of precision. . . .

"The Greek gods I worshiped in youth were false to me," he said aloud. "There is no true lord but the Fire my forebears worshiped on the throne of Persia."

It struck Mithridates that disaster had at least brought him the benefit of companionship. He had no need to hide his plans or worry that those nearest to him were plotting his downfall. Being condemned without hope, meant that he was also without fear.

"Speaking of fire," AE said, "what are . . . those?"

She gestured with her mattock at one of the baskets hanging on a chain from the twenty-foot ceiling. The

pain on her face as she looked up wasn't because the
tool urged her to greater efforts.

The men looked up also. The sex of the victim in
even the nearest basket was doubtful, since all the hair
had burned off and the body was black except where
yellow flames wrapped it. It had probably been coated
with tar before being ignited, but the fire continued
fitfully long after both the tar and the body fats should
have been consumed.

The body was still alive. Its mouth opened and
closed—the lips had been burned off, along with the
eyes and nose—and its charred hands brushed the metal
cage as feebly as the flames licked its writhing body.

"Oh, those were early Christians who chose martyrdom," said the Mandarin as he resumed his desultory
job of putting rubble in his basket. Presumably when
his load was complete, he'd carry it to the hole in the
wall across the cavern and tip it in, the way other
basket-carriers were doing. But as slowly as the Mandarin and the rest of the crew in the excavation worked,
the job would take—

Mithridates froze at the thought. The job might take
all eternity. That was within acceptable parameters.

"And they're *here*?" AE cried in the grip of an emo-
tion as strong as that which drove her to spit in Dauphin's eye. "That's, that's—bestial!"

"Pardon, madam. I was too brief," explained the
Mandarin as he shuffled forward in his stoop, scraping
his load along behind him. "I don't mean those who
accepted martyrdom. I mean those who *chose* it, when
the authorities would just as soon have looked the other
way. Surprisingly few people really *like* to torture and
kill other people, you know."

He looked up at the cadre, gathered at the top of the
ramp. The SS Pioneer in spatter camouflage rubbed the
nozzle of his flamethrower like a giant penis, hoping for
the prisoners to rush up the gravel slope.

"Though there are always enough, of course," the Mandarin concluded.

"They *wanted* to be burned like that?" Mithridates asked in puzzlement. He thought he heard moans coming from the burning cage, but it must have been his imagination. Nothing so soft could have been heard over the sound of tools on rock—and Liszt at the keyboard.

"Yes," the Mandarin agreed, "though I don't suppose they realized precisely what they were wishing for."

He met Mithridates' eyes. "There's a lot of that here, you know. People getting what they said they wanted. What did *you* want, King of Kings?"

"Who are you to question me?" Mithridates retorted angrily. He began to chop at the irregular rock, squinting against the flakes of rock that his blows threw toward his eyes.

Though it was an easy enough question to answer. He'd wanted power, and he'd gotten it. The power to lose *everything* through a misjudgment so slight that he still didn't see how his coup could have failed and brought him . . . here.

Here.

Mithridates straightened and looked at the Mandarin. "I want to get out of here," he said in the same tone of flat certainty as he had the afternoon he'd ordered the massacre of eighty thousand Roman civilians. "Where does that opening lead?"

He nodded to the hole to which basket-carriers staggered to dump their burdens.

"To a glass-edged drop down to a river of fire," the Mandarin answered calmly. "The heat, even for the moment it takes to tip in the rubble, is a pain more intense than anything I've felt since the Undertaker was finished with me. There is no way out."

"There *is*," Mithridates said harshly, glaring around the black walls of the excavation. If he had to dig at a slant all the way to the surface, he *would* get out of this.

In despite of Caesar, in despite of Asmodaeus—

In despite of Satan himself. He was Mithridates, King of—

"Brothers in torment!" called a cracked voice loud enough to echo throughout the excavation. "Sinners! Throw down your tools!"

Mithridates glanced around the excavation. Dust, bad light and the echoes hid the speaker for a moment. A man stood at the hole into which baskets were emptied. He was silhouetted by the faint glow which reminded Mithridates that there was a river of fire below.

"Who's that?" AE asked, nudging the Mandarin to get his attention and nodding in the direction of the silhouetted man.

"Evil damned souls that we are, yet this evil we prepare is worse than our past sins by as much as those sins cringe beneath the loving purity of God, my brothers!"

The Mandarin shrugged. "John, I've heard, but that means little enough. He's called the Preacher here— down here. He does this occasionally."

The Mandarin's face lost its impassivity for a moment. "It makes a break of sorts, you see."

"We are *damned*, brothers in sin," cried the Preacher's cracked voice. "We are lost utterly and absolutely, without hope of redemption. But they *shall* not ask us to rouse the Old Serpent!"

"He's on the basket detail," the Mandarin went on, fingering his own burden and absently reaching for flakes of stone to add, slaking his pain for the moment. "It isn't good for some people. The fire beneath gets to their brains."

"We are sinners, but Satan is the greatest sinner of all, and it is his sin of pride that will destroy him and destroy us all, my brothers. Blast into smoke and memory—him and us and this Hell that was made for our sins!"

"Though from the way he talks sometimes about the

sun glancing from the rocks of the Isle of Patmos," the Mandarin added, "it may be that the damage was done long before he came to be sent here."

"Throw *down* your tools, my brothers, because no torment of Hell can equal the torments of God's tears should we succeed in our mad enterprise!"

"The poor man," whispered AE. "There were so many like that. Especially the ones who'd been gassed . . ."

"Pipe down over there!" called one of the cadre from the entrance. His voice, unlike the Preacher's, was almost lost in the volume of the excavation. "Get back to your work!"

"In his pride and anger, Satan would loose that which he cannot control. Brothers in sin, brothers in degradation, we must no longer be fooled into thinking that the surcease we gain by working is not to be paid for with a terror and destruction worse than even the mad pride of Satan can imagine!"

"Pipe down!" called half a dozen of the cadre in unison. Their linked voices didn't have the authority of the Preacher's cracked demands.

The madman—the Preacher *must* be mad, though Mithridates found his eyes turning uneasily toward the rubble-strewn floor beneath his feet. What was it down there, the thing they were digging for?

But the madman blocked access to the disposal area. Other basket-carriers paused on the slope left in the rock as the diggers ground their way down. Usually the carriers staggered to the top of the ramp; dumped their loads; rested for a moment, out of the glare reflected from the river beneath; and trudged back down for more rock as the pain in the hands gripping their empty baskets became unbearable.

They were clumping now before the Preacher, like sheep huddled at the feet of their shepherd. On the floor of the excavation, some of the diggers had ceased work also.

The Preacher's voice was a whiplash, but its very harshness made the prodding ache of the tools endurable.

"He's never done *this* before," the Mandarin muttered. "How can he stand like that? The heat is agony, pure agony. . . ."

The Preacher wrung his hands together, gripping the handles of his empty basket. Mithridates knew from the burning throb in his own hands that the pain must be hideous, but the Preacher wore an expression of beatific joy.

"There is bliss immeasurable in resisting sin, my brothers!" the Preacher cried.

He was mad, but his words had power; hellish power in these depths of Hell. "God's eternal mercy has given us the chance not of forgiveness—for we have sunk too low to ever be forgiven—but of not sinking lower yet into punishment!"

Dauphin, the state trooper, had drawn the nickel-plated revolver from his holster. He crouched with his legs spread and both hands on the weapon's rosewood grips.

"Oh, no . . . ," AE whispered.

A long shot for a handgun, Mithridates thought. Certainly too far for compressed air to lob the flamethrower's dollops of blazing gasoline. The cadre wasn't armed to fight; only to brutalize. . . .

"Better that we should hurl ourselves into Phlegethon!" the Preacher cried, gesturing into the blazing hole behind him.

"His flesh should shrivel," whispered the Mandarin, staring at his own bleeding fingers. He rubbed them together, his eyes opening wider in speculation.

Dauphin pulled the trigger six times. The *tsk*-clack! of the revolver's lockwork was audible in a ghostly way, because none of the diggers' tools were striking the rock. Orange light glinted on the cylinder as it turned, turned again, again—rotating all the way around to its original position.

None of the cartridges fired when the hammer struck them.

"Lead us, Preacher!" someone shouted from the excavation floor.

The paratrooper and the fencing master took three strides together down the ramp to the excavation floor. A full-bearded Assyrian with the shoulders of an ox turned to face them, raising his mattock high. Half a dozen of his fellow prisoners stepped up beside him like a phalanx in close order.

The paratrooper looked at his scarred knuckles; the fencing master at the deliberately-blunted edge of his weapon. Their eyes met and they backed quickly to the entrance level again, making sure that they stood behind the combat engineer pointing his flamethrower.

"But *far* better, brothers in sin, that we take ourselves out of this pit and through the caves into what will seem the green lands of Paradise compared to the devastation we would release by continuing on this mad path!"

"Dauphin!" thundered the blue-furred demon. "What's going on here?"

Even the Preacher fell silent for a moment while the trooper babbled to the demon scowling down at him. Dauphin's words were inaudible to the prisoners, but the glitter of the revolver as he waved it made his excuse obvious.

And obviously vain. The demon gripped Dauphin by the throat with one hand, lifted him, and with an artist's delicacy slit the state police uniform and the man's belly with a claw.

Dauphin was able to scream when the demon tossed him underhand in the direction of Liszt's keyboard, still holding a loop of intestine hooked on the point of his claw. The demon dropped the guts and sauntered down the ramp without bothering to clamp the trooper properly into the frame.

Dauphin bawled like an infant as he tried to stuff himself back into his torn body cavity. His guts jerked along the ground as he pulled them hand over hand, picking up grit and flakes of sharp rock.

The other members of the cadre looked at the victim—
and looked away, watching the demon uneasily as he
walked across the excavation toward the Preacher.

The Assyrian phalanx disintegrated as soon as the
demon appeared. They'd been soldiers who'd prepared
for death many times—and met death in the end, as
even pacifists must. But the shambling, grinning demon was beyond the willingness of anyone to face, even
the bravest or stupidest of men.

Mithridates turned slightly, offering to meet the demon's eyes from a distance . . . but the demon had
another focus now.

"Even you, thing of evil and child of evil!" the Preacher
cried against the backdrop of lambent Hell.

A prisoner with a pick-axe waited until the demon
sauntered past him, then turned and planted his tool in
the middle of the blue-furred back. The cavern rang as
though he'd chopped at an anvil.

The demon reached back one of his gangling arms
without bothering to look for his victim. His clawed
fingers closed on the prisoner's shoulder and jerked
him forward. The pick dropped to the floor, chipping
the rock slightly.

That was more effect than it'd had on the demon.

"You cannot repent, thing of darkness," bawled the
Preacher, pointing a long, bony finger at the demon
who strolled toward him. "But self-interest alone should
prevent you from aiding in this doomed enterprise.
Come with us! Join us as we seek the mercy that can
never be offered you!"

The demon's jaw opened wide. He bit off the head of
the prisoner he carried in his left hand. His tongue,
blue and as furry as the pelt on his back, forked out and
cleared his broad lips of debris.

"Come down from there," he said as he chewed. He
crooked the index finger of his free hand without apparent rancor.

Tall as the demon was, the Preacher loomed above

him with the advantage of the ledge on which he stood.
The clawed blue arms might *possibly* reach the Preacher's ankles. More likely, the demon would have to walk
up the slope cut into the side of the excavation, just as
the humans did with their loads of rubble.

The other basket-carriers huddled on the slope beneath the Preacher, awaiting an outcome that could
only be disastrous for them.

The demon took another bite of the prisoner, like a
shepherd boy munching on a scallion. The blue jaws
could open amazingly wide. One of the prisoner's arms
flopped to the ground as the shoulder to which it had
been attached vanished into the demon's maw.

"Brothers in sin, creature of darkness! We have denied Satan. Now all that remains is for us to leave this
place of greater damnation—"

The demon set his arms akimbo and began to laugh,
drowning out even the Preacher's cracked ravings. The
raucous bellows echoed from the curving walls and the
rock ceiling vaulted high above, filling the chamber like
bubbles in slime.

The Preacher waited in silence, glaring down into the
demon's foul hilarity.

The demon tossed away the nub of the prisoner he'd
been eating. He burped a gout of blue-white flame as
hot as the core of a star.

The jet of fire enveloped the Preacher from knees to
bald scalp—dimmed the reflected light of Phlegethon
as it flashed through the opening—and glanced upward
along the wall of basalt that glowed white and crumbled
at the touch.

The Preacher's scrawny calves **stood** upright for a
moment, sheared off at the angle at which the flame
had spurted from the demon's mouth. Swirling flecks of
carbon and calcium were all that remained of the parts
of the body wrapped in the momentary blaze.

The right leg toppled over. The left continued to

stand, mummified by the intense heat. The demon began to laugh.

A thirty-ton chunk fell from the basalt dome, crushing the demon like a fly in a drop-forge. One hand projected from beneath the edge of the fallen rock. The fingers twitched spasmodically.

Mithridates looked from the prisoners stunned by the impact of the falling rock, to the cadre cringing in horror at the top of the ramp.

"Follow me!" he roared, once king and a leader again. He swept his arm toward the ramp and the exit beyond it. "We're getting out of here!"

* * *

As he strode for the ramp, his silken trousers flapping at his ankles, Mithridates didn't have time to be surprised that AE was the first of his fellow prisoners to fall in step with him. The woman was quicker on the uptake than the heavy-muscled peasants, swinging tools as they once had swung swords—

And she was at least as brave.

Prisoners fell in behind them, drawn as much by the movement as by the orders he'd shouted. The Mandarin looked at Mithridates, then up at the head of the ramp where the cadre bunched together like sheep behind the bellwether.

The SS Pioneer was at the head of the group, kneeling behind his flamethrower.

The Mandarin stepped aside, letting ex-soldiers rush past him in the mad hope of becoming ex-prisoners.

"Look, we can drop them now," said AE; and did, tossing aside her mattock to clang and dance as it hit the ground.

Mithridates' hands didn't throb as they had, even when he stood transfixed by the Preacher's voice. Whoever the man was, he'd had a power over his listeners.

Enough power to damn himself to Hell, at any rate. If Mithridates had still been in the Administration, he'd have checked to see where the fellow was reassigned.

But for now—

"Get back!" shouted the guard with the flamethrower.

The state trooper, Dauphin, was crawling toward the group of his fellows. He was trying to keep his intestines in with his left hand as he crept forward on the other three limbs, but the tear in his belly was too long. Loops slipped out above and below his hand, tangling with his knees.

Mithridates dropped his tool. The muzzle of the flamethrower was only twenty feet up the slope from his chest now. The pick would have made a dangerous weapon under the proper circumstances, but it was useless here. He'd win not by some physical act, but rather by regal majesty—

Such as remained in this hidden basement of Hell.

"One more step and I'll crisp the lot of you!" the pioneer shouted. "Nothing's different for you, dog turds!"

But a great deal was different for the cadre. They were terrified: by what had happened to Dauphin; by what had happened to the demon . . . and by what might happen to them, now that things were changing in a place where nothing changed for the better.

Mithridates waved the woman back with a quick flick of his hand. This was for him to handle alone, using his personal authority.

"It's over for you," he said forcefully, taking a step forward—though a short one. "Put that down. The flame is my god. The Flame will stand by me."

Mithridates stepped closer, remembering the sounds at Cabira—rending metal and the screams of horses dying.

The guard looked beyond the ex-king to the dark mass of prisoners, hulking and lethal. He turned his head away, as if his mind were separate in intention from the nozzle in his hands.

"Pollux, let's go!" cried another member of the cadre in sudden panic—spinning on the heel of one hobnailed boot, headed for the exit.

The pioneer squeezed the double triggers of his weapon.

The hose connection separated from the fuel bottle. Black napalm squirmed out like a beast-catcher's lasso.

A pool of orange flame exploded, engulfing the group around the flamethrower.

Mithridates leaped back, startled by the flash and slap of heat. Members of the cadre bolted in all directions, like ants from a stirred-up nest. In the center of where they'd bunched, the pioneer was dancing in a growing rope of flame that stripped his clothes and flesh as he screamed vainly.

"Get 'em!" cried an Assyrian, lunging past Mithridates. He'd kept his shovel and used its broad blade as a spear by thrusting under the rib-cage of the fencing master who stumbled in his direction. He pitched his victim sideways off the ramp; certainly a mercy, since the guard's face was melting in its wrapper of napalm.

Like a wedge bursting a hostile shield-wall, the released prisoners swept past the king—and the woman—who'd led them to that point. The cadre provided no opposition. Most of the one-time guards were afire, and they'd always governed the prisoners by moral superiority rather than direct force.

When their pretense of superiority vanished, there was nothing left to oppose the picks and bloodlust of the men they'd dominated.

The flames themselves should have slowed the onrush, but the leading prisoners ignored the pools of gasoline. After the first scores of booted feet had tramped through and scattered the napalm, there was nothing left but smoky trails on the rock—

And sputtering flames to mark the mangled bodies of the guards.

Liszt continued to play. Mithridates glanced at the keyboard; but there was nothing he could do for the men there, and they were no responsibility of his.

The ex-prisoners, by virtue of the fact they had followed his lead, *were* his royal responsibility now. He hadn't the faintest notion of what he could do for them—or for himself.

"Did you know that was going to happen?" someone asked, AE asked, from beside him. "Can you really control fire?"

The woman was so tall that when he turned, their eyes were on a level. For a moment Mithridates considered alternatives: boastful agreement; regal disdain for a personal question asked by a commoner—and a female beside; or—

"In life, my god never offered me such a sign of approval," he said. "None of my gods. Here—well, prayer fails even more often than tools do, weapons . . ."

He looked across the excavation at the Preacher's legs. Both had fallen over. "What I thought," he said, "was that I could face them down, the guards."

"You almost did."

"Yes. And I almost became Ruler of Hell."

The Mandarin was approaching with a bland smile. His arms were crossed, and his hands were tucked into the opposite sleeves to hide their injuries. Mithridates gave him a wintry smile, though he'd been an old man himself before he decided that it was a king's business to *lead* his armies.

"Have you decided what you will do now, noble sir?" asked the Mandarin with a hint of superiority in his voice.

His careful gaze around the milling prisoners was a gesture of its own.

"Of course," Mithridates said. "We'll go back up the canyon the way we were brought here."

He knew that was a hopeless plan; but he knew also that by stating it with assurance, he prevented the Mandarin from turning his special knowledge into control of the situation.

For the Mandarin obviously *had* special knowledge.

The regal certainty took the Mandarin aback, as it

was intended to do. "Why surely, noble sir," he protested, "you realize that there will be more convoys coming this way before we could possibly reach the surface. Even if an alarm hasn't already summoned an armed force that will restore us to captivity."

AE looked from one man to the other. Her eyes were noticeably cooler when they rested on the Mandarin.

Mithridates shrugged, as if he hadn't come to the same conclusion about the only escape route he could imagine. "Alarms don't work here," he said in idle disregard. "And as for more prisoners—we'll take over all the convoys we meet. We'll *ride* back with a real army."

It would be impossible to turn trucks around between the walls of rock, and Bellerophon himself couldn't edge the vehicles up the narrow switchbacks with their steerable axles in back.

Mithridates turned as if to call an order to his milling 'army'. He glanced over his shoulder at the stricken Easterner. "Why?" he asked. "Do you have another idea?"

"Indeed, noble sir," the Mandarin gasped in relief. "To put ourselves under the protection of the mighty Zahhaq, whom we can reach through the caves themselves. I—have had the honor to present myself to the magnificent Zahhaq several times in the past, and I've been impressed each time by his nobility and the splendor in which he keeps his retainers."

"You've been *here* before?" AE demanded sharply. "And escaped?"

"Madam, I misspoke," the Mandarin said with a deep bow. The flash of fear that marred his impassive visage proved that he had misspoken indeed. . . .

"It was because of my endeavors on behalf of Zahhaq— and on the behalf of other unfortunates whom I led to his protection—that I was imprisoned here myself," he continued, calm again. "Personages as high as Satan himself fear Zahhaq and his ability to protect the weak from their oppressors."

"He's a god?" Mithridates pressed. "Imprisoned here by other gods?"

"He is . . . ," the Mandarin said, pausing to look over his shoulder. The claws of his fear tore momentarily at his placid expression. "Zahhaq is, I think, a man, noble sir. But here—" he shrugged "—labels matter little. He can protect you, as he's protected others. And I can lead you to his palace through these caves."

An Assyrian—Mithridates recognized the man by his bloody shovel, though he didn't know the fellow's name—shouldered the Mandarin aside, then braced to attention facing Mithridates.

"Sir!" he said in the clipped shout of a veteran non-com. "Section Leader Kalhu reporting for orders!" He wore a scar which traced its way from his forehead to his chin, where it appeared as a white streak in the full beard.

"Fall the men in, section leader," Mithridates ordered crisply. "We'll be leaving at once, through the caves." He nodded toward the Mandarin. "We have a local guide."

Kalhu saluted. "Very good, sir!" he said in obvious relief that he had somebody to give him orders again.

"I'll lead, then, noble sir," the Mandarin said. He too was relieved. "I'm glad that—"

"Column of fours, you misbegotten whoresons!" Kalhu bawled. "Get your thumbs out of your butts and fall in!"

"With your permission, noble sir," said the Mandarin after an instant of lost composure. He bowed, then scurried to the head of the column forming at the entrance.

AE watched in mild amazement at the speed with which the freed prisoners did the thing old soldiers know best how to do—form lines and wait for further orders. She glanced at Mithridates. "Do you trust him?" she said, quietly though the Mandarin was well out of earshot.

"The Easterner?" Mithridates replied. How many times had the King of Pontus ordered an army to fall in? And how many of the men who'd obeyed his orders had lived to fall in the next time?

"Of course not," he said. "But—"

He met the woman's eyes squarely. "Asmodaeus was very angry when he sent me here. Now that—this has happened—Satan himself will be equally angry. I don't know what the Mandarin has planned, but I'm sure that it can't be as bad as what we'll find if we wait for Satan to react."

He grinned coldly to rob his next words of the cold truth they stated. "Besides, I was always one to take a chance."

"Sir! Section ready!"

"Then move them out, section leader!"

Whatever it really was, Mithridates thought as he watched the column step off on its right foot—a trifle ragged, but they were a scratch formation; they'd settle in. . . .

Whatever it really was, it felt like escape at the moment.

THE GARDEN
OF
BLOOD NARCISSUS

Brad Miner

"Absolute freedom mocks justice.
Absolute justice denies freedom."

—*Camus*, THE REBEL

This was the great Gestas, world famous criminal, the legendary Bad Thief himself, the one and only man who ever stood up to God, Jr., and spit right in the big man's eye. Or so said the thief to anyone in Hell who'd listen. Usually that was nobody. Nooo-body. But just now it was the Reverend John J. Ryan, S.J., late of the archdiocese of New York, who was the thief's captive audience. You see, as long as office hours prevailed, the office door was sealed tight as a coffin. No breaks for coffee or the lavatory. So sorry. Them's the rules.

The thief and the priest were working on a high floor of the Bureau of Error and Illusion. It was their job to review applications for exit visas (a form in triplicate,

Claim of Wrongful Damnation: white copy, applicant; pink copy, Satan; yellow copy, wastebasket). It was a simple process really. The applications were either summarily denied or, in about half the cases, ultimately denied. Because them's the rules! Complaints? See us at the Last Judgement.

"Them rules" had recently become important to Gestas. The Powers That Be (and they be b-a-d, *bad*) had . . . *persuaded* him that obedience is right up there next to, yes, ungodliness. He and another Bureau employee, Origen, the long-suffering Christian heretic from Alexandria, had been given a little R&R of sorts and undergone a very thorough dis-orientation, you might say, and now Gestas was a regular Young Pioneer. No more dreams of escape. No more Bible smuggling. No more kind words for the preacher from Nazareth. And when Ryan asked after Origen, Gestas simply shrugged. Don't know; don't care. But Ryan had sat through enough confessions to know a lie when he heard one. Not that Father Ryan was much concerned anymore with your fine distinctions between a lie and the so-called truth.

Ryan was mostly concerned with his own very active suspicions. Gestas had probably been turned, and Ryan was determined not to get caught making any imprudent professions of either faith or despair. The best thing was to trust no one, and it was the one thing the priest did best. This was the chariest Jesuit in Hell.

He was scared too. Something had happened to Gestas—something harrowing. The thief had visited the Hell that is beyond the pale of simple damnation, and, whatever other intrigues might be simmering inside, Gestas was trying really hard to give up hope. Those . . . fellows, the ones who, well, *catechized* him, had showed him that the sorriest of the sorry down here were mostly grinding their teeth because of hope. And while they were at it, his tutors had given him chapter and perverse about the opposition. Ryan had a hunch most of the propaganda Gestas was lately spouting was intended, indeed carefully designed, to torment both of them. Such is the economy of perdition. The two of them spent most of their working hours shouting at each other about Jesus Christ.

However, *this* was too much. It really was. Gestas was up on his feet pointing at Ryan and demanding (*demanding*, can you imagine?) that Ryan never, ever again refer to you-know-who as the Son of God.

"You Romans!" Gestas hissed. (No matter how often Ryan tried to disclaim Rome, Gestas insisted on associating him with the ancient oppressors.) "First you crucify us; then next thing you know, you're hanging idols of *him* in your synagogues and scribes like you are shaking them little ones at our Prince whenever he's up in the world. You know what I mean . . . them whajamacallits—them *crucyfixers*. Never stopped the Prince from liberatin'. Don' know what they's s'posed to *fix*. Don' fix nuthin'.

"Let's us jus' be sure we's sure 'bout who the bastard was. *And if*," he shouted as Ryan started to object, "if you will shut up for one minute, maybe I can set you straight."

Ryan sighed. And now, he thought, Inferno Films proudly (and do we mean Pride) presents, *The Greatest Lie Ever Told*. I need this. More preprogrammed blasphemy. Bassackwardness in Hell's grand tradition. But until the whistle heralds closing time . . .

"Okay," Gestas began, "now listen careful. Here's how the big man *really* got born. Weren't no angel come to his mamma back then, but a kid from the next village came *in* her. Well, wha'd you think happened? Lemme talk! These was my times, you know, and I can tell you, buster, this girl's in some real deep camel shit, because her little strumpetin' will get her stoned, she gets caught. Not to mention the deal's been made with Ol' Joseph and her folks. Ol' Joe figures he's bought hisself a virgin, and a deal's a deal. These is your old timey Jews, Ryan. Righteous—and I mean *vicious*.

"And lil' Mary knows it ain't no easy matter of sneaking a little pigeon blood on the matrimonial sheets.

She's knocked up, and the weddin's six months off. 'Oh me, oh my,' she whines, 'whatever am I gonna do?' And then it hits her. A plan! And it's so good she'll never have to diddle Ol' Joe, who was her parents' choice anyhoo.

"Now all her people was a real bunch of fanatics. God for breakfast. God at lunch. God when you sit down to supper, and God when you go to beddy-bye. ('And good morning to you, brother. Followed any good Messiahs lately?') And who's the biggest eager believer of 'em all? Why, Ol' Joe, who else. Wasn't it him been tellin' everbody 'bout her cousin Lizzie? Wasn't he just absolutely sure it was all true what they been sayin'?

"See, this Elizabeth woman, Mary's cousin on her mamma's side, really her auntie, she's an older lady. Mary, she's all of fifteen, but 'Lizbeth's, I don' know, thirty-five or forty, which in them days is like eighty for gettin' pregnant, which is what happened to her too. Her and ol' Whatshisname . . . ah—"

"—Zechariah," Ryan said.

"That's the guy. Liz and Zech are married twenty-five years and one day he's in the temple where he's a janitor or somethin' and (so *he* says later on) up pops an angel and tells 'im his ball-and-chain is gonna drop a little bambino just like that. Just (if you can remember it) like that other angel told Abraham. *Just* like it. And just like ol' Abraham, Zech laughs right in the birdman's face. So says Zech. Nobody else saw nuthin'. Ain't *that* always the way. And Zech says the angel's pissed and zaps him and makes him mute till the rug rat's born. But, of course, this is all just a lot of holy roller hoo-ha.

"Yeah, yeah. She got pregnant. Great! But they just *had* to make it like it is in the Scripts. How else they gonna get in the next edition of the Book? You wanna go down in history, you gotta make up a little history of your own.

"So, lil' Mary hears all this and figures, what the hell.

If Lizzie's brat can be the Messenger, which is what Zech says the angel says lil' Johnnie's gonna be, well, Mary thinks, why can't my little lamb be the Message?

"Now she don' like to fib, but a little taradiddle's lots better than stonin'.

"And did the others buy it? Hook, line, and stinker. At first, Lizzie's fumin', but that's because *she* hadn't thought of it. 'My son, God.' But then Lizzie gets into it. It had to be a virgin, she says. It *had* to be. That was the genius of it. It was like when the time came and the kid's born in a stable, they said *that* was the way it had to be. Where else would the king of that-other-place-I-won't-mention be born? Where else? Well in a palace of course, but these folks did love their irony. What else poor folks got? And nobody ever even bothered to ask how the Whole Ball of Wax could, let alone would, squeeze Hisself into one little ol' baby, but they just *knew* he had to come from a virgin!

"And then every day of the kid's life, his ma's sayin', 'You're the one, kiddo. You're the one.' Bible verse flash cards in the morning and magic lessons at night, and then as soon as he's bar mitz'd, zoom! Off to high school in Tibet. Now don' act surprised. Where'd you think he got all them wild notions?"

Gestas walked around the office nodding his head.

"And don' you get me on the subject of how *he* suffered. Ha! There's some foolishness. Compare what he been through to what I been through—you wanna talk 'bout a world of hurt!

"Now *my* dear ol' papa split the day I was born. Mamma (she was a whore) called me, 'Curse'. 'Yo, hey Curse,' she'd yell, and I'd tottle over and she'd smack me upside my head. I never even knew my own, real name till I was ten. . . . Nice name for a kid, doncha think? 'Curse'. Oh she was some piece of work, my ma. I'll betcha not one single, solitary day went by she didn't whack me one good till the day I run off on my twelfth birthday. Only pleasure I ever got was stealin' her whore money she kept hidden under a loose floor tile. Well, she can 'curse' my ass.

"I went into the mines at thirteen and was a galley slave at seventeen. All this was on account of some petty thievery. I killed some whoreson bastard when I was sixteen, but that's another story. But I'll tell you it wasn't no crime. Because there are some really and truly deserves to die and come sit right where you're sittin'."

Gestas had narrowed his eyes to reptilian slits, and not for the first time did Ryan see the deadly intent lurking behind those lids. As a young priest, Ryan had made one pastoral visit to the Riker's Island Correctional Facility. One was all he could endure, and he'd left early that day. He'd seen this look of uncomplicated malice. To these men the Commandments were dust beneath their feet. They sinned without guilt. He could never admit that he believed in Evil, but he'd seen it at Riker's. He told himself they were sick, that *they* were victims, but his heart knew better. And for all the blustering Gestas blathered about dying next to the Saviour, for all his former willingness to memorize the Psalms Origen patiently taught him when Gestas thought it might be a means of escape, for all the antique charm the Bad Thief could ooze, Ryan had to remind himself that Gestas was neither comic nor pathetic. He was a liar, a robber, and, by his own admission, a murderer, and he was right where *he* belonged.

But then why, Ryan wondered, why in God's holy name am *I* here with him? Gestas was still leveling snake eyes at the Jesuit as he went on.

"Oh, and all my miserable life, when I come walkin' down the street, folks like *you*'d cross to the other side. You upright and unctuous types. Funny now, ain't it? Us stuck here together.

"And I don' reckon there's five years I'm a free man between when I stopped pullin' them oars and when I got nailed up beside your former boss. And even then I live on a good hour after he gives up his holy ghost, his parakeet—what have you.

"Now here's my point. The preacher's stepdaddy loved him. His mamma loved him to pieces. He had twelve—make that eleven—good pals, and after three years of celebrity, he had one bad day. A few lashes and a couple hours on the tree. Well, hell's bells, *Father*, one time in the mines, after I split open some Syrian's noggin, they tortured me for a solid week. You wanna talk stripes? Another time, the Romans picked me up for pickpocketing and whipped me twice a day for two weeks. I can show you the scars!

"Only do *not* gimme this hoo-ha about how the Son of God suffered! Sure, he hurt like hell—for three stinkin' hours! I suffered non-stop for thirty stinkin' years, and you say *he*'s the king of Heaven? For what I been through, I oughta be God-stinkin'-Almighty hisself!"

Well sure, the Jesuit thought, you want to be God. Who doesn't? How do you think we all got into this mess?

Then came the siren blast. Whoo-weee! At last. There was the sound of a vacuum unsealing, and the office door swung open.

"Quittin' time!" Gestas shouted, and he was out the door in a flash.

Ryan waited only a moment and then went after him. He was determined to follow Gestas wherever he went. Ryan wasn't confident Gestas would lead him to Origen, but following the thief who died on our Lord's left hand seemed like a good and proper way to pass a little eternity. No?

The truth is, Ryan enjoyed behaving like a spy. Okay, okay! So this was inappropriate according to the standard he'd professed in life, but he hadn't made up his mind for whom he was cloaking-and-daggering. He was ashamed to even consider doing the Devil's work, but he wasn't getting any marching orders from Above, now was he?

The truth is, he never felt more like a Jesuit, and it felt damn good. Of course, like every other felicity in Hell, the pleasurable feeling was probably a setup. But he'd burn that bridge when he got to it. You could worry, but you had to grab these moments anyway, because they were a cut above the ordinary torments; even if they were, themselves, a snare for greater agonies.

Ryan was, after all, a man who could easily have been in the employ of a Grand Inquisitor or a Richelieu; a man to shadow heretics, blasphemers, and unbelievers. He was a Black Robe, a soldier . . .

But he was behind enemy lines now, and not dropped there on a mission, but abandoned by his own army. Court-martialed, dishonorably discharged, and defrocked. God knows why. The enemy has me, and even if I wanted to be a double agent, I don't know if the Good Guys would take me back. So it makes sense to collaborate, doesn't it?

Because, he'd tell you, damnation's a helluva reward for years of loyal toil in Jehovah's vineyard, and, frankly, if Jesus Christ the Lord came on another Harrowing and personally came up to Ryan and apologized, the Jesuit wasn't sure he'd let bygones be bygones just like that. Well . . . maybe. In any case, he wasn't holding his breath. That only made things worse. In lucid moments, which were blessedly few, Ryan knew the reason he 'burned' in Hell was because he hadn't been on fire in life. Well, he was very tempted now to throw himself into the flames, if that's not too dramatic a phrase. To do, in other words, exactly what Satan wanted and maybe more. The time for commitment had come; the time to be extreme. Just between us, Ryan told himself, I think the Boss likes me. I think he can use me. I know the other team's playbook.

So. Ryan sneaked out the office after Gestas and began to tail the thief down the litter-strewn steps of the fire exit. Neither of them was about to use the Bureau of Error and Illusion elevators, which by now would be crammed with workers leaving the various departments and which were apt to break down between floors. Repairs could take a while—hours, weeks, months, and even years, and those stuck in the car, shoulder-to-shoulder, could be heard calling for help and cursing one another and weeping with rage. When Ryan had discovered the elevator problem and begun taking the stairs, he had trouble understanding why anyone could be so foolish as to use the elevators, but he came to realize, well, to suppose (being more a man of opinions than insights) that the damned bring their laziness and impatience with them from life. You were tempted to say that old habits die hard, until you realized they don't die, period. Being trapped in an elevator is Hell, and some people couldn't avoid it no matter how often they got stuck.

But Ryan went on tiptoes down the fire stairs, staying well back so Gestas would not sense he was being followed. The old wounds in the Bad Thief's feet nearly always gave him pain and he moved slowly. Ryan could hear him grumbling and grousing as people bumped into him as they passed. Ryan would stop at each floor and listen for the distinctive shuffling footsteps. Every one of the landings was a mess of crumbling concrete, rusted metal, and graffiti. "I'd rather be living"—that was one you saw almost everywhere. "Support Soviet freedom fighters in Afghanistan"—that's choice, Ryan thought. "The Devil is dead"—somebody would pay for that one. There was one very precise rendering of an erect penis. Above it were the words, "Remember this?"

At the ground floor, Ryan pushed open the door and stepped into the crowded alley behind the Bureau. The usual pushers were hawking their stuff to the bureaucrats, and Ryan had to do a bit of shoving to break through to an open spot. He caught sight of Gestas just as the thief was turning on to the avenue that led straight downtown. Nuts! Ryan scuffed his shoe in disgust. Not downtown.

The Jesuit's sojourns into New Hell were never pleasant. It was an awful, stinking, brawling slum. Your life wasn't worth a plugged nickel. Well, you weren't alive, but your . . . well, your whatever—your being, okay? That was worthless.

Gestas was limping along like he was walking over hot coals, and Ryan tried to concentrate on blending into the crowds as they came into the city proper. He didn't want Gestas to see him and he didn't want to look carefully at what was going on around him. Talk about your bad dream. Ryan couldn't help but notice that a circle of toughs was attempting to sodomize a young woman on the steps of the utility company, Infernal Power and Dark. The woman was probably a feminist. She was screaming for help, but what could you do? She pleaded for assistance, but she also cursed her attackers for their impotence. She knew that their failure to consummate their lust would enrage them to the point where they'd simply give up on the raping and get on with the dismembering, and she, like just about everybody else, feared the Undertaker's table more than anything. Death hurt, but reanimation was worse. Ryan knew. Not long ago he was walking in the hills on the outskirts of the city, minding his own business, when some damned barbarian attacked him, tore out his heart and then made moccasins from his lungs. Yet here he was now, skulking after Gestas. Somehow he'd been put back together—healed, if not exactly resurrected. Like his memory of his first, real death, images of his time on the Undertaker's slab were hazy. Surely it was impossible, but Ryan could swear the surgeon with the bulldog face poised over him as he gained consciousness and then passed out again was . . . well, *resembled* J. Edgar Hoover. But what would *he* be doing wielding a scalpel in Hell?

Ryan saw that Gestas had stopped at a restaurant,

Chez de Sade. Good heavens, was he going to eat? Wouldn't that be just like that low-life! Ryan knew about this place. It had a menu that put you in mind of Tour d'Argent in Paris, but the food put you in mind of the sewer sludge in Cleveland. The trick was to place your order, soak up a little of the topside ambience, and then split before you were served. But you'd better not get caught bolting, because you might end up as the plat du jour. Ryan sat down on the curb across the street to wait. Knowing Gestas, the thief would probably linger over each course and then order dessert.

The Jesuit glanced around and saw one of New Hell's most infamous torments. It was the Infernal City's only movie house, The Pandemonium. Now showing: MYRA BRECKINRIDGE. A writhing line of tortured souls was being driven by demons past the box office and herded into the theater. There would be no intermission.

The movies. Ryan missed them down here, but not enough to buy a ticket to watch Racquel and Rex . . . Rex—well, you know, that movie critic guy—to watch them cavort in Vidal Sassoon's . . . no, not *that* Vidal, but some other faggot's transsexual pipe dream. What the hell's wrong with my memory, Ryan wondered. What was I just thinking about? Oh, the movies.

When he was a kid, he'd loved to sit in the back of a dark theater and watch the smoky white light flicker out from the projection room to splash images on the big screen. Now he looked up at the marquee and squinted at the lights that were bright with an intensity uncommon in Hell. When he turned back to check on Gestas, there were spots before his eyes. He blinked a few times and saw that a waiter was just taking the thief's order.

The Jesuit chewed on a fingernail and felt the marquee lights on the back of his neck. Those lights and the memory of the projector beam reminded him of something. With a jolt, he felt his heart begin to race. He was terrified, but he didn't know why. He thought if he could turn around and look up at the marquee he might remember, but he couldn't look back now no matter how he strained. And *that* reminded him of whatever it was he . . . couldn't . . . quite . . . recall. What *is* wrong with my memory?

Then he thought, Of course! It's like a movie; what I can't remember is like a movie! He closed his eyes and tried to flash back.

There were certain stock scenes in dozens of pictures he'd now forgotten. Ryan could imagine actors' faces, but he couldn't recall their names (even when he ran into them down here—which, of course, was Hell for the stars). He remembered plots but not titles. His head was filled with cinematic images, and while most, he was sure, came from real movies, he suspected others were jazzed up memories of his own life or even figments of his restless imagination which, as we know, is the playground of demons.

He squeezed his eyelids and concentrated. He saw a man on horseback galloping along a mountain road. Suddenly thunder and lightning make the horse rear. For a moment a castle can be seen on a distant crag overlooking a steep drop to a boiling sea. Well sure, Ryan thought, that's the start of a horror movie. But what does that have to do with the price of rotten eggs? What's that got to do with my death?

His death? My death, he wondered? What does my death have to do with lightning and movies? Well, what?

He closed his eyes again. A soldier is in No Man's Land at midnight. A flare explodes overhead, and for an instant the soldier sees he's crawling among corpses. Okay, a war movie. An explosion. A revelation.

Now that reminded him of something. He remembered what the boys in 'Nam used to say. Being a Marine chaplain in Southeast Asia was all of Hell he'd ever expected to see. "Hey, Padre," the boys would say, "I don't like this movie. Tell God to change the channel, okay?"

If only I could change the channel now, he sighed. He grabbed his side when the pain struck. It was the most basic torment of them all, this stitch that doubled you over every time you thought, If only. If only . . . *If only!*

Sweat beaded on his forehead and upper lip. Change the channel now. Look back at your real life, he ordered himself, not at B-movies. Let me see one decent night . . . Just one.

And this is what came back:

It was long ago in the world when he was alive. Ah, it was Christmas, and he was on his grandfather's farm. For days he and old Eamon had been cooped up in the house while a blizzard raged, and when, finally, the snow stopped and after the night's dinner dishes were put away and the radio programs signed off and Eamon was asleep by the fire, Ryan laced on boots, bundled up, and went to stretch his legs along the road that snaked around the lake behind the farm.

A silent night it was. The stars were diamonds scattered on black velvet. The moon was a pearl. A pearl, the young Ryan thought, of great value. Wasn't the sky without end? And couldn't you practically hear God breathing? This was the night he found his vocation to the priesthood.

He walked on that night, his eyes raised to the heavens. He was relaxed for once. He was a city boy and the country usually unsettled him. During summer visits, he never went out at night. Oh, no. There were bats that might swoop down on you and snakes that might strike up at you. But in the dead of winter these beasts slept.

The wind blew the snow in deep drifts over the ditches at the sides of the road, so Ryan was careful to keep to the center where the snow was just deep enough to cover his ankles. The crunch of his footsteps was the only sound.

But then he paused. He cocked his head and listened. He heard an automobile some distance off. He heard its shifting gears and, by the modulation of the engine noise, he figured the car was accelerating, braking, and skidding in the snow. When he heard the sparkle of distant laughter, he was sure of it. Kids from one of the nearby farms, no doubt—out for a winter joyride. Just exactly how close were they? He listened carefully. The winding road and the stiff breeze made it tough to gauge, but he was pretty sure they were coming his way.

He'd put his hands in his pockets and trudged on. He was trying to remember a hymn to whistle but his head was filled with carols and swing tunes. He stopped and listened. The car wasn't behind him, was it? In these hills, on a cold, windy night like this and on this road, you couldn't tell. But it was definitely coming closer. Then—

—Yaah! Suddenly an animal leapt in front of him! Yaah! Then almost before he was aware of catching his breath, of his heart pounding, he was laughing out loud at the sight of a bunny rabbit hopping up the road ahead of him. It stopped just twenty feet from him and stuck its twitching nose straight up in the air.

Ryan knelt down and made kissing noises at the bunny. On a magic night like this he could probably charm a rabbit just as St. Francis had.

"Here fella," he called. "C'mere Bugsy boy."

The rabbit twisted its head and thumped a rear foot, but it stayed safely away from the noisy, foul smelling human.

Ryan was making more kissing sounds when he became suddenly aware of the automobile straining at the bottom of the hill just ahead. The driver gunned the engine, popped the clutch, and came spinning in first gear up over the crest of the hill so that when Ryan saw the black roadster, he saw its rear fenders and the chrome hubcaps of its back wheels gleaming in the moonlight. Then the rear tires caught and the car spun around and the headlights flashed in Ryan's eyes like lightning. Like lightning. For several seconds he was blinded. He shielded his eyes and heard the engine rev up and the tires spin and then he felt the car rush past, missing him by no more than two feet. The kids in the car shouted and laughed as they drove over the next hill and began spinning in wild circles along the straightaway that led past Eamon's house.

Ryan was blinking in the darkness with white and yellow spots before his eyes. He had fallen to his knees. God saved me, he had thought, and with his heart still racing, he'd clasped his hands together and offered up a prayer of thanksgiving.

"O, Lord," he whispered, "I promise I'll become a priest."

He made the sign of the cross. The stars were brightly shining. To the right he could see where skid marks were burned in the snow. He followed the path of the tire prints that came directly at him and then miraculously veered away at the last possible instant. He followed them left until he saw the rabbit.

The car had run the bunny down, crushing its midsection and rear legs. Its entrails were smeared in the snow, a glistening black smudge in the moonlight. Steam was rising from the flattened body. The bunny's tongue hung out and Ryan had seen the moon reflected in its lifeless eyes.

Gestas had his nose stuck into a bowl of soup. Ryan couldn't tell if the thief was enjoying it or was simply eating real fast to avoid tasting it. The idea of food, delicious or atrocious, left the Jesuit cold. He wondered if Chez de Sade had a nice *lapin écrasé en route*. Road kill cuisine was about it.

Ryan had often told the bunny story. "How'd you

become a priest, Father?" And Ryan would joke that he knew he'd be a priest when the rabbit died. The blessed event. Well, in the era of abortion and early pregnancy tests, the story had lost a lot of its punch. In the end, it was just macabre. But it did get a rise out of animal activists.

Those headlights had been like lightning. Why were death and lightning welded together in his memory? He wondered about this and remembered something else.

A penitent had once confessed adultery. There was nothing very strange about that. Some people do still think it's a sin. But this fellow had wept bitterly and was so pitiful that Ryan could almost have forgiven him. But that was God's job. God was the forgiving one. Then as now, Ryan was a bureaucrat. He dispensed the Sacraments like food stamps. For all he knew (or needed to know or cared to know), he'd never really witnessed contrition. If I had, he thought, I wouldn't have heard the same confessions over and over and over from the same penitents, now would I?

But this one fellow, at least, *had* seemed heartily sorry, and Ryan was happy to do the remitting, the saying of the formula, which he always heard first in his head in Latin before he spoke the words in English. *Te absolvo* . . . "I absolve you." But I don't have any other answers.

Ryan recalled how vividly the man described his sin. Whew! Ryan had been on the edge of his chair with his ear pressed to the screen just inches from the sinner's lips.

"Bless me, Father, for I have sinned. It's been ten or twelve years since I made a confession. Sorry. But I really don't think I had anything important to confess until now. You'll say I should have been here anyway, and maybe you're right. Maybe if I'd come to confession I wouldn't have done what I did.

"I'll get to the point. Father, I committed adultery. What is that, the . . . the seventh Commandment? I . . . I don't know how contrite I really am. I mean, if we hadn't been caught *in flagrante* by her husband, I don't know if I'd be here now. I'd like to believe I'd have come to my senses, but I guess I'll never know.

"I'll tell you how it started. We—our company—has a big Christmas party in the office every year. The woman . . . the one I, well, the one I sinned with . . . she's in accounting. I'm in sales. She's a couple of years older than I am, but we've both been at the company for about the same length of time—about ten years. And I've danced with her at every Christmas party since we started, but nothing happened until now.

"What happened is I felt her thighs against mine, and I got a boner. She'd never pressed against me like that before. See, I think it's that she's doing aerobics now and she loves her body. She ground against me, and when the music stopped, we looked at each other for a minute and then burst out laughing. She was staring at me with her eyes wide, and I heard myself ask her if she'd like a cigarette.

"She joked, 'Do you always smoke afterwards?' and that got us laughing more.

"Then I said, 'Come on to my office and I'll give you a cigar.'

"We stood together at the window and looked down at Fifth Avenue. I had some cigars in my desk. I gave her one and began to unwrap one for myself. She put hers, wrapper and all, into her mouth and moved it in and out a few times, giggled, and asked me if I'd ever had an affair.

"Father, I've been married for twenty years, and I swear I never even came close. I told her so and she said, 'Me neither.'

"She took the cigar from my mouth just as I was about to light it. She walked to the door and closed it.

" 'Listen,' she said, 'I'm probably crazy for saying

this, but I want you. If you want me, you can have me right here, right now.'

"When she said that, Father, it was like she'd taken twenty years off my life. I've stayed in pretty good shape, but I don't feel young anymore. She made me feel twenty-five. I missed the sexual revolution, you know, by maybe a year at most, and I'm thinking to myself that this is it. Finally! This woman with a firm body is asking *me* to make love to her right there on my desk.

"Twenty years I've been married and no woman *ever* said anything like that to me. Here I thought I was dead, and she's offering to resurrect me. Aw, hey, I'm sorry, Father. I didn't mean to be sacrilegious. I guess this is my week to break the Commandments, huh?

"I'm telling you, Father, I love my wife. She's a super lady, but I never even considered saying no to this other woman. I never thought of my wife. It was like I was back in the days before I was married, and the fantasy that never happened then was happening now. I just walked over and kissed her and it all happened.

"Anyway, I won't go into all the gory details . . . What? Well, of course, Father, I'm sure you *have* heard it all . . . Yes. Of course, if you think it'll be better for me to tell it all and get it off my chest . . .

"Well, she—we undressed each other. First she was down on her knees, you know, giving me . . . ah, head. And then I pushed her down onto the floor and went down on her. God, Father, you don't know what it's like . . . Ah, anyway, then we did it missionary style . . . Gee, Father, I can't seem to keep from insulting you. I . . . Huh? Right. Okay, I'll just press on.

"For once, I did everything right. We stood up and I went in her from behind while she had her hands on the window. It was like we were flying over Fifth Avenue. But then she stopped me. She turned around and sat on the sill and jerked me off until I came in her face, like in the porn movies. She even turned on my desk lamp so she could watch me squirt. That was that.

"My God. I listen to myself tell this, and I can imagine how awful this must sound to you. I really am sorry to have to put you through this. But you don't know what it's like out there now. Nobody really thinks these things are sinful anymore. Unless they get caught . . .

"First day back at work after the holidays, I called her up and asked her out for lunch. We ended up doing it all over again, with variations, in her office between twelve and one.

"Well, we decided this was definitely a bad idea— doing it in the office, I mean. So we started going to the Hilton. But one day she suggested we take a cab to the Village, and it turns out she and her husband keep a place in the city. They live up in Westchester, but they use the apartment here for when one of them has to stay over in the city on business. I didn't like it, but she said there was nothing to worry about.

"So we began to lie to our spouses, telling them we had to work late and stay over in the city. We did this so we could spend whole nights together. I don't think my wife ever suspected. But her husband did.

"Last night, we—the other woman and me—were lying in bed going at it, the covers thrown back and naked as jay birds. We were making so much noise that we didn't hear her husband and his lawyer and a shutterbug come into the apartment. I don't know how long they stood there in the bedroom doorway, but suddenly I heard a voice whisper, 'Do it.'

"I looked up. There was just enough street light coming in through the living room windows for me to see the outline of three forms standing at the bedroom door. Light glinted off the photographer's camera, and for an instant I thought we were about to be gunned down.

"I held up my hand as though I could stop the shot, but then the flashbulb popped. I shut my eyes and then opened them again, and there was the ghostly image of my extended arm and hand floating in the darkness before me. I'd blink and it would fade to black and then the image of the arm would reappear. The woman was sobbing. She knew what had happened and so did I.

"Oh, Father. I've probably broken my wife's heart. I have to tell her, don't I? Oh, God, I've done a terrible, terrible thing. If only I'd thought of what I might lose . . .

"Help me, Father. Tell me: what do I do now?"

Ryan remembered thinking, How the hell do I know? Give me the woman's phone number. An aerobics instructor, you say? Maybe I can comfort her . . . But you? You go eat shit and die.

Of course, what he told the man was the usual. God has already forgiven you. You're only human. Blah-blah-blah. He reached into his bag of platitudes and, like the old Wizard, he did his best to make the man believe he'd done nothing worse than cheat on his taxes (tell that to your wife!). Everybody does it. And the man had asked Ryan if he could shake his hand. So the Jesuit stepped out of the isolation booth, as he'd liked to call it, and glad-handed the poor wretch. He imagined that, for the man, it was like when Bennett Cerf and the other stumped panelists on "What's My Line" removed their blindfolds and met the mystery guest. And now, here's this afternoon's confessor . . . Father John J. Ryan! Big reaction from the crowd. Oh! And I thought it was Father Mahoney. Well, the man embraced him, and Ryan was quite moved. He couldn't resist a parting word or two or ten.

"Listen," he said, grasping the man's shoulder paternally, "men are men. These kind of goings-on are as old as the Bible. Don't get all worked up over it. As sins go, a little 'strange,' as we used to say, is pretty far down on the list."

And the man left walking on air. And Ryan had thought, Am I a priest or what?

But that was then. Back in the real world. Sitting here now on a curb in front of a movie house in Hell, Ryan couldn't shake from his memory the man's description of the flashbulb and the retinal image of his arm hanging in the darkness like his guilt. And this was like the headlights that blinded him just before he found the flattened rabbit. And all this was like something else. But what? He'd thought of it before. Of course! It was the lightning that had struck at the moment of his death. It's hard to remember dying, but he remembered the lightning. He knew he'd seen something in the flash; something he could not describe. Whatever it was that had been illuminated refused to take form now in his mind. Perhaps, he thought, I don't want to remember.

Ryan covered his face with his hands. He pressed hard against his eyeballs and made colored lights blaze in his brain. Then he looked up and blinked. He glanced across the street and saw that the waiter, who was an enormous fellow, was standing over Gestas now and shouting at him. Ryan heard the waiter's voice all the way over on the other side of the street but only in muffled tones; he couldn't make out any of the words. But the giant waiter was shaking a check in front of the Bad Thief's nose and Gestas was desperately shaking his purse, from which fell not a single penny. Ryan gathered that the management was demanding payment for the swill they'd served and that Gestas was a bit short. You don't want to be short.

Money's hard to come by in New Hell, most labor, after all, being slave labor, but when a big guy says, "Pay up!," you'd better give him something, anything. And there are other species of exchange. You've got sex, such as it is. And violence. Hope's a kind of currency too. And, speaking of hope, the dissidents love to come by real dollars and rubles and pounds and francs that, one way or another, get smuggled into the dark kingdom. You can't spend the stuff here, but the point is they hope to take it with them when (and *if*) they escape. "Orphean jack" it's called. But Gestas was flat busted.

So the waiter picked him up by the ankles and carried him to the door. The world famous Gestas was then drop-kicked into the street.

The addled thief sat in the dirt for a moment. He peered around to see who'd witnessed his ignominy, then he shrugged and, when the waiter turned his back, shot him the bird. It was, Ryan reflected, an affecting sight—seeing this man of the first century using a gesture of the twentieth, but that's the kingdom for you. Heaven, one supposes, must be of a unity—one people in one time. But this place! Here everybody's going this way and that, struggling to justify themselves in the idiom of their own time but freely borrowing from every other era too. It put Ryan in mind of those discomfiting subway rides when he'd hear a couple of South Bronx spics jabbering away in their rapid fire gibberish *and* lapsing into King James English too. Poly- . . . poly-something or other. A man needs to be rooted in one time, but nobody here belongs anywhere anymore.

What a world, Ryan thought. What a world. Oh, I'm melting . . . melting. Now what movie was that? Grrr, it's maddening not to remember! I wonder, he thought, does a man burn because of what he remembers or because of what he can't remember? Well, give the Devil his due; you're damned if you don't and damned if you do. Hey! I'm a goddamned poet and don't know it.

But I do feel like I'm melting; like I'm out of control. I can't stop it. I can't change, no matter how much I want to. What was it Cardinal Newman wrote? "To live is to change; to enter the kingdom of Heaven is to have changed often." But that won't wash down here. Down here the only theologian worth his salt is Alfred E. Neuman—not John Henry, the cardinal.

Ryan recalled the postcard he'd bought in a motel gift shop outside of Pensacola. On the glossy side was a color picture of the smiling idiot from *MAD Magazine*, and beneath his famous, "What me worry?" were the words:

Why worry?
When you die, you'll either go to Heaven or to Hell.
If you go to Heaven, you'll never worry about anything ever again.
If you go to Hell, you'll be so busy shaking hands with all your old friends,
you won't have time to worry!

MAD Magazine . . . Now *that*'s a significant bit of evidence. He should have recognized it as such at the time. But that's just it. He didn't. I didn't, he thought. All around me all the time there were signs, but I couldn't interpret them. I thought I could, but I misread everything. Why did God hide all the ways and places of His Presence? Why? Because He wanted us to fail? Well, He shouldn't have allowed us to choose. That was stupid. That was cruel. And then when you die you're struck by lightning.

Ryan shook himself from woolgathering just as Gestas was limping out of sight at the end of the avenue. By the time the Jesuit caught up to within fifty yards of him, the thief was heading up into the hills. But this was great! Ryan knew these hills quite well. He came often to walk and think, and he knew shortcuts that allowed him to save time and effort climbing. He usually went no higher than the rock formations that jutted out just below the crest of the hills and formed a barrier he was loathe to cross. He had no desire to venture over the summit to discover what horrors lay on the other side, but to his disgust (*naturally*, he thought), Gestas disappeared right over the top.

But how? The ridge was impassable. At my age, Ryan thought . . . whatever age I am . . . I certainly can't go gracefully scaling these rocks. Impassable, I tell you. But how did Gestas manage . . .

And then he saw it—a pass. There was a narrow gap between two enormous boulders, and (cripes!) scrawled on one was a directional arrow that he recognized as the Sign of the Fish. Great. He was carp bait for sure if he went on. The Sign was the symbol of the ancient acrostic that used the letters of the Greek word for fish, *ichthys*, to stand for Jesus (*i*) Christ (*ch*), God's (*th*) Son (*y*), Savior (*s*); to stand, in other words, for t-r-o-u-b-l-e. Ryan had memorized the code when he was a seminarian. He was sorry he had. Now he was sure Gestas was still counted among the religious dissidents and Bible smugglers and chasing after him was undoubtedly a really rotten idea that was only going to get him into some really deep shit. And yet he squeezed between the rocks and went on in spite of himself, eager to see what lay beyond.

He was shocked. What lay before him was a vast field of dark purple lilies. Imagine! Flowers growing in Hell. There were tall street lamp-like Gro-lites encircling the field, and from the long, perfectly spaced rows, Ryan surmised that these weren't wildflowers. This was a garden.

He started down the hillside, lost his balance and went into a tumble. He rolled ass-over-elbows all the way to the edge of the garden. His head struck a sprinkler jet and he lay there for a moment seeing stars. Then he sat up. He could have reached out and picked a lily, but he was willing to bet that doing so would surely violate some damned ordinance. He didn't want to anger the gardener, whoever that was. But he did lean over to catch a whiff of their scent. They smelled like rotten eggs.

He got to his feet and brushed himself off. Just then the sprinkler system came on and he was spattered. He stepped back to avoid getting soaked and wiped the water from his face. But when he looked at his hands, he saw it was blood that had sprayed him. He drew back and nearly lost his balance again. He stood for a moment, swinging his arms to keep from falling, on the edge of a long, deep irrigation ditch. He teetered and was about to fall when another man came scrambling up out of the ditch and knocked Ryan back. The man's eyes were wild and he was covered in blood. He stared at Ryan. He shrieked and ran off. It was Gestas.

"Gestas!" Ryan called after him.

Gestas looked over his shoulder, shrieked again and kept on running until he ran—smack—into a man sized rock and fell like a timbered tree. Ryan ran after him and, when he got to him, fell to one knee and began to shake the thief, hoping to revive him.

Gestas moaned.

"Is it you?" he mumbled. "Is it you?"

"Yes. It's Father Ryan, Gestas. Are you all right?"

"Huh!" Gestas barked, opening his eyes. "Who's that?"

When he recognized Ryan he jumped up and stumbled behind the big rock. Ryan could hear him whispering. The Jesuit frowned and shook his head. What a golem. Ryan walked around the rock and saw Gestas kneeling before the stone with his head cocked as though he were listening to it speak.

He was. The rock was Origen. Ryan saw the Egyptian's grey face and one grey arm protruding from the stone. So this is what had become of the heretic. Satan had turned him into a sculpture. A monument. It reminded Ryan of the blocks of marble lining the long gallery leading up to Michaelangelo's David at the *Accademia* in Florence. The blocks were unfinished works, and the figures emerging from them were like characters snatched from the *Inferno*. Ryan had looked at those incomplete statues and knew he was seeing the condition of souls in Hell. Some other priests with whom he was travelling noticed that Ryan's eyes were wide and his breathing labored. He'd begun to clutch his throat, and his companions (and himself) were sure he was having a heart attack. But it was only (and this he could not tell them) that Ryan knew then that he would one day be turned to stone.

Gestas was wiping his blood-stained hands on his trousers and eyeing Ryan distrustfully. He glanced at the rock and then said to Ryan:

"He wants to talk to you."

At first, Ryan figured Gestas, being Gestas, was talking to the stone, and he thought, Well, I'd like to talk to Origen too, Gestas, but I'd just be talking to myself, now wouldn't I? The way I used to when I said prayers at the statues in the church. *You* may be—no, you *are*—nuts enough to talk to a slab of granite, *but not me*.

"He wants to know how you found us here."

Ryan looked at Gestas.

"What?"

"I said, 'Origen wants to know how you found us'. As if that wasn't obvious, you stinkin' snoop. Aw, shit! Origen, dammit . . . I'm really in for it this time."

Gestas collapsed against the rock and grimly pounded a fist against Origen's flinty forehead. It was then that Ryan noticed something very eerie. Origen's left eye was animated. A real eye! My God, Ryan realized, he's fused in the rock.

Ryan felt profoundly enervated. He knew this was what it came down to. Satan owned them and would countenance no rebellion. Hell was the worst thing imaginable, but it got even worse if you got out of line. No doubt about it. He *had* to toe the line.

And yet he couldn't escape the almost sickening addiction to compassion that made him want to reach out

to Origen in some way. What had this man done to
deserve such a destiny? He loved his Lord, even if he
didn't understand Him. Was being wrong such a terrible thing? Origen never did the Devil's work. Not in
life, but that was no distinction, Ryan realized, neither
did I. Did I? But Origen held true to his faith even in
Hell. How many others could say that? How many . . .

But you'd better walk away, Bucko, he told himself.
Or your ass is grass . . . 'which today is in the field, but
tomorrow is cast into the furnace' . . . Why is it I never
paid attention to that passage?

He decided to beat it. What could he possibly do to
help Origen anyhow? But he simply couldn't stop himself from asking:

"Is there anything I can do?"

Gestas put his ear near the line that etched Origen's
lips and listened intently.

"He says, 'Pray for me.' "

Ryan shook his head and almost laughed.

"Ask him what *else* I can do. I'm fresh out of prayers
today."

The Bad Thief's face became quite relaxed. He looked
up at Ryan and the Jesuit saw that the thief's eyes had
become clear and calm. Those are Origen's eyes now,
Ryan thought. Well, Origen's mind is behind those
eyes.

"Wait a while, Father," Gestas said softly, and Ryan
recognized the voice as Origen's.

"Wait for what?"

"For the end."

Ryan made a sweeping motion with his hand.

"What would you call this?"

"This? This is what you might call the oven. But not
far from where we are is what you might call the
refrigerator. Are these the correct words? The lids . . .
no, excuse me, the *doors* of both appliances are open.
You must wait until they close."

Ryan was nodding his head.

"Right. Well, I'm glad you cleared that up. That explains everything. Eternity's a kitchen, right? Fine. Well, *I* do not want to be baked or frozen, and I don't want to cross the Chef."

Ovens, refrigerators, kitchen. Pots and pans. Broken china and dirty glasses. Frying, searing, baking. But wait, if the door of the frig is open, won't the ice cream melt? Melt . . .

The body of Gestas rested limply against the rock. The light of Origen's intellect shined in the thief's eyes, possessing him.

"I am," the Egyptian said, "uncomfortable in the idiom of your time. Try to understand. This rock impedes my thought and, as you can observe, my ability to speak. Please listen and understand.

"The oven you can comprehend. The other is the . . . *interim refrigerium*. How should I translate?"

Interim refrigerium, Ryan thought. The pause that refreshes? He shrugged at Gestas and then glanced at the rock's one good eye. Where *do* I look, anyhow? And he shrugged again.

"After the first death," the voice of Origen explained, "there is waiting. Until the Last Judgement, the oven, Hell, and the *interim*, what you call Purgatory, are simply antechambers."

So what's that mean? Ryan wondered. Some—I guess—are in the first class lounge at JFK waiting to take the Concorde to Paradise and others are sitting on benches at Port Authority waiting to take a Trailways to Hell. What's the dif if we're here and our tickets are stamped?

"Our tickets are bought, aren't they?" Ryan mumbled.

"No. None is lost. We remain as free today as ever we were in life."

Ah, Ryan realized, the old heresy. Of course.

"But Origen," he said sanctimoniously, "*we* aren't free. *We* are prisoners—the condemned. Our failures are final. We'll never escape. Never."

Gestas smiled weakly and as the thief's lips moved, Origen said:

"No. God is more powerful than you can imagine—so mighty. So very mighty that He made Himself humble to love us. He made us free, and so He made Himself weak. He allows us to choose, knows every choice we could make, but He chooses not to know—He cannot know—what we *will* choose.

"It is a paradox, no? To be free yet seem to be a slave. But until the end of all, all may change. We come and go.

"Did not Satan go forth from Heaven? He left with his angels and fell here to the dark kingdom. It was a very long time ago, but their falling goes on.

"And now, demons are going forth from here. They go among men and whisper into human imagination all the unspeakable sins we master."

"And good angels go forth as well, guarding us from the demons and protecting us from ourselves.

"In the end, all the . . . upwardly mobile souls in the *interim* will go forth, patched and polished, into the eternal and immutable Kingdom of God. No one will remain on the earth. All will have come to one moment . . . one idea. A yes or a no.

"We come and go because we are free. Men and angels. Living and dead. Some are good because they choose to be. Demons and the damned are evil because that's what they want. This is the law, the law of liberty.

"When the Last Judgement comes, *then* will the law be repealed. Then the choosing will cease, and love will no longer be diminished by hate. The oven will rage. There will be everlasting conflagration—no dreams, no comforts.

"But, my dear friend, the oven may be empty."

Ryan steadied himself against the rock.

"All around us now," Origen continued, "especially . . . above us there are souls watching us and praying for us. Do you know that in Purgatory, in the *interim*, the prayers of the Church militant fall upon the suffering souls as rain? Did you know that? Someday, I believe, it will rain tears here. It will be as though the earth were collapsing and the oceans had begun to seep through, but it will be the Church triumphant weeping for us, welcoming us. Purgatory leaking . . . weeping for joy."

The body of Gestas went limp for a moment, and then the Bad Thief roused himself and began to shake his head vigorously. He looked up and recognized the Jesuit spy and groaned. Then he sighed. He looked at the grey stone face of Origen sticking out of the rock and, with great solemnity, said:

"Aw, Origen, dontcha see? All this hope is hopeless."

But Ryan wasn't so sure. He wasn't sure at all. I mean, it makes sense, he thought. I'm lost, but that doesn't mean I'll never ever be found. They're searching for me now, and as long as I . . . well, like Origen said, as long as I'm . . . free, as long as I can choose, I'm holding the last trump!

Ryan was rubbing his hands together.

"Hey, Black Robe," Gestas, the real Gestas, said coldly, "the Egyptian says, 'Don't make the same old mistake.' "

Gestas hadn't even put his ear down close to Origen's mouth. Ryan doubted that Gestas was relaying a message from Origen. Still it would be injudicious not to hear him out.

" 'The old mistake'," Ryan sniffed. "Whatever does that mean?"

Gestas looked at Ryan with loathing.

"He means don' wait for the stinkin' cavalry. He means don' go bein' no good boy. He means don', for Crissakes, succeed."

Were these Origen's words or simply the thief's spleen? The great Gestas. Hah! Well, Ryan smiled to himself, it doesn't really matter. This little drama isn't over after all. There's going to be a reversal of fortune in the last act. It was exactly as he'd thought when he'd first found himself down here. *If you can hope, this can't be Hell. And now I've done it! I've found the proof.*

He was about to clap his hands and dance a little jig, when he noticed that Gestas was running away as fast as his wounded feet would carry him. Ryan looked at the rock and saw that Origen's one good eye was now grey and still.

And then he was aware of the shadows lurking behind him. He tried to look around but, as in a dream, couldn't budge. He heard two sets of heavy footsteps approaching and then felt himself being lifted up. He knew he wasn't being carried off by angels. *Not yet, anyway.*

The Jesuit's feet never touched the ground all the way to the nifty little dacha Satan kept on the outskirts of the city. The two bullyboys held him up by his armpits and paraded him along as though he were a common felon! As the trio passed by, onlookers would either avert their eyes or grin ghoulishly at the sight of a priest being led off to face the Muzak. Ryan was terribly embarrassed. *So what else is new?*

They reached the gates of Satan's mansion and were admitted along a winding drive lined by incinerated pines and other dead fauna. His escorts left Ryan at the big front door and walked off without ever having spoken a word. Presently the door opened and Ryan was ushered into an entrance hallway by yet another of the Boss's mute lackeys. The servant led him through room after room of the most advanced communications equipment you've ever seen. The screens of ten thousand televisions were lighted with images from all over the world and Hell too. Ryan heard the din of hundreds of languages and assumed this must be the headquarters of Satan's intelligence network. He wondered if any of the sets was tuned to a New York station. *Can you pick up broadcasts from Heaven down here?*

After walking for quite a while, Ryan was delivered to a door that opened into the back yard. The servant pointed to a small outbuilding and then left. Ryan walked towards it and saw that the land here was part of a bluff of sorts overlooking the shimmering lights and orange glow of New Hell. It was almost beautiful.

Ryan went to the door of the outbuilding, knocked twice, and waited. Nothing. He knocked again. He waited several minutes and then opened the door just a crack. He turned the knob carefully and gently pushed on the door as if he expected an explosion. He tiptoed inside and saw the Evil One, dressed in chinos and a polo shirt, sitting upon a stool before a workbench on which there were clay pots and bags of soil and a number of the lilies he'd seen on the far side of the hills. Gro-lites were focused on the plants and there were gardening tools hanging neatly along the walls. It was a tidy little potting shed.

John J. Ryan, S.J., who once had vowed to defend orthodoxy and to guard his own purity, stood with his arms at his sides. This was only his second encounter with the Prince, and he was filled with fear.

At last the Devil spun around on his stool and brushed the soil from his hands.

"Do you have any hobbies, J.J.?" the Devil asked.

Ryan managed to shake his head. "J.J." had been his mother's pet name for him, and it made his testicles shrivel to hear the Devil use it. Hobbies? Not really—unless you wanted to count the movies and maybe masturbation. But that was then. The Jesuit shook his head again.

"Too bad," the Prince of Darkness sighed. "It helps, believe you me. My *fleurs* help take my mind off the Work. I love the Work, but I need *this* time too."

Satan stretched his arms over his head and yawned. He looked lovingly at one of the potted lilies and smiled.

"You know, it took me more than five hundred years to create this hybrid."

He stroked the stem of the flower with the knuckles of his right hand.

"Know anything about botany? No? Shame. This beauty is a cross of amaranth and belladonna. I could regale you with genetic nuances, but I gather the details would be wasted on you. Besides, we haven't the time, you and I, do we? I call it the blood narcissus. I take it you've seen why. Yes?"

"Blood narcissus is the rarest flower that flourishes in Hell. That blood we use to water the plants is fresh and comes straight from your old world—mostly from 'Revolutionary Kampuchea' these days. We've tried using the cat's piss and cherry syrup that passes for blood down here, but it's no damned good. 'Course, that's not a big problem. We get all the surface blood we need. And I'll tell you, the best hobby's the one that compliments your job. Our surface Work is very much a blood business, so the two dovetail quite nicely."

"You know, J.J.—and this'll surprise you—I often think the flower's the most significant achievement of my long, long existence. I know, I know. You wonder how that can be. What about that first Garden? The way I bamboozled your great-great-grandparents. What about famine and pestilence and war? Yeah, yeah. Those things are very fine indeed, but in my old age . . . and as the time grows short, I think all the evil we've achieved in the world is important only for the bloodshed and the bloodshed's important only for plant food.

"But look, you're probably thinking I had you brought here for punishment." The Devil shook a finger at Ryan. "You've been rubbing elbows with the optimists again, haven't you? Hey, it pisses me off, okay? Really. But . . . I've decided to look the other way for now—if (and that's a big if) *you*'ll play ball with me from this moment on."

Satan walked over to the Jesuit and patted him on the shoulder. Then he pointed to a lawn chair and Ryan sat down. Satan remained standing and leaned back against the wall. He put his hands in the pockets of his chinos and crossed his legs at the ankles. Ryan saw that he was wearing no socks inside his Topsiders.

"Father Ryan," the Devil began. "I'm going to tell you a few things that only a few folks have ever heard. I think you've got what it takes to do the Work. Jesuits, especially those with qualms about being here, are still a novelty in Hell, you know, and you're just the sort of fellow I think has the right instincts for an opening we've got in Surface Intelligence."

In spite of himself, Ryan felt his heart swell with excitement and pride. A job? For *me*? And on the surface!

"And frankly, although Origen's pretty much out of action for the duration, I'd love to have you on our team just because he and his bunch expect to have you on theirs."

"I have a feeling it won't be too long before the old Egyptian becomes a regular Mount Rushmore. And to be perfectly honest, I don't give a care. Hey, they wanna piss and moan over a block of granite, that's their beeswax. I'd better have the stone moved, though. I don't want those boobs tracking through my garden or, worse—picking my flowers to lay at their precious monument."

Satan pushed himself off the wall and began to pace as he spoke.

"Now the last time we met, I gave you a little lecture about freedom, am I right? Uh huh. I was eloquent, wasn't I? . . . *I was eloquent, yes*? Well, thanks a heap. So. Have you been thinking about what I said?"

Ryan nodded. He'd been thinking about little else.

"Good. That's good. Given a chance, Ryan, and a little loosening up, I think you can think with the best of them. And if you succeed, it'll be because (and only because) you've understood one simple fact. Now what's that? Well, let's do a little catechism, alright. Okay.

Here it is: evil and freedom are two faces on a single coin."

Satan raised his eyebrows at the Jesuit. Got it? Ryan didn't seem to.

"Look at it from the other side," Satan went on. "Good is synonymous with obedience. Your Heavenly Host are citizens in a totalitarian state."

And then the cobwebs were swept from Ryan's brain. Clear thoughts clicked on just as if a switch had been thrown.

"What is Hell," he asked, catching himself and holding down a sarcastic tone, "a *democracy*?"

Satan smiled and slapped a hand against his thigh.

"Good question. Excellent question! The answer, of course, is no. Freedom does not thrive in a democracy any more than in a dictatorship. Anarchy, which is freedom squared, doesn't work in your old world (or in mine) because earthlings, like angels, are incurably bourgeois. That, as they say, is life—certainly not our problem. Because here chaos is perfected. Or should I say, 'is perfecting.' "

"But Hell is one great, lugubrious bureaucracy," Ryan said heatedly. He was warming to the argument. "It's rules, rules, rules. What kind of anarchy is it that has so damned many rules?"

The Prince nodded.

"The rules, my friend, are an agitation, nothing more. They are a source of torment, and torment (damnation, if you like) is the means by which freedom is realized . . . not that many have realized it yet."

Ryan was shaking his head again, his confidence growing.

"But what," the Jesuit asked with a splash of his old pulpit manner, "is the end at the . . . end of those means? What is the point of freedom? Is there no peace? No love?"

Satan sighed. He narrowed his eyes at the priest.

"Have I overestimated you? I wonder . . . Peace and

love, Ryan? Oh come on. How can there be peace in a free world with competing ideas—of different strengths and weaknesses? Ryan, be real! How can love overcome self-love? You and I are selfish. And I mean we *are* selfish—selfishness itself. And that's what you must accept. *Must.*

"But look. I'm not going to repeat myself. You've heard all this. God made us free. The freer we are, the more as God made us. Rebellion and anarchy are the acts that make us like God.

"So you can see why mischief is critical to my work. If we are to win souls—well, *steal* them—we've got to be as devious as possible. You can help. I want to send you back to New York. Not to haunt but to observe and report. You won't be your old self, of course, and there will be hardships, but I think you'll find the challenges greater than those in the Bureau of Error and Illusion.

"You're unsure, I can see. Uncertainty is nature. To act with assurance, to choose to treat one among the many uncertainties as a certainty, *this* is to be alive. Paradoxical, ain't it? Now that you're dead, you've got a chance to be really alive!"

Manhattan! To walk the streets of the city again— even if only as a shadow . . . Wow! Ryan thought. I'm having a pretty good day.

But then he recalled all that Origen had told him. And he thought of the warning Gestas had relayed. Don't succeed, the thief had said. Ryan felt the full tension of the possibilities Origen and Satan were presenting. He realized he couldn't be excited about both. Could he?

"I *am* uncertain," he admitted to the Devil. "I'm especially fuzzy about the end of all this. I suppose you intend to go out in a blaze of infamy—"

"—What do you mean, 'go out'?"

"Well, at the Last Judgement . . . when we'll no longer *be* free."

Satan sighed a long, angry sigh.

"So that's it. You're afraid of getting stuck in the elevator, aren't you? You think a time will come when you'll get on a man-sized lift and the doors will shut and there you'll be—in the dark struggling to draw your last breath; struggling eternally. But, Ryan, this is just Origen's old apocatastatic heresy in a more orthodox shade. Your Last Judgement gets everybody off the hook, doesn't it. Freedom didn't work (it was a nice idea but it didn't work), so God, being a Big Man, decides to roll up the rug and have a real big party. Some are invited and some are left out. But nobody chooses. Just dance or weep, and that's it.

"*You* are hoping, of course, that you'll get an invite, right? If you do then, whew! it was tough but it's over. No more hard choices. No more choices, period! The great, good God has decreed you're either in or you're out but, above all, you're done. Freedom goes on to the ash heap along with polio and the internal combustion engine and all the other interim calamities and inventions we use and then abandon when blessed progress delivers us to a higher truth. And isn't He a good God! He's finally done what we've always wanted Him to do. He's absolved us of responsibility!

"Sorry. God doesn't uncreate what he creates. That wouldn't be kosher, and He's a kosher kinda guy. Oh, there *may* come a time when all this passes away, but there'll never be a time when you and I won't have to tie our *own* shoes."

Satan raised his eyebrows at Ryan: Got it? Ryan nodded: Got it.

"Okay, Father," Satan said, taking Ryan by the arm and showing him to the door, "the ball's in your court." He patted the Jesuit on the back. "My advice is be what you are. Hope is just an excuse to avoid the rebellion that's human nature. Even a Jesuit can be a natural man, can't he?

"Think about it. Say the word and we'll put you in

the Work. The Big Apple wouldn't be such hard duty, would it?"

When Ryan was ushered out of his confab with the Boss, he knew he had some rugged thinking ahead of him and some very woeful decisions to make. He could have gone back to the rectory he shared with some other failed clerics. That was probably a good idea. It would look good. Maybe he'd finally agree to concelebrate a Black Mass in the church, Crowley Cathedral. He might have a lie-down after and try to relax. Sleep was out of the question, but sometimes it was soothing just to close the old peepers. Other times it was terrifying. With his eyes shut, he could see things. He could see where he really was. Is. The pleasant pretense of imagining he was somewhere else would fall like the blade of a guillotine.

No, not the rectory. No, he thought, I believe I'll go back to the hills and stretch my legs there. A little exercise is recommended for clear thinking.

Of course he knew this was a bad idea, not because he despised exercise, which he did, but because he knew he'd be unable to resist visiting Origen. And that would surely be noted and probably punished. Why don't I care, he wondered? I *do* care. But Origen's the only friend I have down here. A man needs friends.

So up to the hills he went. He squeezed between the boulders marked by the Sign of the Fish, slid down the tall bank and then walked carefully around Satan's garden of blood narcissus. He came to the rock and the man trapped inside the rock. He sat on the ground and looked up at the granite death mask. Perhaps Origen would hear his confession.

"Can you hear me? I do wish I could hear you. I've just come from the Devil, you know. He's offered me a position in his service. I don't want to accept, but I don't know how to say no. I want to believe that, as you said, someday it will rain tears here and that some day the Lord will come harrowing again and take us with him to Paradise, but Satan is awfully convincing on the subject of freedom. He says things are as they are and always will be. He says the end will never come.

"My soul's a desert. If there's an oasis down here, I wish you'd show me where it is. Without clear, cool water to drink, what can I find to quench this thirst *except* blood?

"I know you'd tell me to have some faith, but I never even had a little. I never cared for anybody but myself, and Hell's a lousy place to begin to learn to care for others. I'm more likely to be struck by lightning than I am to learn to be patient and love."

Lightning? Now he remembered! He knew exactly what it was he'd seen in the lightning when he died. It was God's Face! He knew it, and he knew he'd always known it. God as He is had flashed before him. And Ryan had recoiled. He couldn't look. He'd *hated* the sight.

And then the Jesuit felt the Presence. God's eyes were on him even now.

And then—CRACK!—lightning struck behind him. Ryan felt the fear crawling up his back like a current. Look! he ordered himself. Look at Him now! But even as the thought formed in his brain, he was desperately trying to crawl beneath the soil. He wanted to cover himself with rock and dirt, to hide, but escape was impossible. It was the one true impossibility.

Oh, he wanted to cry out, if only God did not exist! And he clutched his side. "If only" was *Verboten*. He was burning up. He'd not known the fires of Hell could be so intense. He had not known those fires were shame.

Thunder sounded above him, and he heard a sound like wailing. It began to rain. The raindrops beaded in the dust that covered the rock that was Origen. Ryan turned his face up into the rain and caught a drop on his tongue. It was salty. It was a tear.

The rain swept down in sheets from above the sur-
rounding hills. All over the garden, steam was rising as
the prayers of the faithful rained down on molten rock.
The raindrops made streaks on Origen's face and left
trails the color of flesh.

Ryan jumped up and began rubbing the Egyptian's
face. He cupped his hands to trap the raindrops and
then threw the precious liquid onto the stone. He was
rubbing the rock, feeling it becoming flesh, when he
looked up at the top of the hill overlooking the garden.
Satan stood there beneath an umbrella watching Ryan's
attempts to revive Origen. The Devil shook his head
sadly.

Ryan's arms dropped to his sides. He wanted to help
his friend, but he didn't want to cross the Boss. It was a
dilemma the Jesuit might have resolved with a choice,
but the rain stopped. The hot porous ground sucked up
the tears and soon the only moisture was Ryan's own
sweat. He wiped some from his forehead and discreetly
massaged it on Origen's cheek, but it had no effect.
Origen was solid rock again.

Ryan glanced up at the top of the ridge. Satan was
closing his umbrella. The Devil held out a hand, palm
up. He smiled.

When Ryan returned to the Bureau of Error and
Illusion, it was because he knew he had nowhere else
to go. As far as *he* was concerned, his options remained
open. He didn't know on whose team he'd finish the
season, Christ's or the Devil's, but he knew he'd play.
And this is not a decision you make lightly or quickly!
He needed time to think it through. Yes, yes. I know,
Ryan told himself: "He who hesitates is lost." Well . . .
that'd be some very serious "lost" that would outdo the
lost I already am.

Ah, ambivalence, Satan might have sighed.

All in all, despite the incident in the rain near the
garden of blood narcissus, Ryan was feeling pretty sunny

about his prospects. He thought the best thing he could
do would be to report for work as usual and use the less
than taxing office hours to begin to formulate a plan for
making up his mind. Should he stay true to the old
school, or should he take the plunge? The truth was, he
hadn't the foggiest notion which way to go. He wasn't
even sure he *could* go whichever way he *might* choose.
In fact, he was so damned confused, it was all he could
do to put one foot in front of the other.

Which is why he decided to take the elevator instead
of all those stairs. He got on in the lobby. He pushed
his floor. The doors closed and the car soared up; the
bell dinged and the doors opened. He stepped out into
the dark hallway and let out a satisfied sigh. Now that's
a very good sign, I think, he thought. I have the feeling
the Boss is watching over me. Of course, I *am* a few
minutes early, and nobody's ever early. There's probably no economy in having the lift break down with just
one soul stuck in it. On the other hand, I've already
been singled out for special treatment, so it's probably
Satan reminding me what it's like to be a part of the
. . . the Work. Unless it was the Lord who made the
elevator work. But I haven't seen His hand in things
down here any more than I did up top.

Ryan was turning over these possibilities and options
as he felt his way down the dark corridor towards the
office. He could see the office doorway up ahead. Just a
blush of the red glow from outside was hanging there in
the threshold. Once inside, Ryan would find the chair
at his desk, sit down, and wait to see if the great Gestas
would show up, which he very much doubted. Ryan
had a feeling Gestas was currently being fitted with a
granite overcoat.

So the Jesuit planned to sit and wait until the door
was shut, prison-like, and sealed, tomb-like, and until
another period of form-sorting came to an end. Ryan
was looking forward to a session in solitude, when he

stumbled on a body that lay stretched out in front of the office door.

The man groaned. Ryan stepped back.

"Gestas?"

The man groaned again. It didn't sound like the Bad Thief's groan. Ryan moved towards the recumbent figure and gave it a kick in the ribs. More groaning but nothing else, so Ryan gave another scornful boot and then stepped over the body and went into the office.

Ryan wished he had a copy of the *New York Times* and a cup of hot black coffee. That would make even a morning in Hell tolerable. He longed to know the news from home. Well, he thought, take Satan's offer and go and see for yourself. Still, I hate to think what sort of honeycombs and spider webs I'd be expected to make of people's souls. Satan hadn't said what duties a fellow doing surface Work is given, but they couldn't be pleasant—not if you had scruples anyway. Ryan was just beginning to realize he didn't have too many of those when he became aware that the man outside the door was trying to rouse himself and get up on his feet. Was he drunk? Or was he just new? A lot of the newly damned go about in a kind of daze; they can't accept what's become of them, so they struggle to dream away the horrors of Hell, only to find that repression makes them worse.

It wasn't compassion that forced Ryan from his comfortable musings about demonizing but the aggravation that the man's slipping and whining was giving him. The Jesuit was in no mood for distractions. In just ten or fifteen minutes, the lights would come on and the door would shut and the lovely glow and soothing quiet would be lost. Ryan meant to shove the man to the fire stairs and then give him a push.

He grabbed the poor man by the collar of his jacket and began to drag him along. The wretch thought a kind soul had come to his aid and muttered:

"God bless you, sir."

He *would* say that, Ryan thought. Here I am about to send him tumbling over the railing of the fire stairs, and he takes me for the Good Samaritan. I guess the Lord is here . . . having His little jokes.

Ryan had the man out on the landing, ready to give him one last kick, when he was aware of the sweetness of the man's embrace. The man was holding on, trusting. It was the feeling Ryan wanted to feel when he was a priest in his parish in New York City, but he hadn't felt it then, because his wealthy, successful parishioners hadn't needed him and had kept him at a safe, if also occasionally respectful, distance. No one had ever leaned on him as this fellow was now. So, Ryan tightened his hold on the man and hauled him into the office. When the man was settled into a chair, he began to come around.

He looked up into the dark room and out at the red glow beyond the windows. Ryan could see the recognition strike the man with a jolt. He knew where he was all right. He buried his face in his hands.

Ryan would have offered him a shot of whiskey, but . . .

"Is this," the man mumbled, "the place where I can see someone about a mistake that's been made?"

John J. Ryan, S.J., did not need to ask the man what mistake he thought had been made. Oh no.

"You'll be wanting Form 7-11-Z, *Claim of Wrongful Damnation,* but I'm afraid it's not going to do you much good. I'm not saying you're stuck here forever," the Jesuit said, noting the man's crestfallen expression, "but the administrative resources of New Hell will get you nowhere. Sorry."

"And now, my son, you must get on about . . . about your business. Our office doors are about to be sealed. I'm sure you don't want to be stuck in here with me."

The man sat in the shadows with his head hanging down.

"Where will I go?"

Ryan never had much patience with lost souls.

"I don't know," the Jesuit said; "just go."

But the man wouldn't budge. If Ryan were wearing a watch, he'd have been looking nervously at his wrist.

"Look, I'm sorry you ended up here, but it's not my fault, is it? I really do not want you hanging around here. Here's a copy of the form. Take it with you *as you leave.*"

Now Ryan had the man by a limp elbow and was shoving him towards the door, but—Soosshhh—the door was sucked shut, the lights came on, and it was Ryan's turn to moan.

He let go of the man's elbow, turned in a huff, and stalked back to his desk. He sat down heavily and began riffling through the exit visas.

"Excuse me," the man said; "got a pen?"

Ryan looked up at the man and scowled. He saw the man's face clearly for the first time. He squinted to get a better look.

"Don't I know you?" he asked the man.

The man was staring back at him and trembling with rage.

"It's you, you lying son-of-a-bitch!" he shouted.

Ryan recognized him! It was his favorite adulterer—the man with the floating arm.

"*You,*" the man growled between clenched teeth. "You *told* me I was forgiven."

He was coming across the room with murder in his eyes. Ryan began backing up.

"Please . . . please!" the Jesuit pleaded. "*I'm* not to blame. I was just doing what *they* told me to do."

But the man was not listening to excuses now. The quaking snake in the black cassock was *his* murderer, and he was going to have his revenge.

He grabbed Ryan by the neck and then grabbed Ryan's crotch. He lifted the Jesuit over his head and stepped to the window. With all his might, the man hurled his victim at the glass. The glass broke, and Ryan went hurtling towards the ground. The adulterer stood at the shattered window and watched the priest, who'd absolved him and told him there were worse sins than adultery, fall to yet another death. The man heard the priest cry out:

"Damnation!"

And the man thought, You should have told me that the first time.

DEATH FREAKS
Robert Sheckley

"Is the new one ready yet?" The Undertaker asked
one of the Morticians who worked under him.

"Yes he is, sir," the Mortician said. "We've just gotten through sewing him up. Did a good job on it this
time because we knew you had an interest in him."

Usually, The Undertaker's job was routine: greeting
the newly-animated dead after the Morticians had finished sewing them up and preparing them for another
round of infernal misery. The Undertaker liked to be
there when the dead awoke, standing right over them,
his long, terrible cadaverous face just inches from theirs.
How comical it was to see the newly-awakened dead
open their eyes and look at him, and then past him at
the bloodstained horrors of The Mortuary.

The first-time dead were sometimes pretty cute.
"What? I'm in Hell? Thank God, I thought I was in
Jersey City."

And the Old Dead were even better. They were the
ones who had already lived through Hell at least once,
been killed, and now found themselves reborn to another round of agonies.

The Undertaker liked the look on their faces when they realized the game—another round of infernal misery, then death again, and then rebirth, and so on and so on until the end of time or the beginning of forgiveness.

This particular reanimee was an old acquaintance of The Undertaker. He lay on the white marble slab, fully dressed in the black clothing and knee-breeches worn in the days of the French Revolution. He wore his famous red silk cravat tied just so. His long terrible face with the pallor of the madhouse upon it, except for his cheeks, which burned with the hectic flush of criminal insanity. Then his eyes opened, slate-colored eyes in which danced flames of perversity similar to those observed in the eyes of Satan himself. He sat bolt upright on his slab and looked at The Undertaker.

The Undertaker waited for the usual reaction, the look of sick dismay when the newly-reanimated realizes where he is.

But of course there was no dismay in this one. The Marquis de Sade—for that is who was on the slab—had been through too many deaths too often to find even waking up in the Mortuary of Hell an unusual experience.

He looked at The Undertaker and smiled. "Alphonse, my dear fellow!"

"That's not my name," The Undertaker said.

"But it's what I decided to call you, the fifth or sixth time I came back to life here in your amusing little abbatoir." Sade took a lace handkerchief out of his sleeve and touched his nose.

"It's good to see you again, Donatien," said The Undertaker.

Sade looked around. "Actually The Mortuary is a lot neater than last time. Cleaned the place up a bit, haven't you?"

The Undertaker liked and admired Sade. The guy really had a lot of cool. And it was gracious of Sade to notice the improvements in The Mortuary. The Undertaker had gone to some pains to fix the place up. Not he himself, of course; his flunkies, the ghouls had done the actual work. They had scraped the accumulation of blood, pus, and rust from the walls. Then they pigged out the floor, which was thigh-deep and squashy in chunks of bloody severed limbs and maggoty heads with tongues sticking out, and the pale corpses of half-human creatures with ruined worm-eaten faces.

The mess had begun to bother him only recently, at the Hell Senior Officers Ball. Before that, The Undertaker had grown used to blood and limbs everywhere, just part of the job, and, aside from ordering his Morticians and ghouls to shovel a dry path through the really nasty stuff (because he hated to get blood on his clothes) The Undertaker had never done much about it.

But then he had met Queen Astarte.

She and the Undertaker had gotten along well. The Undertaker had asked her to come visit him.

Astarte, Queen of the Dead, showed up a few days later. The delicate-featured goddess wrinkled her retroussé nose as soon as she entered the Mortuary. "Why does it smell so?" she asked.

The Undertaker had been annoyed. "It smells like it's supposed to smell. I mean, this part of hell is *supposed* to smell. What's it like where you come from, a bouquet of roses?"

"This place is like some stupid horror movie," Astarte said. "All these heads and torsos lying around. Just because we're in Hell doesn't mean we must be tasteless. Thank you for inviting me for tea, but I prefer to leave at once."

With a haughty toss of her head she left.

"Stuck-up bitch," The Undertaker thought. But it got him to thinking. Maybe he *was* getting a little careless. He'd been keeping house for himself for quite a while, and men, especially weird semi-mythical men with many crimes on their souls like the Undertaker, tend to be careless about keeping up appearances if they don't have a woman around.

Years ago The Undertaker had been married to Me-

dusa, and they'd been good together, but then Medusa
had decided that she was not fulfilling herself; it wasn't
enough of a life for her, just hanging around watching
The Undertaker reanimate corpses. "My art form calls
me," she had said to The Undertaker, and departed,
never to return. The Undertaker had never understood
what was so fulfilling about turning people into stone.
But then, he had never claimed to be an artist himself.

Now he wrenched himself away from such bitter-
sweet thoughts. "It makes a difference, doesn't it? Well,
Donatien, I'm glad you like it. You come through here
often enough to remember how it used to be."

"Yes," Sade said, with a low laugh, "I do come through
here a lot, don't I? People in Hell keep on killing me.
It's amazing how many moralists there are, even in
Hell. Especially in Hell. No matter what *they've* done,
when they see me they say, 'There's Sade, he was
really bad; let's have a little fun with him, the bastard.'
And often as not the 'little fun' ends up with a knife in
my guts or a rope around my neck. And then I come
here and start all over."

"Yeah, I know it's not so easy for you," The Undertaker said.

Sade patted his waistcoat and found his snuff box. He
took a good sniff of the special mixture Lucrezia Borgia
had prepared for him the last time he was here. "It
would be bad enough if it were just a matter of being
killed over and over again. But sometimes, when they
have the time, the *leisure*, so to speak, the moralists
around here take most savage and painful revenge on
me, drawing out my agonies as I am said to have drawn
out the agonies of others, and claiming justice by
reciprocity."

"Well," The Undertaker said, "boys will be boys."

"True enough," said Sade. "Tell me, Alphonse, how
are things in Hell these days?"

"About the same as usual," The Undertaker said.
"Another day, another dollar. A few nice people come

though from time to time, like yourself, but aside from that it's just the same old grind.''

Sade grinned his crazy grin, a smile so warped it made even The Undertaker nervous. Then the Marquis swung his long legs to the ground, tipped his long black hat, and started toward the elevator.

"Would you like me to arrange any transportation?" The Undertaker called after him.

"Don't bother. I can find my own way around here." He paused, a tall, theatrical figure. "And perhaps, Alphonse, with a little luck, I can liven things up for you in the days to come."

And then Sade was gone, and The Undertaker was left wondering what he'd meant by that last remark and deciding that whatever it was he probably wouldn't like it.

You know how it is when you get back home after being away for a long time. You want to stroll around, look at some familiar sights, talk to a friend or two, lift a glass in your favorite cafe, take a meal at the local greasy spoon. You want to do all the old familiar things. That's why Sade always came back to East Hell each time he was killed. It was where he felt at home.

East Hell wasn't much to look at. Bleak desert sort of a place. Tin shacks and a couple of two-story frame houses. One corduroy road running through town. About four stores and a livery stable. Pokey sort of place. Although at the corner drugstore you *could* get several Paris newspapers. This was in deference to Mr. Sade, who was a big man in these parts.

The local boys respected Sade, and treated him well, except when they got liquored up and killed him. Sade never held it against them. He knew all about killing people out of *pique*, as he called it. He considered it a very French thing to do.

They had kept his room for him, above the Last

Chance Saloon, within sight of Boot Hill and the witches' coven.

It took Sade a few days to get used to things again, the dusty streets, the drunken swagger of the damned as they staggered down the narrow plank sidewalks, pushed along by the gritty south wind that blew forever. And Sade had forgotten about the Indians. They must have been *really* bad to get reanimated here rather than in a proper Indian's hell. They never did anything, just stood around like wooden cigar store Indians from an America before living memory.

The Marquis liked Indians on principle. He was European enough to get spiritualized by any Indians at all, even cigar store Indians.

Just as he was settling in, the door to his room burst open and a burly, shaved-head man entered. He wore tiny glinting glasses. He had on a salt and pepper suit and a stiff celluloid collar. A mean little necktie was pulled tight around his throat. He wore a gold Rolex, and its watchstrap was made of mink. He was Count Leopold von Sacher-Masoch.

"Leopold!" Sade said, instantly recognizing his old friend from Hell (they had never met on Earth). "How pleasant that we had the good fortune to be reborn together."

The famous Leopold von Sacher-Masoch could claim an eminence equal to Sade's, since he, too, had an ism named after him.

Yes, masochism was his very own invention. But it had taken a while before it caught on. Some of that was the fault of the advertising agency. First they had called it sacherism, and that hadn't caught on. Then they tried sacher-masochism, and that was a little better, but still not mainstream.And then he himself had come upon the perfect name for his psychological propensity: masochism. And the world had been ready for it.

Not that most people knew much about it. It was Sacher-Masoch's opinion that whining hypochondriacs like Woody Allen were the sort of people who gave masochism a bad name. Because after all, masochism wasn't really about whining, or your nasty head cold or your problems with your mother, any more than Existentialism (which Sacher-Masoch had studied with Sartre in The Pit) was about sitting alone in a room feeling sorry for yourself, as a lot of people seemed to believe.

"My dear Sade," Sacher-Masoch said. "How pleasant to be reborn in Hell at the same time as your illustrious self! Have you had a chance to study recent history? Our names are linked together in the great doctrine, Sado-Masochism! Eternal glory, my master, eternal glory!"

Sade wasn't sure how much he liked Sacher-Masoch. But Sacher-Masoch certainly liked him. The eponymous sadist rented a room in the hotel and announced his decision to stay until, in his words, "certain dispositions have been made."

Sacher-Masoch found a room in the Last Chance Saloon in East Hell and moved right in. It was difficult for him, because he had to get along without his pornography collection, his furs, and his leather tuxedo. Still, he managed. He was a puritan at heart, something no one would believe.

"One thing about Hell that I've always admired," the Marquis de Sade said to Sacher-Masoch later in the week, "is the way the Devil provides the means for destroying one's body and mind. He's really quite a puritan about the virtues of self-destructiveness, isn't he, Leopold?"

"I hate it when you talk like that," Sacher-Masoch said sulkily, sitting down in a window seat. "And must you puff on that opium pipe? You know you get quite silly when you smoke that stuff."

"Leopold," Sade said severely, "how I *get*, as you put it, is no concern of yours."

Sacher-Masoch looked gratified—he'd really been needing a good put-down lately. Hoping for another snub, he said, "How do you like the way things are going in Hell?"

They were taking dinner together in the dining room of the Last Chance Saloon Hotel. It was a low, dimly lit place, smoky with the smells of chunks of meat turning on greasy spits. It is not generally appreciated how smoky a room can get when ten chefs are simultaneously turning joints of meat over glowing charcoal, especially when you consider what the ventilation's like in Hell.

"Oh, it's nice to be back, I suppose," Sade said. "Not very interesting, not terribly amusing, but nice. Boring but nice."

Sacher-Masoch admired Sade's boredom. Leave it to the French! What could be more decadent, more trenchant, than Sade, bored in the heart of Hell. Sacher-Masoch was sure there was a philosophical concept lurking there somewhere. He would have to talk with his friend Mr. Sartre about doing an article together, a collaboration, something to do with the banality of evil.

That would come later. Presently, he had to tell Sade the big news. But it was difficult to know just how to go about it. Sade seemed a changed man. Capable of viciousness, no doubt. Nastiness, no doubt. But evil?

Or had the repeated punishments taken their toll, had the leader's soul finally been purged? Had he gone soft? Given into the Big Fellow? What the hell was up with Sade, anyhow? He seemed changed somehow, different.

Sacher-Masoch needed an answer. He had to make up his mind. He knew it might become his unhappy lot to have to kill Sade if the inconceivable had happened and the Marquis de Sade had gotten religion.

The Devil's week is made up entirely of Mondays, so the Marquis de Sade wasn't sure how long he'd been back in East Hell when Leopold brought the other Frenchman to visit him. The newcomer was a tall, handsome, square-shouldered man, dressed in the style of the Court of Henri III. Leopold bustled around making introductions, sweating unpleasantly and emitting his involuntary little whining sound that made him so especially objectionable.

"Donatien!" Sacher-Masoch exclaimed in his overfamiliar manner, "look who I've brought!"

De Sade looked over the man. From his manner and bearing, the stranger had to be of a high order or nobility. Higher perhaps than that of the Marquis himself. Ranks and degrees of nobility were matters that people in Hell paid careful attention to.

"I do not believe I have had the honor," de Sade said, incling his head in the merest sketch of a bow.

"Nor I," the stranger said. "Though I am some centuries your elder, I look upon you nevertheless as my spiritual mentor, the man whose life and writings most and best expressed what I felt but could not quite accomplish with my deeds."

"Sir," said Sade, "who are you?"

"The Comte de Rais, at your service," the tall Frenchman said. "Though I am best known to posterity, as Gilles de Rais, also called Bluebeard."

Sacher-Masoch sucked in his breath. "Donatien, this is the very man whom more than one notable critic has called 'the wickedest man who ever lived.' "

"They exaggerate, no doubt," Gilles de Rais said, "though one tries one's best."

"Delighted to make your acquaintance," Sade said; his bow deepened.

"No more delighted than I, master," said Gilles de Rais.

When Charles Baudelaire was reborn in Hell, he was accorded special attention. He was taken straight to Satan himself, without being subjected to the usual indignities meted out by The Undertaker and The Welcome Woman.

"Baudelaire," the Devil said, "I just want you to know that I have always loved your *Flowers of Evil*. Those poems really put into words the sorts of feelings that unliterary angels like myself have but cannot express."

"Very kind of you, I'm sure," Baudelaire said. He sounded awkward. He had never known what to say to people who thought he was great. If his only problem during his lifetime had been what to say to people who thought he was great, he'd have had no problems at all. But he had plenty of problems in his lifetime, Baudelaire did, and he suspected, standing now looking into the ominous face of the Prince of Evil, that he was going to go right on having problems after death.

"I just wanted to take this opportunity of welcoming you," the Devil said. "I do happen to have a copy of your masterpiece, *Les Fleurs de Mal*, and I would certainly appreciate an autograph . . . Yes, you can use that pen. Thank you very much. Now I've got a surprise for you."

"I don't much like surprises," Baudelaire said.

"You're going to like this one. I have a special place picked out for you. A region of Hell I think you're going to like."

"Oh, I am sure," Baudelaire said, though he wasn't sure at all.

"You'll really be sure once you get an idea of what general conditions are like here. In fact, maybe you'd like a guided tour of some of the seedier parts of Hell?"

Baudelaire shuddered. "I'm not really up for a guided tour," he said. "What I'd prefer is some quiet place where I can dream about Hell."

"You poets have your methods, no doubt," the Devil said. "Go along now to the Nouveau Paris which I have constructed for you and let me know how you like it."

"I'm sure I will adore it," Baudelaire said.

"If so," the Devil said offhandedly, "I may call upon you at some time to do me a favor."

Baudelaire drew himself up to his full height. His ravaged face lighted up for a moment. He looked the Devil in the eye.

"Of course, monsieur. Any favor that is in my power to grant is yours."

It was the right thing to say. The Devil liked a touch of class. And anyhow, what could one do, what the Devil wanted from a sinner he was bound to get, whether the sinner acquiesced or not.

Baudelaire allowed himself to be led to the Elevator, which brought him to the Châtelet-Les Halles Metro stop in the middle of Nouveau Paris.

He saw at once that the Nouveau Paris construct was very nice. Not perfect, but nice. Baudelaire's acute eye, which had so startled the literary world of Paris when his writings first appeared, noted the imperfections at once. The lighting, for one thing. Only God Himself might hope to recreate the incomparable display of the colors and hues of Paris.

He continued to walk, and his steps led him to the Pont Marie, the small bridge which he crossed over to the Isle St-Louis. This small island in the Seine, at almost the exact heart of Paris, had been his home for some of his happiest years. And he had lived right down the block there, at the Hotel Lauzon.

He walked to the hotel and was amazed and delighted to see his friend, the poet Paul Verlaine, sitting at the cafe outside of the Hotel and sipping a glass of white wine.

"Paul!"

"Charles!"

"I am delighted to see you," Baudelaire said. "What a relief to see a friend from the old days. I don't know anybody here. And I've just had an experience which has shaken me to the core."

"My friend, try to take hold of yourself," said Verlaine. "We're dead, what more can happen? Relax and enjoy this fine Paris the Devil has caused to be built."

"He's coming for me," Baudelaire said. "The Devil. He just told me that he built this entire place for me, Charles Baudelaire. And he spoke rather ominously about calling on me for a favor."

"Oh, he was just trying to compliment you," Verlaine said. "Actually, he put up Nouveau Paris as a monument to all of us, the French Symbolist Poets, for our masterly service in the dissemination of Evilist propaganda while on earth."

"That's not what he told me," Baudelaire said. "He wants something from me, personally. Paul, he's setting me up for something."

"My friend," said Verlaine, "sit down and take some of these excellent drugs. You remember, perhaps, that saying of the Americans, to wit, that life is just one damned thing after another. Well, it could hardly have escaped your notice that death is exactly the same way."

"Then what is one to do?" Baudelaire asked.

"My suggestion," Verlaine said, "is that we throw a party. Like in the old days."

"A party? Here?"

"Yes, this hotel has been remodeled so perfectly, even to containing a replica of our old Club upstairs."

Baudelaire brightened up at the thought of wine, opium, and literary discussion, the three prerequisites of civilized life. "But whom will we ask?"

"The old crowd," Verlaine said. "Most of them are down here somewhere."

The Hotel de Lauzan was located on the Quai d'Anjou on the north side of the Ile St-Louis, almost equidistant between the Pont Marie and the Pont de Sully. Baudelaire used to live there in a little room under the eaves, back when he was alive. There he would watch the Seine stretch and preen itself under the changing Paris skies. He found, in the contrast between its protean mutability and the fixed lines of the quays and bridges, a symbol for art itself. That was at the beginning of the affair with Jeanne Duval. The lost years of despair and madness came afterwards.

Still, that was a while ago, and now, since Baudelaire was enjoying one of his rare fits of sanity, he and Verlaine lost no time in calling a meeting of the Club des Haschischins, where so many notables had assembled in the old days, not all approving, of course, but fascinated by the decadence, the wit, and the style.

The leader of the Haschischins, La Présidente, was Aglaë-Apollonie, a buxom little wench whose renowned debauchery fit badly with her air of country innocence.

The other guests arrived soon after, and the air grew dense with a miasma of smoke from the charcoal fire and from the candles, and from the top-hatted gentlemen sitting on sofas covered with figured silks, long slender pipes in their mouths, talking, laughing, arguing between puffs.

Baudelaire began to find all this mirth depressing, but he brightened when his old friend Théophile Gautier showed up.

"What a delightful idea this was," Gautier said. "Your party is certainly the event of the season. I had to get special permission to come here. Would you believe, they've put me in an antique Chinese hell, probably in punishment for my lifetime interest in chinoiserie. I see that a lot of the others were able to make it. There's Delacroix, holding forth to Debussy, Boissard is wearing his silly hat, and the Goncourt brothers are looking supercilious as always."

"Who's that fat fellow with the coffee cup and the cute blonde?"

"Surely you remember M. Balzac. He used to visit us only for the conversation, since he claims that his consumption of coffee and spirits renders him immune to the effects of other drugs. I don't know who the girl is. You find that type all over Hell."

"And who are those two over there?" Baudelaire asked, because two men had just entered and were looking with stern eyes upon the proceedings.

"The one on the left is Richard Wagner. You can tell by his floppy tie. The other is an up-and-coming young poet named Rainer Marie Rilke."

The evening passed pleasantly. Towards dawn, the guests departed to take up their assignments in other corners of Hell.

Leopold von Sacher-Masoch came over to East Hell to bring Sade to the special meeting he had called. He found Sade in his room above the Last Chance Saloon, scribbling his memoirs.

"Well, Leopold," Sade said, looking up, "how are you today?"

"Well enough, Donatien. But I've been a little upset since you returned to us."

"Why is that, Leopold?"

"There has been some talk," Sacher-Masoch said, "to the effect that you've lost your old spirit. Some even say that you're not as keen on cruelty as you used to be."

"Think I'm losing my touch? Is that it?"

"Some people say so. Not me, of course. My dear marquis, what are you doing?"

The Marquis de Sade had reached out and stroked Sacher-Masoch's porcine cheek. The Austrian flinched back involuntarily, but Sade had seized a fold of his flesh between two fingers that were strong as iron pliers. Tears came to Sacher-Masoch's eyes as Sade tightened his grip. Sacher-Masoch sank to his knees, moaning.

"Please, Donatien!" Sacher-Masoch cried.

Sade's vise-like fingers gave another half turn to Sacher-Masoch's outraged cheek. Sacher-Masoch screamed, tears came to his eyes, his fingers fluttered toward his face like poisoned bats after the cyanide bomb has gone off.

"I believe it is possible," Sade said in a conversational voice, "to twist a man's face right off like this."

"Donatien, please, I beg you—"

"But of course it's easier if you start it by opening up a little slit along the neck." A straight razor appeared as if by magic in Sade's free hand. He bent toward Sacher-Masoch, smiling.

Sacher-Masoch went into hysterics. Long after Sade had released him, he was still rolling on the ground, sobbing and banging his fists together like a berserk chipmunk with an Austrian accent.

"Oh, come on, stop snivelling," Sade said after a while. "I was merely demonstrating that I have not lost my—what is it the Americans call it?"

"Edge?" Sacher-Masoch asked.

"No, it was a word that sounded like *monkey*."

"Ah, you must mean *moxie*," Sacher-Masoch said.

"Yes, that's it. *Le Moxie*. I have not lost it, no?"

"Your renowned rage is intact," Sacher-Masoch said, getting shakily to his feet. "For a while I did have my doubts. But now it is apparent that I won't need this."

Reaching into an inner pocket of his waistcoat, Sacher-Masoch withdrew a slender throttling wire with leather handles. He cast it aside with a contemptuous gesture.

Sade said, his voice gentle, "So you would betray me too, Leopold? And all for a bit of fun, I suppose."

"I was considering killing you," Sacher-Masoch said. "But not out of pleasure, as you must know if you know anything about masochism, my great invention for which I will be eternally famous. I was going to kill you because I thought you had reformed, opted for The Other Side."

"What an unlikely idea!" said Sade. "That would be like asking me to repudiate *sadism*, for which I have received eternal glory and a permanent place in the history books. Many think, by the way, that this *masochism* of yours is merely a subset of the more deeply rooted and fundamental *sadism* which is my own personal invention."

"There's room for argument there," Sacher-Masoch said, remembering that his psychoanalyst had told him he must stand up for himself even when—especially when—he didn't believe in himself and was clearly in the wrong.

"But what I want to know," Sade said, "what concern is it of yours if I *had* gone to The Other Side?"

"I know it must seem unfriendly of me," Sacher-Masoch said. "But I was merely thinking of the morale of the others, those of us who live at the inner core of evil, and who would be dejected if our master, the great Sade himself, were to desert our ranks."

"Desert evil? Never! I have returned, my dear Leopold, and it is my determination to do something of lasting value, to strike a blow for the cause of evil as we know it."

"Ah, it's the marquis I have known so long," Sacher-Masoch said. "And how good it is that you have come back to us! We live in changing times, *mon cher* marquis. Even Hell is susceptible to change. Listen, Donatien, I have some friends I want you to meet. Some you already know, others are new to you. But there is one thing I can assure you about them. They are all truly and sincerely *bad*."

Sade smiled, a dreamy smile that twisted his long, thin lips. Sacher-Masoch knew he need say no more. The great dream was about to begin. Satisfied, Sacher-Masoch massaged his bruised cheek. It seemed almost certain that he would have an unsightly hickey from where Sade had twisted. But what of that? De Sade was back! And besides, thinking back on it, it now seemed to him quite fun.

The Grand Council of Real Evil held its meeting in the Meeting Place, a special room put aside for infernal functions of exceptional importance. The saloon below catered the meals—hominy grits, country gravy, chicken fried steaks, and for side dishes you could have either stewed okra or stewed blackeyed peas or both. The devil knew how to hurt a man, especially if he were a Frenchman.

Sade took the seat at the head of the table. He cleared his throat and called the meeting to order.

"I want to wish you all a very good day," de Sade said. "I see several of our old friends here. And I notice a very distinguished newcomer in our midst, the famous philosopher Friedrich Wilhelm Nietzsche; how good to see you!"

"I really shouldn't be here," Nietzsche said. He was a small man, almost a dwarf. He had large moustaches, twirled at the ends. He wore gold-rimmed pince-nez, a heavy English salt-and-pepper tweed suit. "Hitler and his National Socialists perverted my teachings for a while, and now people think that the term 'Nietzschean' refers to the sorts of dirty tricks they were up to. The same goes for you, Sade, with your vaunted sadism, at the heart of which is just sheer bad manners and hopeless vulgarity. When I sang of Zarathustra and the *Übermensch*, I definitely didn't have you in mind."

"Always a pleasure to listen to a learned colleague," Sade said. "Especially one who saw fit to try to define evil without himself ever trying it out at firsthand. Typical German idealism, if you ask me. But still, you are welcome to our ranks."

"Any common butcher can do evil deeds," Nietzsche said huffily. "It takes a thinking person to consider their metaphysical implications."

"Moving right along," Sade said, "I see some notables here. Gilles de Rais, for example, is a most welcome addition to our ranks. Feeling up to performing some bad deeds, Gilles?"

Gilles de Rais, sometimes known as Retz, was a curious fellow who had tried throughout his life to keep a pipeline open to God. While he was murdering children—estimates of their numbers ranged from 160 to more than 800—he had also been endowing monasteries and having masses sung for the salvation of his soul.

To no avail. After a few rebirths in Hell, Gilles had given up the dream of salvation. It had been a pretty outside chance anyhow. And it was kind of nice to be known as the most evil man who had ever lived, with the possible exception of de Sade.

"God saw fit not to hear my penance," Gilles said. "So I'm ready to do worse than before, and let's see how that suits Him."

"That's the spirit," Sade said. "And I also see the Countess Elizabeth Báthory, from one of Hungary's greatest families. Elizabeth, as the more learned among you may know, is famous for bathing in the blood of her serving maids. Some hundreds of them. After torturing them to death, of course."

"What could I do?" Elizabeth Báthory asked, lifting her beautiful face toward Sade. "They were naughty. Someone had to punish them."

Sacher-Masoch, sitting across from her, thought that the Countess Elizabeth was the most gorgeous thing he'd ever seen. She looked like a lady who really knew how to hurt a fellow, and Sacher-Masoch found that irresistible.

He blurted out, "Darling countess, I know someone here who needs punishing, and who is ready to submit himself to you."

The Countess' lip curled. "Austrian pig," she said, "I am not interested in *men*, among whose ranks you barely qualify. My taste is for young girls. So please direct your vileness toward those who might get a spasm of twisted pleasure out of administering punishment to an inept and stupid creature like yourself."

"Thank you, Countess," Sacher-Masoch said, leaning

back, well contented. Elizabeth was a lady who really knew how to talk to a masochist.

"Friends," de Sade was saying, "there are too many of you here for me to single all out individually. It is lucky for us that this table extends as interminably as it does into the recesses of our meeting room, since only thus could it seat all who desire to be with us today. Now, gentlemen, shall we set a topic for conversation?"

Gilles de Rais said, "You know there's only one burning topic, Sade! I refer to the relaxed and decadent position to which the Devil has brought Evil."

"And that is my theme," Sade said. "Brothers and sisters, for too long have we tolerated conditions in this effete and ridiculous Hell. And what do we find on all sides of us? What are the activities of this Hell? War, with all its shoddy impersonality. And since when has war been considered evil? War is hell, yes, but is war evil? The point has never been questioned. And that is not all we find. We observe that Hell is a pedestrian place full of political parties and differing causes, just like back on Earth. My friends, I put it to you that what we need is a serious-minded Hell, a place filled with unspeakable horror, perversion and cruelty, a Hell far worse than this *laissez-faire* place we find ourselves in."

"Hear, hear!" the assembled shouted.

Sade waited until the applause ended. Then he said, "To that end, my friends, I propose here and now that we form ourselves into an action group dedicated to making Hell really Hellish."

"And what if the Devil doesn't like it?" Oscar Wilde asked from the end of the table.

"Well then, so much the worse for him. If he can't stay up with the times, he must be superceded."

"To take over from Satan in his very own Hell!" Sacher-Masoch mused aloud. "What a magnificent concept!"

"I could expect no less from myself," de Sade said.

*   *   *

Sade and Gilles de Rais were sitting alone that evening after the meeting, on the little balcony that opened out from Sade's suite in the Last Chance Saloon & Hotel. Sade was in the wicker armchair, and Rais was sitting in the armchair which he had pulled to the balcony. It was a quiet evening. Paradise, the fluctuating orb of Hell, had just gone down, a molten mass of fire. An even blueness suffused the sky, darkening to royal purple at the line of the horizon.

"Do you think back much on the old days?" Sade asked Rais.

"Sometimes," Rais said. "And you?"

"Yes. Sometimes." Sade lighted up the clay pipe that Leopold had given him. He puffed for a moment contemplatively. "You know," he said, "these things we did for our pleasure . . . you know what I mean . . ."

"Yes," said Rais, with a sigh, anticipating Sade's next words.

"They can't really be defended," Sade said.

"No," Rais said, with a sigh. "I suppose they cannot."

"But when they say we did what we did merely for pleasure—as if that were an insignificant impulse easily subjected to the will, if only we cared to try—it shows how little they really understood how it is with us."

"Ah," said Rais.

"They don't understand that they have never tasted pleasure, those who judge and condemn us. Their own meagre lusts are easy enough to control. They have never gone beyond the protection of what is lawful, in order to taste what is ineffable."

"True enough, my dear marquis," said Rais. "But it seems that you propose to do something about it."

"Yes. We are in the place at last where the unthinkable is lawful. Let us proceed, my friend, to raise hell in Hell."

The first serious incident involving Sade's forces took place shortly after, in a frontier camp about two hundred miles inland from Nuevo, main port of the Intemperate Zone, and fifty miles from New Capetown. This area had long been disputed between the forces of Che Guevara and Hadrian. Now war had come again to this unhappy region.

Sad testimony to this is the last communication sent out by Hrdçon Ulsimara, commander of the guard for the town of Aris-Simulé, to his commander in the Pentagram:

What in hell is going on out here in nethermost Hell? Who are these guys? I just hope I can get this communication through. The telegraph lines still seem to be up.

The trouble began with these persons who come and go to the various camps, posing as minstrels, bawdies, reprehensibles, condottiere looking for jobs, I mean these people just keep on coming, all over, moving through the war zones. As if there were nothing going on at all.

From time to time, some of them get blown up, machine gunned, mortared, grenaded, napalmed, ripped by short swords, skewered on spears, and so on through the phantasmagorical gamut of weaponry that your Unmerciful Improvidence has provided us with. But not enough of them. The rest—they're the worst kind of urban guerrillas. The kind with no cause. Not even anarchy! Can you imagine it, Master; they have no politics whatsoever. Instead, they're talking religion. They keep on saying, "As long as we're in Hell, let's make the worst of it."

They speak in disparaging tones of your theories of punishment. They say, maybe he is a fallen angel. So what? Once an angel, always an angel.

Whereas we, they point out, have never been angels at all. We don't have a single redeeming feature. Now tell me, frankly, which would you consider more reliable on the subject of damnation? The so-called Fallen Angel, or us, the baddest of the bad?

*This is all pretty childish stuff, Master. Yet it con-
vinces some. And many of our citizens are sick of the
futility of war and death and rebirth and war. The
same old round, they call it. And Sade with his vulgar
legions of bloodthirsty Frenchmen appeals to the popular taste. He gives them a chance, if not to be good,
then to be truly bad, and to be punished for new sins
rather than to continue atoning for sins they can hardly
remember.*

*I wouldn't bring this matter to your august attention,
Master, were it not for the fact that it looks like a trend
is being established. Hysteria infects the crowds when
Sade and his zanies appear. They're presenting a Punch
and Judy show, you know, but it is nothing like the
original. No, it is obscene, perverse and I'm sending
you a videotape of a typical performance so you can
judge for yourself. Such entertainment puts the crowd
into the right mood for the later abominations, the
torturings, the unexpected decapitations, the gruesome
masques and hideous tableaux, the entire Grand Guignol
of Hell presented vivant, in living retchovision.*

*I fear I am getting hysterical. I only hope that this
message goes through.*

*My Lord, they are battering at the door outside my
guardpost. And distantly, I can hear the sound of axes
as they finally get around to chopping down the telegraph poles. I told you we should have put them
underground!*

*They have broken through! Bloody hands are reach-
ing for me. Frantically I work the telegraph key. They
are at me, tearing at my clothing, their long knives
flashing . . . aieeee!*

The message was received in the Pentagram and
given to a special courier. The High Command courier,
Ulr Bruadshaw, thought long and hard about what to do
with Ulsimara's message. Satan hated to get bad news.
He had been known, in his annoyance, to belch a gout

of flame which consumed the unfortunate bearer of evil tidings, frying him to a crisp while the surviving officers applauded, saying, in fear of their lives, "I knew there was something about that fellow I didn't like."

At last Bruadshaw decided to bring the message to Satan. Might as well, he'd be punished for sure if he didn't bring the message. Might as well be hung for insolence as for squelance, he told himself, a little hysterically. As he started toward Satan's Audience Hall Bruadshaw was muttering to himself in his native language, "Harnmins redarter fur. Squelaach!"

Satan turned the tables on the bookmakers of Hell when he didn't do the expected and consume the messenger and his "Squelaach!" but rather accepted the information in a normal fashion.

"Interesting," was all Satan said.

The dignitaries of his court were thinking, Interesting! All hell breaking loose in East Hell and the only thing he could say was "Interesting"? They were indignant, but they knew better than to bother Satan about the Sade problem. Satan liked to think things out on his own. It was what had gotten him into Hell in the first place. Now, deep in thought, Satan did nothing to correct or chastise Sade and his ever-growing band of murderous crazies.

At last the High Command sent an expendable junior officer named Dactis, a recently appointed Lieutenant in the Enemy Secrets Division of the Department of Unintelligence, with a request to the Chief for a military-type miracle to take Sade and his people out of play once and for all.

Satan considered the proposal for a while, then shook his huge, grizzled head. "No," he said, "I don't think so."

"Why not?" Dactis asked. "Hell is your creation. You could do it if you wanted to."

"Tearing down Hell is not part of my plan," Satan said. "If I had to call upon a miracle now, I'd be confessing my impotence to deal with situations in the normal way. No, Dactis. Besides, I find Sade amusing. He's quite a terrible fellow, isn't he? Ho, ho." And Satan broke into an unseemly guffaw.

"But the man is scoffing at you, the Commander in Chief! So far, the troops we have thrown against him have had no luck. Sade's madmen are never where you expect to find them; they merge into the general populace, appear unexpectedly, hit and run."

"Sound, very sound," Satan said. "He must have learned his tactics from Mao."

"He preaches against you. He tells the people that you are not sufficiently evil! He as good as accuses you of being a fellow traveller serving The Other Fellow."

"Does he really?" Satan asked.

"Yes, he really does," Dactis said.

Satan refused to be ruffled. "There's nothing so powerful as an idea whose time has come."

"Oh, wow," Dactis said. "I never thought of that. Let me think about that a moment. Oh, I got it, yeah, but what can we *do* against an idea whose time has come? How can we expect conventional troops to fight against an army of madmen led by a crazy poet and philosopher?"

"That's it!" Satan cried. "You've got it!"

Dactis looked distressed. "I didn't mean to, Sire!"

"The solution to this situation with Sade is apparent now. To control one crazy poet we must send another against him."

Dactis said, "Yes, Sire. Who did you propose to use to control Sade?"

Satan smiled. "Ask Baudelaire if he'd mind dropping by on me at his earliest possible convenience."

"The fact is," Archilochos said to the sibyl, "I'm fed up."

"What's the matter?" the sibyl asked. "Not getting your share of the maenads?"

"I'm not interested in them," Archilochos said.

"They're always sweaty from their frenzied dances, and they don't have any small talk."

Archilochos and the sibyl were sitting on a little bench beneath a sterile willow. In front of them was a dismal plain, dotted with black cypresses and strewn with asphodel, stretched to the low muddy shores of murk-haunted River Phlegethon. To one side was a classical Greek temple. From it you could hear the sound of singing. It was Persephone, leading her class in classical Greek folkdance.

During his lifetime, Archilochos had followed the two professions of poet and mercenary. Naturally, they put him in Tartaros when he died. But he didn't get along. He made up a satirical song about Persephone and laughed at Cerberus. He was a man who couldn't take Hell seriously. He was bored with the classics, and he'd made up his mind to seek his fortune in one of the other levels of Hell.

The sibyl warned him not to even try. "Of course, you can go if you want to. There's no law against it. But Tartaros is your own country. It's not so bad, you know, having a classical Hell of your own."

"I'm sick of those gloomy cypresses," Archilochos said. "I'm sick of always eating souvlaki. I'm sick of hearing Achilles talk about how good he was. I'm sick of Helen putting on airs. I'm sick of there being no war. War is my occupation, and love, and poetry. I think I need to find some more action."

And so Archilochos had taken the passageway that led up past the Corinthian columns and beside which was the archaic statue of Apollo. There was the Elevator. He rode it to New Hell.

On the level of New Hell, Archilochos noticed that many things were mechanized. There seemed to be many efficient ways of killing people.

He passed through an outlying army group. They were Augustus' men, some of them Romans, others Italians from different periods, who had decided to serve under Caesar's colors. They were professional fighting men, and they recognized Archilochos as a brother. When they found out he could recite sharp and biting poetry full of cusswords, and often heartachingly beautiful, he was welcome to every campside. Military poets are always pets of the army, and Archilochos was so obviously one of them, a man with a natural inclination towards arms, and a man who learned new killing techniques quickly, whether these came from Scythian bowmen or from Italian swordsmen. A man who had lived a thousand years after he had died. The hardware changed, but the basic trade stayed the same. Archilochos felt much more at home in this level of Hell filled with armies and clash of arms then he had in the classical Hell of black cypresses and Greek temples and infinite resignation.

After a while, Archilochos was able to sort out the main issues in these parts. He learned enough about Sade, and saw enough of the gruesome work of his followers, to decide to join the other side.

Archilochos applied for a sergeant's position in the Symbolist forces, but he was turned down. "You don't have a modern technical vocabulary," the Republican Guard with the tricolor cockade in his hat said. "We need machine gunners, not ash spearmen."

"I can learn to use any weapon you use," Archilochos told the man.

"Well, come back in a week or so and try us again."

"Can I stay here in New Paris while you make up your minds?"

"Sorry, that's strictly forbidden. Not enough room. Satan only built a part of Nouveau Paris, you see, and there's only room for a few hundred thousand people, until he gets around to putting in some of the outer neighborhoods."

"Whom do you usually let in?" Archilochos asked.

"We tend to favor soldiers and poets."

"Why goddamn it, man, I'm both!"

The guard looked mildly interested. "What did you say your name was again?"

"Archilochos. Accent on the antepenult. Favorably mentioned in all reviews of Greek poetry since the 7th century BC. For centuries, every educated Greek and Roman had me in his library alongside Homer."

"But *we* have not heard of you, m'sieu," the guard said. "Can you at least show us your press clippings, or tell us where we might read some of your works?"

"Hey, listen," Archilochos said, "It's been a long time. Libraries burn down. Even the few remaining fragments of my poetry have been preserved on Earth only as a matter of luck."

The guard was still suspicious. He called for an aide and sent him to bring a Classical Reference Work. He consulted it, and said, "If you are the real Archilochos, perhaps you'll remember the first (and only remaining) line of your most famous love poem, which is also one of the oldest fragments of love poetry in Greek."

"No problem," Archilochos said. "It goes: 'Oh to touch Neobulé's hand.'"

"He's got it right," the aide said, peering over the commander's shoulder.

"But what does it prove?" the guard asked. "Anyone trying to pose as Archilochos would learn that much off by heart."

"Still, what other test can we apply?"

They discussed it for a while. Finally, they let Archilochos in on a temporary visa.

Archilochos asked where headquarters was, got directions, and went straight to the Hotel Lauzon on the Ile St-Louis. where Charles Baudelaire was reputed to be staying.

When he arrived at the hotel, he found two armed guards at the door. They told him that the leader, Charles Baudelaire, was having one of his sick headaches and couldn't see anyone.

* * *

Baudelaire put down the opium pipe. "What are you talking about, I'm supposed to do something about Sade?"

Verlaine said, "That's what Satan told me to tell you."

"There must be some mistake."

"He said it takes a poet to fight a poet."

"He considers Sade a poet? *Mon dieux!* He must have been expelled from Heaven for his literary taste."

"Nice one," Verlaine said, "but the fact is, you're supposed to do something about this madman."

"But why me? I'm no soldier," Baudelaire said. "Once upon a time soldiering might have been individualistic and orgiastic, and then I could perhaps have gotten interested in it, if for no other reason that just for perversity's sake. But now, it's an age of mass armies with vulgar reading habits or none at all, and I want no part of it."

"Satan told me to remind you," Verlaine said, "that you like it here in Nouveau Paris."

"Well, yes, of course."

"And that you might *not* like some of the other areas quite as well. Like East Hell, for example, where Sade lives above a saloon."

"Above a saloon in East Hell?" Baudelaire said. "Can't blame the poor bastard for revolting, can you?"

"Please stop kidding around," Verlaine said. "You've got to do something or we're going to lose Nouveau Paris. You wouldn't like it out there in the rest of Hell, Charles."

"No, I suppose I wouldn't," Baudelaire said, remembering the images of Hell he had been able to imagine even before visiting the place.

"Well, then?" Verlaine demanded.

"All right," Baudelaire said, "I see this is serious. Satan actually expects us to put down this rebellion or whatever it is? Did he put any army to our disposal? What am I to do about air power, bearing in mind that it was unheard of in my day? What about Caesar and the Cong? Will either of them cooperate with us?"

"Those are a lot of questions," Verlaine said. "What you need are some answers."

"Yes, I do. All right, then, Paul, you get them for me."

"Get what?" Verlaine asked.

Baudelaire clutched his forehead. "Don't try to confuse me. Get the answers."

"But what were the questions?" Verlaine said.

"Well, I don't remember either," Baudelaire said. "It's obvious to me that we must find someone who can get things done. Otherwise grand strategy is sure to languish."

Just then a tall, burly man with shoulder-length brown hair held in place by a silver circlet turned, putting down his newspaper as he did so. This took place in the Brasserie Lipp, which, by popular demand, had been moved from the Boulevard St-Germain to a new location on the Ile St-Louis.

"Excuse me," the burly man said. "I couldn't help but overhear your conversation. If you want a practical sort of a soldier who can keep accounts and get things done, I'm your man."

Baudelaire and Verlaine exchanged arch looks.

"And who, monsieur, might you be?" Baudelaire asked.

"Archilochos."

"Archilochos what?" Baudelaire asked. "Or is Archilochos the family name?"

"No, Archilochos is the whole thing," said Archilochos. "I'm from the classical period; we just had one name back then. Plato. Aristotle. Homer. Like that."

"Oh, really?" Baudelaire said. "Am I supposed to know of you?"

"Not necessarily. I was almost forgotten until the mid-20th century. Then my poems once again began to receive attention."

"Yes," Verlaine said, "I've heard of him. Definitely. Around 750 B.C."

"Close," Archilochos said. "You've heard of me, huh?"

"He's a poet as well as a mercenary," Verlaine said to Baudelaire. "This is a fantastic opportunity. This guy is not only classical, Charles, he's class as well."

"Zat is fine by me," Baudelaire said, reverting to the imitation French accent he used when people around him were talking too much. "I suppose people will call him Archie for short. Already the prospect is painful. If I ask about your experience, Archilochos, I suppose you'll recite the *Iliad* to me?"

"Not at all. I'm a professional soldier. Born on Paros in the Cyclades. Been a fighting man all my life. There was plenty of work for a free-lance hoplite back in the late 700s."

"You sound good to me," Baudelaire said. "I see the end of my dilemma. You, Archilochos, must command the counterattack or whatever it is that we must launch against Sade and his vulgar lot."

Archilochos shook his head. "Hey, wait a minute, that's grand strategy. It's not my thing, leading the whole army. Squad Leader, that's what I do. Platoon's all right, too. In a pinch I suppose I could handle a regiment. But the big stuff's for someone else. Why don't you put me in charge of one of your assault squads?"

"With pleasure," Baudelaire said, "once we *have* an assault squad. Can you define an assault squad for me? Never mind, before forming these assault squads we must find someone to lead that of which they are a mere subsumption. I refer, of course, to the army. Someone with a level head, sound strategic sense, a practical man, a worldly man, strong and self-assured, that sort of a man."

Just then the door opened and a man stepped in. He was dressed in 19th century American garb—long black jacket buttoned to the neck, white cravat, narrow stovepipe pants and black patent leather shoes. He was blackhaired, small of build, wispily moustached, delicate of construction, nervous-looking, probably neurotic.

"Excuse me, gentlemen," he said, "I do not mean to intrude, but I was given to understand that I might meet a Monsieur Baudelaire here."

"I am Baudelaire. What do you want with me?"

"Only to thank you for the nice job you did translating my stories into French."

Baudelaire stared. "Then you must be—"

"Yes. Edgar Allan Poe, at your service."

"By the way," Poe said, "you haven't seen Annabel Lee around here, have you?"

Baudelaire and Verlaine shook their heads.

"Helen, maybe?"

No.

"I suppose it's possible they both went to Heaven," Poe said. "Just my luck."

Baudelaire sneered. "You think you know about bad luck? What about me? Even as a very small boy—"

"As for that," said Verlaine, "I could match you both. But first we have a war to fight."

"More to the point," said Baudelaire, "I think we should have a drink to celebrate the arrival of our esteemed colleague, Mr. Poe, who, thanks to my efforts, was resurrected to his full stature in France long after his fellow countrymen spurned him as a mere neurotic scribbler."

They took Poe inside the Hotel Lauzon, introduced him to their friends Mallarmé and Rimbaud, Gaudi and Piranesi, Miró and Debussy, Victor Hugo and Alexandre Dumas. Balzac was there with his stomach, Flaubert with his beard, Montaigne with his all-penetrating eye.

After several glasses of white wine, Baudelaire said, "you're very welcome to stay here with us, Mr. Poe, in this decadent and jolly hotel. Unless you'd rather stay with your own American literary friends."

"What friends? They snubbed me during my lifetime. Hawthorne, Longfellow, Whittier. The old boys' club. Fenimore Cooper was friendly for a while, but then he caught me laughing over a copy of Mark Twain's essay, 'Fenimore Cooper's Literary Crimes,' perhaps the most delicious literary indictment ever written. He hasn't talked to me since."

"Who is this Mark Twain?" Baudelaire asked.

"I haven't seen him around," Poe said. "He's probably down in the pit telling jokes to the worst sinners. That's his style."

"We could use his kind here with us. The fact is, Mr. Poe, we face a difficult situation."

Poe's eyebrows lifted. "Difficult?"

"We have to do something about the Marquis de Sade and his Army of Liberation Through the Willing Acceptance of Pain. The ALTWAP, as they call themselves. There's a war on, Mr. Poe, and we're in the middle of it. The infamous and untalented Sade is tearing hell out of Hell, and the Devil has deputized the French Symbolist Poets to stop him. Or else."

"Or else what?"

"Or else we lose this snug little place we have here and will be obliged to go around fighting and dying in messy ways like the others."

Poe looked around. He could hear the sound of a battle raging. It came from the big TV screen. The Hotel Lauzon kept abreast of the news. Poe watched, fascinated. On the screen, disjointed bodies flew in the air, blood splattered everywhere, and the mashed viscera made ugly sucking noises. It was all very ugly and painful.

"Will you help us?" Baudelaire asked.

"Oh, absolutely," said Poe. "I've always wanted to live in Paris. What do you want me to do?"

"How about taking charge of the whole thing?" Baudelaire asked.

"I was afraid you were going to ask that," Poe said.

"Afraid?" cried Baudelaire. You are a Virginian, Mr. Poe, and it is well known that fighting blood is native to your soil, a gift to its sons from the deep-cut arroyos and shadowed haciendas of that Indian-haunted land."

Poe stared at him for a moment, then said. "The geography of Virginia, sir, although varied in the extreme, does not include such features as arroyos."

"I stand corrected, sir."

"Virginians are indeed a fighting race, however."

"As I have surmised," said Baudelaire.

"If you are really serious about my leading this action," Poe said, "I'll take it on as an exercise in scientific ratiocination."

Baudelaire sucked in his breath. "The ratiocination of an Edgar Allan Poe! We could ask no more."

Poe was thorough, a trait which Baudelaire appreciated. When Poe said he'd apply ratiocination to the problem, he was going to do no less than that. He asked for and received a private office, a supply of quill pens and parchment (there wasn't time for him to learn how to use a computer, or even to learn what a computer was), and a supply of laudanum, wine, black coffee, and sausage rolls. He retired to the den to think the problem through. From time to time, he'd stick his head out the door to ask questions.

"What do you call those things that fly in the air?"

"Aeroplanes, *mon ami.*"

"And tanks are the ones that go on the ground?"

"Correct."

"And the bomb that kills everybody around and then poisons everything for years to come—it is the atomic, is it not?"

"*C'est-ça!*"," Baudelaire said.

"I think I'm getting somewhere," Poe said.

He resumed his introspection. He had asked that the television be turned on to "Infernally Yours," the 24 hour news show. At last, he walked somewhat unsteadily to the door, opened it, strode through to the waiting Symbolist Poets, who had assembled in the Games Room where they played bumper pool while awaiting the outcome of Poe's cerebrations.

"What's the answer?" Baudelaire asked.

"It's simple," Poe said. "Get a really good general."

"Whom would you suggest, specifically?" Baudelaire asked.

Poe shrugged. "Robert E. Lee, of course, but I understand he's tied up with other duties."

Baudelaire turned to Archilochos. "Whom would you suggest?"

"I have no knowledge of the modern world," Archilochos said.

"Well, dammit, man, *someone* has to lead us."

"All right," Archilochos said. "Can I borrow one of those horses stabled near *Les Deux Magots*?"

"Of course. But what are you going to do?"

"You'll see," said Archilochos.

Lizzie Borden had learned a lot from Sade. She had been all shamefaced when she first arrived in Hell. She knew that people looked down on her. But the truth was, she really couldn't remember exactly what had happened that hot August day in 1878 in Fall River, Massachusetts.

She had walked around the central bus station of New Hell timidly, not exactly frightened, but definitely put off by the vast clots of armed and smelly men who surged back and forth looking for transport to various corners of Hell.

She was lost, bewildered, and there didn't seem to be any people around here like her. And then the Marquis de Sade appeared, tall, cadaverous, crazy, charming, and every inch a gentleman.

"Miss Borden," Sade said, taking off his lofty black hat, "I have heard of you, because I make it my business to study outstanding persons in the central libraries of Hell whenever I get a chance to take a break from my other activities. I suggest, Miss Borden, that if you haven't made any other plans, come with me and join my cause."

"Well, I'll come along and see how I like your cause," Miss Borden said. "But no promises."

They rode together on the stage coach to East Hell. Along the way, Sade asked in conversational tones, "And may I enquire how was your death, Miss Borden? Not too painful, I hope?"

It seemed to Miss Lizzy that really cultured people didn't talk about their deaths. But of course Mr. Sade was a foreigner and exceptions had to be made for him.

"Why, I scarcely remember, Mr. Sade," Lizzy said. "In fact, all of the most important parts of my former life are now a blur to me."

That should stop him from asking questions about the Fall River affair.

"You mean you don't remember The Fall River affair?" Sade said.

"No, I do not," Miss Lizzy said.

"Don't kid me," Sade said. "Of course, it doesn't matter a curse whether you remember or not. You did it and you know it."

Miss Lizzy knew she should be shocked by such candor. Yet she felt, instead, refreshed by the way Sade got right to it. She remembered that she was in Hell, the worst was over, and things which had once made a great deal of difference now didn't matter at all.

"I don't remember, but it's possible I did do it. In a moment of madness, I mean."

"You shouldn't back away from it," Sade told her. "Take pride in your monstrousness, girl! Anybody can love their parents. It takes an exceptional person to break societal conditioning and take the axe to them that they so richly deserve."

"But why do they deserve the axe?"

"Victims deserve to die," Sade said in reasonable

tones. "And only those who deserve to die become victims. This is a law of nature. Despite their protestations, victims are drawn to the crime every bit as much as their murderers. They are accomplices together, murderer and victim."

"Are you referring to all people, Mr. Sade?"

"Indeed I am. A characteristic of the human species is our ability to enjoy the pain of others. This sets us apart from the animals, who are still unaware of the possibility of sensations more exquisite than mother nature has given them. You are the bearer of a great reputation, Lizzie, a figure of gigantic folkloric proportions. Don't ruin it all now by repenting just because the going has gotten a little rough."

"A little rough!" Miss Lizzy said with some acerbity. "I'm in Hell! How much rougher must it get?"

"Hell's your new home, my dear," Sade said. "You might as well get with it."

Sade was a zealot on the subject of hurting people. Lizzie thought that sadism was childish. It bored her. All this emphasis on pain. All that French exquisiteness and decadence began to get on her nerves. She was a plain American and she longed for others of her own kind. But they wouldn't even speak to her. And that was unfair.

The hypocrites! They thronged around Lucrezia Borgia, and she'd probably killed more people than Lizzie had even *known* in her lifetime. And they were crazy about Elizabeth, the pretty Countess Báthory, who used to bathe in the blood of young village girls back in the good old days in Transylvania.

Having a title and being foreign made all the difference.

But there was also that other bunch of French people, those symbolists or surrealists or whatever they were with whom Mr. Poe always hung out. They wrote crazy stories and painted crazy pictures, and even this music didn't sound like anything human. But they were fun, always hanging out together in cafés, filling the air with tobacco and wine fumes, and with their shouts of laughter as they scored off each other. She thought about them sometimes. They were decadent, but it would be nice to live in Paris.

Lizzie had died in 1927, at the age of 67. When she came back to life in Hell, she found that she was much younger than that. This was a frequent device on the part of Satan, who didn't want Hell filled exclusively with old people, and had an interest in seeing some of the famous ones at their prime.

She figured she was about thirty years old. Maybe late twenties. But, although Satan, or rather, his helpers, those terrible Morticians and their boss, The Undertaker, had taken old age away from her, they had not given her any more beauty than she had had during her life. Rather less, if anything.

She studied herself critically in the mirror. Was her nose perhaps a trifle larger than she remembered it? And that little whitehead behind her left ear, had it really been necessary for them to reproduce that? And why, she thought daringly, instead of just taking off years, didn't they add a little to my—bust!

She was pleased with herself for having allowed herself to think the naughty word. After all, she was in Hell now. Vulgarity was no doubt the norm here. Not that she was planning to stoop to it on any regular basis.

The more she saw of Sade, the less she liked him. The Massachusetts spinster was repelled by Sade's twisted, bitter, crazy face, his habit of cackling and rubbing his hands together, his general air of nearly uncontrollable mania. As for Sade, Lizzie didn't even exist for him as a woman. She wasn't at all like Juliette or any of the other heroine-victims of his written works.

Lizzie found a nice room in a boarding house on the side of town, away from Sade, run by a pleasant French lady named Charlotte Corday.

Miss Corday was an enthusiastic French lady who talked frequently about her fiancé, somebody named Dantin or Dantawn. Miss Corday's accent was a trifle thick, and her fiancé was never around.

Miss Corday seemed too nice to be in a place like this, but Lizzie knew that appearances could be deceiving. Not many of the people she had met so far in Hell looked like the sorts of people she would have expected to find. And she was disappointed to notice the large numbers of clergymen of all faiths and denominations, still dressed in their worshipful uniforms, walking around with no show of shame at all.

It was nice at first in New Hell, because Lizzie found that she was a celebrity among the locals. It was difficult for her to understand why, but that's how it goes with stardom; you never know when it can strike.

For a while it looked like she'd made a friend in Miss Bonny Parker, but she just couldn't stand Bonny's boyfriend, Clyde. Everyone else on the block was worse. People like Pretty Boy Floyd, Machine Gun Kelly, Father Cooghan, Joe McCarthy.

Just about everyone on the block had been a criminal or done something notorious in his lifetime. Lizzie had never considered herself a criminal. She'd certainly never stolen anything, and she secretly thought that stealing was a worse crime than murder.

There was nothing much to do in East Hell. The time stretched on, a ruin as far into the future as Lizzie's eye could see. But that changed the day she attended the annual picnic given by Sade's Benevolent Protective Brotherhood of the Criminally Insane.

De Sade adored theater, loved to put on plays, spectacles, and his buddy Rais was just as bad. During his lifetime Rais had almost beggared himself by staging massive, elaborate stage plays on edifying subjects, in some of which he acted. The picnic gave them a chance to put on their theatricals. For the townspeople of East Hell, it was a chance to eat fried chicken and corn on the cob and dance square dances to the music of a jug band.

It was then that the tall young man came up to her and enquired if he could bring her a plate of chicken and a glass of lemonade. Lizzie hadn't wanted to go to the tables herself because there were too many drunks in the way, and those Hell's Angels people, on their huge motorcycles, wearing helmets with horns and feathers.

"That is very kind of you," Lizzie said. "Frankly, those large, hairy young men on those *motorcycles*—I believe that is what they are called—are rather intimidating."

"To some," the young man said, implying, clearly, that he was not one.

"I wonder how they get such mechanisms here—the Bad Place." For she could still not bring herself to say Hell aloud.

"I've heard," the young man said, "that Satan makes special arrangements with a factory on Earth. I would like to introduce myself. I'm Jesse Woodson James."

"The famous Jesse James?" Lizzie enquired.

"I reckon I am. And who might you be, ma'am?"

"Miss," she corrected. "I'm Miss Lizzie Borden of Fall River, Massachusetts, and I suppose I am not unknown, either."

"I'm afraid I died before you were born," Jesse said, "So I haven't heard of you. I'm trying to keep up on all the people I meet in Hell; but it's tough, you meet so many people."

Jesse was of medium height and slender and nice to look at. He looked about 25 years old, and he probably didn't have to shave more than once a week.

The afternoon wore on—the long, long afternoon of Hell filled with the infinite expanses of boredom that open out on an endless August day in East Hell, when not even the Devil can find mischief enough for idle fingers. Lizzie and Jesse talked on.

Toward evening, Jesse James asked Miss Lizzie Borden if he could take her out to dinner that evening.

"Why, Mr. James," Lizzie said, "That would be a waste of your time. Why do you not go out with one of the many beautiful ladies I see all around us."

"Well, ma'am," Jesse said, "those are mostly foreign ladies you are referring to, people with aristocratic titles. Not my kind of folks at all. I'm a country boy, Miss Borden."

"But I am not a country girl. Fall River was a city in my day. Not at all your sort of place, Mr. James."

"I doubt our backgrounds are all that dissimilar, Miss Borden. You look and talk like a country lady, not one of them Boston or New York folk."

"Well, I should think not!" Lizzie said. "My parents *were* farm-bred, after all. I used to help with the canning and putting up preserves."

"I sure would like to eat some real food," Jesse said wistfully. "It don't appear like nobody bothers farming in all the parts of Hell I've seen yet. They're too busy fighting each other to have time for anything but foreign quick-prepared food."

Jesse felt better when he was with Lizzie. It was hard to figure out why. Though she looked only a couple years older than him, still, she was no looker. Plain. Maybe even homely. And not what you'd call a sexy lady. But Jesse felt great peace when he was with her. She seemed to make such sense. And ever since he'd died and come back to life in Hell, Jesse James had wanted to find something that made sense.

He couldn't find any of his brothers. He didn't blame Satan for that. He understood that that was just the way it had to be. If everyone was reborn with his kin around him, and then maybe their friends and *their* kin, there'd be no time to meet the new people who were always coming in.

Jesse felt ill at ease among these people. They all seemed to think so much of themselves. Always walking around braggin' about how great they was. Especially them Frenchmen. In Jesse's sly, hard, country view, *they took too much on themselves*.

But they were the prevailing fashion, the trend of the times—loud-mouthed bullies, shrill voiced French crazies, and as fine a collection of riffraff selected from the dyings of five thousand years, or from even further back, from one million B.C. when the first intelligent cave man with an actual soul, somebody who looked like Victor Mature, raised his head and threw the bone into the air that marked the beginning of recorded history.

But now he was able to spend a lot of time with Miss Lizzie, and they could talk about country things. Sewing bees and horseshoe pitching. Haying and harvesting. Eating Thanksgiving turkey and mending fence. Hayrides and sleigh rides. Corn for the chickens, slop for the pigs. Not so much difference if you're country-bred.

It was at this time that Sade was organizing his shock squads, and collaborating with Jean-Paul Sartre to write propaganda that would inflame the minds of the damned and turn them to the path of *utter* utter damnation.

Not that Sartre believed in the Marquis de Sade or his doctrines. Sartre was mentally and morally opposed to everything Sade stood for. But Sartre was also curious, and he had that weird detachment of the intellectual that permitted him to take on the coloration of the world around him with no nonsense about moral approval or disapproval—just the artist learning his material. Sartre was intrigued by Sade's project, interested to see how this contest between different connotations of evil would come out. He considered himself a sort of foreign correspondent of the infernal, and, since disengagement was alien to his nature, he was happy to work for his keep by writing broadsheets for Sade.

Jesse watched these developments with bleak, expressionless, slate-gray Missouri eyes. He knew that soon Sade and his bunch would have to pull out of East

Hell. They weren't strong enough yet to hold territory. But East Hell would remain the center of the resistance.

One way or another, war was about to start soon.

It would be time then to make a decision.

Miss Lizzie Borden was a light sleeper. She had frequently been troubled by bad dreams during her lifetime, and this became more frequent after her death. Her dreams came in three varieties: nervous ones filled with mice; major ones of drowning; and odd dreams in which she danced with a man whose face she could never remember upon awakening.

It was this latter dream that bothered her most. And this was the dream that awakened her in the darkness of the night.

Just after she awoke, she heard the light tapping at the window.

Lizzie got out of bed, pulled a robe around her and went swiftly to the dresser. There was the two-shot derringer that Sade had given her. It was loaded. She pulled back the hammers, cocking them. Then, as the tapping came again, she walked to the window.

It was Jesse James outside, his small-featured face ghostly and shadowless in the moonlight. She was both alarmed and thrilled, because his attentions over the recent days had not gone unnoticed, and had in fact been recorded word for word and look for look in the *tabula rasa* of her heart.

She opened the window. Jesse said, "Miss Lizzie, kindly excuse me for barging in this way at this hour of night. But I found something out. I learned there's going to be a big fight right here in East Hell. I was figuring to get out of here, since that Markwess Sadey doesn't impress me as a leader to be proud of. I don't know nothin' about those other fellows, the ones doin' the attacking, but they got no claim on me, nor on you, neither, it seems to me, so I came here to offer you my most loyal and respected protection."

"Your protection is most welcome, of course, Mr. James," Lizzie said. "But what do you propose to do?"

"Miss Lizzie, I can't think of no better way than for you and me to skedaddle out of here right quick. Like now, immejiately. Because in a couple of hours ain't nobody going to come in or out of East Hell except in a body bag."

"My goodness!" Lizzie said. "But I can't just *leave*. I'll need time to pack. And I'm not as assured as you of the urgency."

"Miss Lizzie, tell you what. You just get dressed and take a little bag and come with me to the top of Eagle Pass. I've got a sulky all hitched up. If by dawn nothing's happened, I'll admit myself the biggest fool in these parts and take you back to your hotel."

Lizzie went behind a screen and dressed hastily. She was still by no means convinced that the danger was as imminent as Mr. James made it out to be. It seemed to her that Mr. James might be exaggerating in order to increase his own importance as her helper, and so put her under obligation to him. Still, prudence dictated that she give him the benefit of the doubt, at least for the moment.

"I'd appreciate your gettin' a move on, Miss Lizzie," Jesse said after a while, as she was lacing up her corset and having trouble finding the proper stays in the dark.

"I think, Mr. James," she said, "you are being somewhat familiar. Have you informed Mister Sade of your suspicions?"

"No, Lizzie, I haven't."

"And why, pray? It seems a shoddy way to repay his hospitality."

"Well if that don't beat all," Jesse said. He banged his fist against his thigh, then grinned and shook his head. "This nice Mr. Sadey is feedin' us because he considers us part of his army. He expects us to fight for him when the other fellers come ridin' over the hill.

Honestly, Lizzie, you don't know whatall about politics in these parts."

Well, Lizzie thought, he *is* being cheeky. She knew that she ought to administer a strong rebuke, because this sort of presumption was not to be permitted, especially in one who, say what you will about him, could not be considered to have been gently raised. He was in fact what they called nowadays a *redneck*. The sorts of people who are beneath consideration by well-raised New England spinsters who . . .

There flashed before her eyes at that moment, an image of a small axe, its ash handle dark with blood, its steel head coated in blood, in the hand that held it, the small hand, that, too, was covered in blood.

"Come *on*, Lizzie! Time we hit the Owl Hoot Trail."

"All right, I'm coming," said Miss Lizzie Borden.

The Undertaker didn't like to think about going on strike because he was loyal to management, namely, Satan. But this latest trouble had increased his workload immeasurably, and he felt he was not being suitably compensated. The bodies were coming down the chutes like peas in a hopper. What was worse, the bodies were coming through in such terrible condition that the Morticians had to spend a lot of extra time sewing them up. Sometimes, parts of people came down the chutes in logjams of trunks and heads. Sometimes, there were showers of fingers, blizzards of kneecaps, hecatombs of toes. Sometimes, the Morticians were so overworked and so behind schedule that they couldn't put aside all the partially reassembled torsos in order to wait for a matchup on just exactly the right foot or hand or whatever it was. They just had to patch with what was at hand.

It was in this time that a new class of dead came into existence, The Mixed Dead, composite bodies who were unsure of which of their many physical components was predominant. "A generation of mumblers," The Undertaker called them and tried again to reach Satan on the emergency line. He didn't want to go on strike, but something had to be done. However, it appeared that Satan wasn't answering his calls. Not even the twenty-four hour Curse Line was open. Not even the switchboard to the Pentagram answered. Looked like those fellows were pretty busy, the Undertaker opined.

Poe said, "Someone is treading on my tail."

Baudelaire looked up. "Did you say something, old man?"

Poe smiled a twisted smile. "Oh, never mind. I was just trying out the first line of a poem. Where was I? Yes, the campaign has gone well so far. We owe it entirely to General Robert E. Lee, the finest flower of the southern Confederacy."

"But we do not have the famous general here," Baudelaire pointed out, hating his role of straight man and wishing there were someone else around to do it.

He was getting a little sick of Mr. Poe, the strutting little fellow with the uncertain temper and the huge, easily wounded ego. It was a lot easier to translate Poe than to get a straight answer out of him.

"Of course General Lee is not here in person," Poe said with his know-it-all air. "But I went down to the Circulating Library of East Hell yesterday and was lucky enough to find a book outlining Lee's campaigns. Through ratiocination I was able to make a quick study of the strategems and strategies of this mashter stratishtrician."

"*Comment?*" said Baudelaire. He saw at once that Poe was drunk.

"Sorry, *strategic tactician* was what I meant to say. Applying hish prinschiples—" Poe pulled himself together with an effort. "General Lee's, I mean, I saw that I had to push our troops through Apache Pass and direct them to fan out on either side of East Hell in a double envelopment movement. With Huysmans leading the left wing and de L'Isle-Adam the right, our success will be assured: each man carrying through his orders with that cold indifference that wins battles—but only so long as the sun of sentimentality remains in recession."

Orders were given and the movement of troops begun. The High Command, Poe, Baudelaire, Verlaine, Rimbaud, Mallarmé, a few others, sat around with glasses of white wine, cigars clenched in their hands, waiting to hear the results.

The early returns were favorable. On the basis of them, Poe announced, "I think we can safely assume that the back of their resistance is broken."

Just at that moment, Sade's riposte broke in all its fury on Poe's troops, who were sitting around drinking white wine and writing verses and so were caught completely by surprise.

Fiendish berserkers in clown makeup and fright wigs roared into battle behind Elizabeth Báthory. Facing them were a few frightened platoons of critics and editors who had been talked into making common cause with the poets in the name of culture. They wavered, then ran for the hills as the crazed kamikazes of Sacher-Masoch's Pouting Brigade thrust through the perimeter defence with short gasping cries. The poets, alas, had spent too much time considering vintages rather than machine gun installations, and had worried more about who was in charge of catering the snacks than who was to lead the counter-attack. The right flank, compositers, mostly, held for a while, thrusting back the assaults of Gilles de Rais' Carnival Rioteers. But then Rais assembled his men once again, and said to them, "Once more, my braves, and this one is for Jeanne d'Arc, the glorious vision that uplifted me throughout my years of doing evil!"

The poets retched at the hypocrisy, and so, weakened, gave way at last when de Rais' assault was backed up by the final charge of the Marquis de Sade himself, at the head of his chosen companions, the five hundred hard cases known as *Les Piquants*.

The battlefield broke up into a hundred individual combats. Soon it became clear that the forces of French Symbolist Poetry were on the verge of a crushing defeat. And suddenly, it was no laughing matter for anyone, least of all Satan, who immediately started answering his calls again.

"This is difficult country," Miss Lizzie Borden said, allowing Jesse to help her up onto a rock ledge.

"Yes, ma'am, it is," Jesse said. "This sure looks to me like some country I passed through down in Texas."

"Texas is probably above us now," Lizzie said.

"I mean Hell Texas. Stands to reason there'd be such a place."

"I don't know if that's levity," Miss Lizzy said, "but I can do without it."

"Suit yourself, Lizzie," Jesse said equably.

"Excuse me," a voice, speaking English in a heavy Greek accent, said.

Lizzie and Jesse both jumped. The owner of the voice, Archilochos, was standing on a ridge some ten feet higher than theirs, and set back some thirty or forty feet. The repeating Winchester he held in his bronzed hands looked capable of enforcing his will, reflecting, as it did in its brightly polished walnut with brass facings, the indomitable will of its holder.

The three stood and stared at each other for a moment.

Then Archilochos broke the silence. "Hi. I'm Archie."

"I'm Lizzie," Miss Borden said.

At last Jesse said, "I'm Jesse."

And then the moment of tension was over, and it was as if they had been old friends for a long time.

"The news is very bad indeed," Archilochos said. "The French Symbolist Forces have been defeated in front of East Hell. Nothing now stands between Sade and the final onslaught on Nouveau Paris."

"My goodness!" Miss Lizzie said. "Isn't there anything we can do?"

They were camped at the time on the bank of a dry wash. Jesse, an accomplished scrounger from his days riding with Quantrill in the Border Wars, had managed to stone a couple of incautious gerbils, and now they were boiling in the black hat he used, when need arose, as a pot. Archilochos, from a different tradition, was equally provident. His snare had taken in a lapin and a scottle hen. He had them bubbling in the pot his helmet provided. Both men saved the choice bits for Miss Lizzie.

"We're just sitting here," Lizzie said, "and those terrible men are marching on Paris. Archilochos, don't you have any ideas?"

Archilochos looked up from the bit of greasewood he was whittling. "Of course I have ideas. But what good is that? I know a way to pin down Sade's army. Look here."

He quickly sketched out the positions in the sand; Paris here, Sade approaching from the only practicable route. But if we could interpose a force here—and lead Sade's men toward it . . ."

"Yes, I see," Lizzie said. "You could ambush him!"

"If I had a large force of men," Archilochos said. "But I don't. Everybody's spoken for."

"Oh, I don't know about that," Jesse said. "I know a fellow out this way might want to help."

"What's in it for him?" Archilochos said.

"He likes to fight."

"A sadist?"

"No. That sort of term doesn't apply. Let's say he's a man with a grievance."

"What's his name?"

"Tishwin."

"That's a funny name," Lizzie said.

"Oh, he's a funny fellow," Jesse said.

In 1877, Jesse James had left Missouri and gone to Chicago. From there he entrained to Oglalla, Nebraska. And from there he had travelled by horse to Santa Fe, making several stops along the way. The purpose of this visit was never revealed, and any efficacy that it might have had was erased by the guns of the Fords when, not long after, they put Jesse James in his grave.

Now Jesse was on the trail again, the Owl Hoot Trail, he called it, and he was trying to finish after death what he had been unable to complete in his life.

They journeyed all day through a flinty desert. At nightfall Jesse saw a trace of smoke on the horizon. They steered for it, and soon came upon a solitary Indian sitting before a fire.

The Indian, a tall, impressive man, rose. "How," he said.

"I'm fine," Jesse said. "How you?"

"Fine, too. Long time no see, Jesse."

"Yep, I reckon it is. Too bad that little plan of mine about making an alliance with you and your Apaches to fight on the side of the Confederacy never came to nothing."

"Indians know what it is like to dream in vain. What brings you to these parts, Jesse, and who are your friends?"

Jesse introduced Archilochos and Miss Lizzie Borden to his friend, whose name was Geronimo.

"As for why I've come," Jesse said, "it's to invite you and your friends to come fight a war with me."

"Are you kidding?" Geronimo asked. "Me fight with a bunch of palefaces? And French symbolic poet palefaces at that?"

Geronimo had been practicing mortification for a long time. Hell had no surprises for him. It was rather less painful and disgusting than he had expected.

"I've got a reason for you," Jesse said.

"What is it?"

"Just a chance to kill a few more palefaces. For old time's sake."

"Your statement lacks logic," Geronimo said, "but it appeals to the Indian in me."

"That's what I was hoping for," Jesse said.

Sade's troops were sighted in St-Germain-en-Laye, and so the weary symbolist poets marched out of Nouveau Paris again to do battle.

Outside Paris, they ran into difficulties. This level hadn't been too fully thought out. There were difficult features, slate desert piled on top of a rain forest, like Satan was storing his nastiest natural effects here. It was treacherous country, all the more so when combined with the fluctuant and unpredictable operation of Paradise, now popping up and down on the horizon like an enraged Jack-in-the-Box.

Poe's troops tried to form a line of battle. Suddenly the rain began. It dampened everyone's spirits. And Sade's forces drove in from the flank. It looked like the end.

Then Archilochos rode in with news. "Help is at hand! Me and Jesse did it! Pull back your formations to the left and watch what happens."

Doubt, uncertainty among the High Command. Poe desperately searching through his journals. What would Robert E. Lee have done? Many different things, but it's obvious that a move to the left is madness. Who knows what this fellow Jesse James is up to? And has anyone actually heard this so-called Archilochos speak classical Greek? What is there on the left, anyhow? Just a lot of hardscrabble, granite plain, a little grass here and there coming up in sunny tufts. Just that and the sour slough of the wind. To go there would be madness, Sade could slaughter us there without effort.

"Still," Baudelaire said, "let's do it anyhow, maybe

something good will happen." Orders were given; the movement was effectuated.

It was a great sight when Sade's forces were all assembled on the endless plain outside of Paris. Among those who passed in review were Mongols, Turks, Tartars, Tatars, Huns, Visigoths, Lithuanian Knights, Esthonian Afternoons, Moldavian Morning Arquebusmen, Sadduceean Khedives. They paraded past Sade's reviewing stand, barbarically splendid in their furs and silks. They chanted their new motto as they marched past: "Kill for the hell of it!"

Sade, standing on the reviewing stand and taking the salute, remarked to Rais, "Quite a good turnout. Where did you turn up so many fine fellows?"

Rais said, "First we sent out loudhailer men and they went to the endless pockets and fringes of Hell where the lost peoples of the past reenact their endless feuds. We offered them glory and loot, palahan and chanduanga, those usual things."

"Who are those fellows in ostrich feathers?" Sade asked.

"A couple of Zulu *impis*, may it please your grace. Good spearfellows those, and ample to the measure no matter how strait it may turn out."

"Splendid," said Sade. "Let the madness begin."

As Sade's forces rush after the Symbolists out into the open, the Indians attack. Led by Geronimo they pour in from behind the pitcher-topped mesas, they come galloping in from the arroyos, they arise from the gulches and dry washes. And there seems no end to them. Even more Indians come tumbling down from the cottonwood trees. There are Comanches, strong for battle, and the noble Dakotas, game for one more try. Here are the Iroquois, here the Sauk and Fox, here are the Apache, and on the other wing we have Pawnee, Ute, Cheyenne, Blackfoot, Crow, Cherokee, and a host of others.

They fall on Sade's forces, one last throw of the dice against the whites. Their war cry is: "Reform the Reservation System in Hell!" And on they come.

The forces of Sade fall back in disarray. Sade's last words are, "Old sadists never die. They just fade away. I shall return."

The last of the loyalists, Leopold von Sacher-Masoch, escapes from them all. He takes refuge in a cave on a mountainside. He is panting, out of breath, exhausted beyond human measure. He has been wounded; he doesn't know how many times, because for each wound he receives another opens up in anticipation, a mirroring stigmata which is his alone, and no man can say whether the bullets of his pursuers killed him or the more potent ammo of his imagination. We do not know. But they have recorded his last words.

Lips peeled back, he snarled, "Th-th-th-that's all, folks." And that was all. For him. This time.

Jesse and Lizzie moved to Paris and were given a free apartment by a grateful Baudelaire. Their apartment had ten bedrooms and was right on the St-Germain-des-Prés. That's class. Archilochos came by to visit, and told them he was on his way again.

"Why not stay here?" Jesse asked him.

"Yes," Archilochos said, "it's a fair city. But I never stay long in one place."

"Well, I can understand that," said Jesse.

"Goodbye, Mr. Archilochos," said Lizzie, and waved to him with her lace handkerchief as he rode off.

By morning, Archilochos was at the head of the pass leading into the unexplored territory beyond the Intemperate Zone. Here he stopped. Someone was waiting for him, a man on horseback with a slouch hat pulled down over his face. But Archilochos knew him anyway.

"Jesse!"

Jesse took off his hat. "I thought I might as well go along with you for a while."

"What about Lizzie?" Archilochos asked.

"She likes to run things her own ways," Jesse said, "And she doesn't approve of gambling, drinking or bad grammar."

"I don't think much of bad grammar myself," Archilochos said. "But you're mighty welcome anyhow, Jesse. Let's go!"

They rode on beneath the lurid beams of Paradise.

"PROFITS IN HELL"
Bill Kerby

Executive VP:

We stood in the hall because it was cooler. It was just another cheap but prevalent irony, the airhead secretaries were nice and comfortable while the movie studio executives sweltered in their offices. But the halls were wide and deeply carpeted (a restful mauve), so we decided to hold the staff meeting right there. The bimbos got us some chairs and a table and a few extra tubes of Gelucil and we were off to the races.

"All right," Darryl Zanuck said, "I want a run-down of all the pictures on the slate, inverse order." He twirled his well-worn polo mallet expertly. "In case we pull any plugs down the ladder, we may be able to piggyback some pay-or-play people up into our more important projects."

There was a murmur of appreciation in the hall. This short, balding man with the razor eyes had not gotten where he did on a lottery ticket. Every day with him was a learning experience and, so far, I'd had twenty-two years of them. Still, he was breaking me in; still, I was the New Kid; still, I was in charge of the 'B' pictures and it was my turn to start the meeting.

"D.Z., we have a few labor problems—"

"It better not be the writers!" he roared. "Those hacks. I'll get Nunnally Johnson or one of the other real writers in here so fast, it'll wilt their pathetic little keyboards."

"No, sir," I replied. "It's the Teamsters. Again." There was a silence in the room so real you could have sent it out for more coffee and Danish. "They're talking about wanting profit participation," I went on. "And apparently, they're fairly specific. Not net: they want gross. From dollar one."

"First I'll see them all in—" He stopped and grinned that grin, the cold, sly one that Jack Nicholson copped from the photographs. "This is war. And if they want it, I'm just the man to give it to them. They're not getting a cut," Zanuck said simply. "They're cockroaches. And while they may survive us all, that doesn't mean we have to reward them for it! Go ahead with the report."

"Well, sir," I went on, "actually, we're in pretty good shape, considering. *Mud Wrestlers from Mars Vs. The Aztec Mole Men* is on schedule even with the hijack of the weapons truck. *The Oklahoma Backhoe Massacre* looks good in dailies if we can get the lab to print two stops hotter. *The Dildo As Big As the Ritz* unless we replace the lead with his wife Zelda, who I talked to last night on the phone, and, mirabile dictu, seemed to be clean and clear. Next . . ."

I went on, running down the projects in order, Zanuck's eyes sparkling at my Latin bon mots and general scholarship. He was a life-long sucker for all things erudite and I could see a clean, smooth tunnel leading straight to lunch where I would order a little-known French white burgundy and then send it scornfully back as fit for only salad dressing while my boss looked on, proudly.

Everything was going fine, until Harry Cohn (sitting at the right hand of Himself) got up and told us in quaking tones what had happened yesterday on *Hell's Gate*.

"There was an accident," he said, "and, gentlemen, we are in deep shit."

There went lunch.

Portable Dressing Room Owner-Operator:

There are two sides to every story, I'll tell you. Sometimes more than two, once the sleazy land-sharks in the suits get through with their version; teaching common sense and truth to jump through hoops and then bend over for them. This is why I got my face in here. So that you would at least have a shot at what really happened.

See, I saw it. The whole enchilada. But first, there're a few things you should know. For background. For instance:

It *wasn't* war. It was simple justice, David and Goliath style. Although there are always those who think what we do is like war. Because the making of a movie is about equal chunks of hate, skill, exhaustion, love, fury, jealousy, and pain that get marched out like some military band fueled on LSD and the explosion in the center of the football field sometimes will look a whole lot like combat.

It was that way on our movie. I was there. And I don't have a clue why I wasn't killed, too.

Here's what happened. It was the third month of shooting Part XXVII's big battle scene and nothing was going right. Dar Robinson had damn near quit, there were so many stunt men getting banged up.

That Sadderday, we were supposed to have a big fly-by; a multi-camera shot that took the coordination of a slew of assistant directors, production managers, and I don't know what-all. I do know that the shot itself was rumored to be costing in the outskirts of a hundred million. Give you some idea of how complicated it was?

Anyway, things were going pretty good: This battalion marched into position, that oil convoy blew sky high, the battle raged to the howling song of every weapon and pyrotech in the business. It was quite a spectacle, we all agreed.

Then, all hell broke loose. The Chinese Bandit backfire retro-jets came in way too low as they screamed over the top of the ridge, dumping two camera positions and scattering cameramen and assistants everywhere. The half-snockered rookie stunt pilots (we found out later at the hearings who'd got them drunk and why) had overflown the check point and, instead of releasing their white phosphorus and napalm high over a secured area, they cut loose at about a hundred howling feet over a mob of extras in full battle drag. By the time the Chinese Bandit jets tried to pull up and get out, it was too late.

Two of them creamed into the mobile dressing rooms, vaporizing the location bus, a double articulated prop truck, and the second shift lunch at the caterers. The crashed Bandit jets' unused ammo and rockets kept detonating until it looked like Fourth of July forever while the cameras kept rolling. When the w.p. smoke finally cleared and they could get the gurneys and Med Techs in, over five hundred people lay in parts of wholes, dead or wounded. Two hundred and eighty of them eventually bought it. It was the most horrible thing I have ever witnessed, which includes a war, the deaths of my wife and son, and all that's gone before on this endless goddamn nightmare show which I have been on since Day One. *Hell's Gate,* is named just right, let me tell you, or will be if it ever gets in the can. That afternoon, it almost went belly-up, what I heard.

You can lose your stars, you can 86 your director, you can set fire to your negative, you can do anything in the course of a movie . . . except fuck the Teamsters. And

that day, in the big battle scene, the Chinese Bandit
retro-jets crashed and decimated nearly a hundred of
them at one time. Not even Bobby Kennedy had been
able to do that.

Movies are hard work for those who actually have to
make them, believe me. And once you've earned your
living (ha!) doing it, you have struggled and pounded
and suffered enough so that a couple of back-to-back
eternities in this asshole place seem like two weeks, all
expenses paid, at the Kahala Hilton.

Why anybody'd want to do this if he knew how to do
anything else, is beyond me. To send a little strip of
film about half as wide as your forefinger through a
camera for a couple hours on a big show like *Hell's
Gate*, it takes the intricate planning and perfect execu-
tion of at least fifteen hundred people, maybe more.
And that doesn't even count your proverbial Cast of
Thousands.

"Below the Line," we're called. It's a budget term,
no one knows where it came from. We're the people
that come in the credits after the movie's over. Our
brief moment of fame is seen by the backs of heads as
audiences put on their coats, walking out, and start to
argue about where they left their cars. Grips, gaffers,
costumers, stunt people, editorial, wranglers, greens-
keepers, the sound crew, the guys in foley who make
the footsteps that you hear down the hall, the drivers,
the camera crew, props, special effects, the caterers,
and (like me) the honeywagon guys with the portable
dressing rooms and bathrooms. A thousand people, all
trained by years of struggling on commercials, indus-
trial films, low-rent tit flicks; trained by decades of
scuffling to get jobs that would gag a Mexican donkey;
jobs on wimpy educational films, on National Geographic
shoots in East Jesus, Morocco, on beach-blanket biker
cheapies, on student films so cancerous they drove from
setup to setup in the director's dad's station wagon
while the cameraman was off begging for tiny rolls of

leftover film from famous artsie German directors like what's-his-face Fast-binder who thinks everything down here is so jerkoff it's cool. But hey, we only *make* the picture after the fame and the big fees and the publicity are doled out to—

The "Above The Line" People: the executives, the stars, their friends, their personal managers, producers, screen-writers, and *The* most over-rated job in movies— the director. So okay, here's your basic traffic cop who can follow a plan (sometimes); usually this guy has a strong ego and a weak back and he sags around in his hand-tooled leather director's chair trying to look tortured yet in command for the "Entertainment Tonight" crew; a guy who is the total focus of everyone's attention for the length of the shoot, who has no idea of what he's doing until he looks down at the page to see what the writer said or until he ambles over, all fake buddy-buddy, to talk to the stars to see which way their wind is blowing. Yeah, these overpaid college grad dorks who scowl real creatively, you know, these are the "Above The Line." And until recently, they got most of the front money and *All* the juice at the end, the all-important PROFIT PARTICIPATION.

Did I tell you? Movies are big, big business.

And since time immemorial, it was a real screw-a-rama. We were being hosed and for years, we knew it. But until the Chinese Bandit jet accident on *Hell's Gate*, there was nothing any of us could do except give it our best Gary Cooper grin and get on with finishing the show. We worked hard, partied hard, slept hard, and took beaucoup pride in knowing that we had made the movie while others, who knew they hadn't, would take all the credit when it was over. It made us strong, this feeling of brotherhood. And, in the end, it nearly got our dicks knocked off.

My grandad used to say, "if you want to know how something went wrong or who's responsible for it, ask yourself, who profits?" That one simple question was going to lead me to the light, even if it had to take me into a night black as ten feet down.

Executive VP:

Oh, I mean, you could just throw up, reading that outrageous drivel! Here is clearly a man with little or no regard for the facts, careening around in some impotent union leftie's blue collar wet dream. Those kind are always referring to some mythic "granddad" or nonexistent "uncle" who had all these ridiculous all-purpose folk sayings.

At the trial (there seem to be more lawyers down here than any other occupation), they tried—unsuccessfully, I might add—to prove that the whole unfortunate accident was *Our* responsibility. Here is their tortured logic: since we had terminated all their veteran stunt pilots for repeated insubordination, and had forced them to hire untrained replacements to fly the scene, which we could not reschedule for economic reasons, that it was our fault that the rookies all got drunk at our Welcome Aboard luncheon, the day of the flyby, the one at which I was able to secure a hundred cases of ice-cold Dom Perignon at considerable cost to the studio.

Laughingly, they connected the fact that all cameras accidently did keep rolling and in the final cut we did feature quite a bit of that very footage, tragic as it may have been. There was a tense moment in the courtroom (even I turned my face away) as their lawyer, that ludicrous communist Pekinese, Allard Lowenstein, brought in huge color blowups of some of the more unfortunate and grisly aspects of that sequence.

Fortunately, the judge, a man known far and wide for his respect for loyalty as well as the law, was a friend and political colleague of Darryl Zanuck's, and—without the boss's ever asking for even a dollop of extra fairness—we were acquitted of all charges. In perpetuity.

You would have thought from their outraged bellowing in court that the union and its symps had lost their minds. Their lawyer was an absolute embarrassment. We strode out and went to a late lunch at "22" and they slunk off to some prole diner, I suppose, to whine and lick their wounds. And I'm sure they'll never work with us again, ever. Until we offer them money and tell them where to show up.

Haw, haw, boys. Life in the big city.

Portable Dressing Room Owner-Operator:

Goddamn sonofabitch bastard, if I could get my hands on that prissy wimp lackey, I'd smack the chrome off his trailer hitch!

He's right about one thing, though: we were fit to be tied that day in court when the judge found them innocent of any wrongdoing. And we were all set to appeal it—Al Lowenstein was set to lead the charge again—until we found out that the same black-robed Nazi had just been promoted to head the Appeals Court. We knew we were hosed.

And oh, how the bastards strutted. We were given exactly one hour off to make the memorial service and the front office never even answered our request to put a title card on the show recognizing the victims' efforts and sacrifices.

The last straw was an executive order for another champagne lunch for the new rookie stunt pilots who were to fly the same formation (this time in B-17s, in a dream sequence) in the same part of the same movie! Hey, you can only rub people's noses in it so deep. Know what I mean?

I don't know, but I think I had the idea for the chili.

Executive VP:

Since the party was my bailiwick and I knew it would look good if I came in on time and under-budget, I accepted their offer of homemade chili at the luncheon. Many of the below-the-line folk are either generally inclined toward this type of dining or are actually from Oklahoma. In either case, they are what they eat. Still, I knew it would lighten my duties as a supplier and might make the newly employed stunt pilots more at ease, especially in light of what'd happened with their predecessors.

I ran into Zanuck in the men's room. He was checking the soap and paper towels. Nothing escapes this man's attention where running a studio is concerned.

"I hear everything is back on track again," he said.

"It is, D.Z.," I replied with my helpful grin.

"And are we going to need reshoots on the big battle scene?" he asked.

"No," I lied. "Editorial says they have enough, that audiences will love it. I saw a rough cut. Unbelievable." There was no need for the boss to know that we were going to have to shoot some of the more difficult stuff again. Not after what he'd been through. Part of my job is to run interference, to handle this kind of shit detail. Everybody does it. Somewhere in their career.

Besides, I had a party to think of. I had some boys to get drunk. Before their first stunt flight.

Portable Dressing Room Owner-Operator:

We had it covered. There were three pots of steaming, homemade chili. One was labeled, "Wimp." Another was "Normal." And the last was "Five Alarm, Men Only." We knew which pot the executives would make a big show of eating. It's part of how they are: they out shit-kick us. Today, we would let them. Because in that last pot, the chilis were barely masking the telltale flavor of the Ex-Lax.

My honeywagon, conveniently located to the back-lot set where the lunch was, was the designated revenge vehicle. We had sort of retooled the septic system for our little surprise and a couple of ol' boys from special effects had come up with this no-smell, quick-bond, clear glue. It went onto the toilet seats with no problem.

I made sure the Cuban cigars and good Frog brandy was in plain sight and I cleaned the unit extra good. I even gave it a shot or two of Giorgio's men's cologne on the way out. And on the door, I hung a sign. Executives, it said.

Executive VP:

Even though I despise mariachi music, I had hired the band to sort of keep spirits high in all senses of that phrase. And it seemed to be working. Pretty soon the new ones were talking and laughing with the old ones, you heard the same old stories, and got the same old movie crew feeling (which, in spite of the people involved, is actually quite appealing).

I must say the old crew was taking their defeat in court with real equanimity. There seemed to be no hard feelings or hidden agendas, no taut jaws or the smoldering glowers that that type has perfected. It was just music and beer and laughter and tequila shooters.

I lined up with some other of my fellow executives behind the "Five Alarm, Men Only" pot of chili. I love to see their faces as I outdo them at their own childish games.

Portable Dressing Room. Owner-Operator:

We all knew to stay away from it, of course. And it seemed to hit all at once. You should have seen their twitching faces and glazed eyes as they realized what this strange feeling was. As the conversation and laughing went on hold, only the mariachi music played on. We had all turned to watch them. What a sight: studio executives in the starting gate of the Diarrhea Derby!

That pusbag assistant brown-nose of Zanuck's was the first to hit the bricks. The howl built out of him as he ran, heading straight for my trailer of bathrooms.

Executive VP:

That bastard sonofabitch, I knew he was involved somehow! The pain was excruciating as I turned the corner, bounding up the stainless steel stairs to the honeywagon. Thank God for portable toilets, I remember thinking.

Sitting down, the seats seemed especially warm (a new advance?) and when one is where one is supposed to be in a situation like this, a comforting feeling comes over one, not really experienced since youth.

It did not last long. I heard some squeaky, high-pitched howling below me. When I tried to get up to see, I was stuck fast! I couldn't move. And the howling under me became shrieking and as I peered down into the darkness—as much as I was able to—I saw the glint of two horrible, hungry little eyes.

And then it began.

Portable Dressing Room Owner-Operator:

We had not fed those weasels in nearly two weeks. And, bubba, they took to the honeywagon's sewer pipes like it'd been home all their life. The first uh, rain must have made them real angry. Until they saw those moon dinners up above them, fat and puckered and stuck and waiting.

Ho, boy . . .

To Whom It May Concern:

1. After lengthy negotiations with various unions (including, of course, my beloved Teamsters), henceforth, all those allied below-the-line personnel will receive participation in our profits, gross from dollar one.

2. No more than one hour will be taken for the executive memorial service.

3. And Bill Kerby, former portable dressing room owner-operator on Unit 6, will be relieved of his duty. And will be installed as my new assistant, effective immediately.

D.Z.

TERMINAL

George Alec Effinger

"All right, buddy, end of the line. Everybody out."

The bus driver was shaking Rusty Cope by the shoulder. It seemed like a good time to wake up. "We here?" asked Cope.

The driver was a demon, and he gave the young man a demon's black-toothed grin. "*I'm* here, anyway," it said. It turned around and headed back up the aisle. "Move your ass."

Cope yawned and rubbed his eyes, then stood up. He wondered where he was. His last memories were of a vicious barroom brawl in a rundown saloon in New Tombstone, where he'd died for at least the twentieth time. Then there was the horror of the Undertaker's table. He didn't remember getting on the bus. Through the grimy windows he could see the back side of a Hellhound bus station. The other passengers were already standing on the sidewalk, waiting for the bus driver to open the baggage compartment. Cope yawned again and stepped down out of the bus, into the warm, overcast afternoon. "Thanks for riding with Hellhound," he thought. He felt curiously let down; he wondered what he had expected, maybe beautiful native girls handing out flower garlands? He joined the others and waited for the red-eyed demon or some other employee to dig his knapsack out.

There had been six other passengers on the bus, all young men about his own age; they all seemed to be in their early twenties. Cope got his knapsack and put it on the sidewalk. He stretched and rubbed his scalp and looked around. Across the street was a small flower shop, a lunch counter, a magazine stand and a bank. The sign on the bank said FIRST INFERNAL BANK OF NEW SPRINGFIELD. He had never heard of a section of Hell called New Springfield. He knew from experience that the first order of business was to learn the local rules. Cope squinted his eyes for a moment, then turned and gathered up his pack. The others were already trooping slowly into the bus station. Behind them, the demon driver climbed back into the bus, closing the door with a mechanical wheeze. He gunned the engine, and the bus pulled away from the curb. "End of the line," the driver had said; Cope supposed that was meant to be an ominous remark. Everything that came out of the mouths of demons was meant to be ominous. After the first hundred years or so, you stopped paying attention, or you went crazy. Cope watched the bus roll away. There didn't seem to be any other traffic on this street, and no pedestrians, either.

"Watch it," growled the boy ahead of him. Cope hadn't been paying attention and hadn't realized that the others had bunched up in the doorway of the terminal.

"Sorry," he muttered.

"What the hell *is* this?" said someone. Cope couldn't see what the trouble was.

A moment later, they were all inside the bus station. Or what had once been a bus station. The high-ceilinged waiting room was deserted. The paint on the walls was peeling in long strips and the paneling overhead was crumbling and now littered the floor, ankle-deep in some places. The air smelled damp and stale. Dust covered everything: the plastic molded chairs, the abandoned counters, the dark and smashed pinball and video games. A corrugated metal grate protected the small newsstand, but the grate had itself been breached and now hung opened on one side, sadly and uselessly. It was dim, the only light coming through the broken windows high up on the walls. Despite the dust, every footstep echoed. The place was dead, long dead, and frightening.

"The goddamn driver let us off at the wrong bus station," said one of the others, a tall boy with a curly halo of blond hair.

"Must be new on the route," said a short, heavy, freckled youth.

"Ought to know where the station is, though," the blond complained.

"I don't even know where I am," said Cope.

"I don't, either," said the heavy boy.

"Then why did you come here?" asked the tall blond.

Cope shrugged. He didn't remember getting on the bus in the first place.

"Anybody know where we are?" asked the blond.

Cope looked from one face to another, but everyone was shaking his head or frowning. "Nobody knows anything about New Springfield?"

"It wasn't my idea coming here," said a tall boy with short red hair.

"One minute I was attacking this villa with the Khan's men screaming all around me," said a young man with huge hands and a beard in need of trimming. "And the next thing I know, I'm on some damn bus."

"So no one knows where we are or how we got here?" asked Cope.

"I was just tagged by the Undertaker," said the blond.

"Me too," said Cope.

"And me," said the bearded boy. Everyone else was nodding in agreement.

"Great," said the heavy boy with a sigh. "What does that tell us?"

"That we're not here by accident. That somebody in the Administration wants to prove a point." The blond boy looked around with his eyebrows raised, daring someone to disagree with him.

"Well," said a young man carrying a shopping bag from *Auntie Maim's*, "even if that's the case, we're going to have to go out and see about food and shelter."

"Have you noticed that we haven't seen another person since we got off the bus?" asked the heavy boy. "Not on the street, or in the stores, or in here. No traffic, either."

The blond boy shrugged. "This is obviously the low rent district. We're just going to have to find out where the action is."

"I just came from the Undertaker's," said the red-haired boy with a shiver. "I don't want to find any action so soon."

All seven former passengers crossed the lobby of the decrepit bus station and headed back toward the street. "We'll search the immediate area," said the blond boy, who seemed to be taking charge, "but we'll use the bus station as our home base. Worst comes to worst, we'll just wait for the next bus out of here."

"Have you ever heard of the Hellhound Bus Line?" asked Cope. "Have you ever *seen* one before? I haven't. They may only exist when the Administrations has a point to make. There may never be another one through here, not for years, if ever."

The blond boy shrugged. "You're all free to do what you want. Me, I'm hungry." He marched out the exit. He didn't pause or look back to see if anyone was coming with him.

Because there wasn't much point in staying in the bus station any longer, everyone followed him back out to the street. They stood on the sidewalk, looking up and down the avenue. The stillness was almost supernaturally perfect. The air was warm and dry, with only the smell of dust on it; there were none of the common city odors: garbage or exhaust fumes or cooking food. The longer they stood there, indecisive and bewildered, the stranger the place seemed to become. Finally, Cope said, "I'm going to go down to the corner and see where the hell we are." He walked half a block and glanced up at the street sign. He ran back to the others. "You're not going to believe this," he said, his eyes wide. "That's the corner of 6,212,589th Avenue and West 4,236,572nd Street."

"That's a joke," said the boy with the shopping bag. He didn't sound very confident. He spoke English with a heavy accent. Cope wondered if he might be one of the Old Dead, one of the damned more accustomed to speaking Greek or Latin.

"We could check it out," said the red-haired boy. "We could scout out the neighborhood, see if the street signs are like that on every corner."

"And what if they are? What does it mean?" asked the short, heavy boy.

"It means we're not in New Hell or anywhere else I've ever heard of," said the blond. "We're someplace much larger."

"And emptier," said Cope. "Where are all the people?"

"Uptown," said the heavy boy. "Downtown. Maybe they have the afternoon off."

"Right," said Cope, shaking his head and smiling cynically.

"We have to scout out the neighborhood anyway," said a dark-skinned boy with a neatly trimmed mustache and a hawk nose. "Let's just see if that street sign was some kind of local joke."

A moment later, they spotted a green road sign. One arrow pointed back where they'd come from. It was labeled "West Side Bus Terminal." Another arrow pointed across town, and it said "East Side Bus Terminal." "I'll bet that's where the goddamn demon was supposed to take us," said the blond boy. "This whole area looks deserted. I'll bet there's more activity on the east side."

"Then let's head over there," said the boy with the shopping bag.

"Fine," said the blond. He started walking at the head of the group, once again assuming leadership. It didn't seem worthwhile to Rusty Cope to make an issue out of it. It was better if they all stuck together, at least until they found someone and could get some answers to their questions.

They walked for hours without coming to anything except more abandoned buildings, burnt-out tenements, wrecked hulks of automobiles, and shops either stripped or almost completely stocked with aging merchandise. In one stationery store, the blond boy found a pistol, and tucked it away in his waistband. In a hobby shop, two of the other boys found .22 rifles and ammunition. "You never know who you're going to run into," explained the boy with the shopping bag. He shrugged. In Hell, that was a basic truth that didn't need much elaboration.

They walked east from 6,212,589th Avenue to 6,212,504th Avenue. They were all getting hungry and tired. The boy with the beard and the boy with the hawk nose went into a building to look for something to drink. They came out carrying bottles of water and some torn blankets. They spread the blankets on the ground, faced the veiled Eye of Heaven in the sky, knelt, and began praying. "I testify that there is no God but Allah," they chanted, "and Muhammad is the Prophet of Allah."

When they finished, the blond looked at them and frowned. "This is Hell, you know," he said. "Praying is something the living do so they won't end up here. You probably prayed all your life, and you still ended up here. What do you think praying is going to do for you now? God isn't listening anymore. He can't hear you here."

Cope expected the two Muslims to leap on the blond in a rage, but they were remarkably placid. "Our faith

promised us life after death in Paradise," said the hawk-
nosed boy. "If we're not now in Paradise, it must be
because we have sins that must still be worn away. We
will be in Paradise eventually, you may count on that,
because we still have faith, even in Hell. It is not for
you to determine what Allah can and cannot do. He
hears us, even here."

The blond boy shrugged. "I'm open-minded," he
said. "You can practice whatever foolishness you want.
I just don't want to hear anything about it."

"We have no interest in discussing our faith with an
infidel," said the bearded boy.

After they'd all had some water, they continued walking along West 4,236,572nd Street. Half an hour later,
they came to an empty place where an apartment building had been torn down. A little neighborhood park had
been built on the vacant lot, with some swings for small
children, benches, and a basketball goal against one
wall. "Look," said the tall red-haired boy, "there's a
ball."

He went over and picked up the basketball. He
dribbled it experimentally, and it seemed to be fine.
The shorter, stocky boy joined him, and they began
taking shots at the netless rim. The others sat on the
benches and rested. The two boys began playing a
game of Twenty-one. The red-haired boy narrated his
moves as if he were announcing them on the radio.
"Willis takes the ball out, dribbles it once, twice, looking into his opponent's eyes, then with a quick burst of
speed—" Willis flashed by the shorter boy and drove
for a layup. "He really put a move on him that time.
The crowd loves it. Now Willis takes it out, moves
down the right side of the lane, back out, spins, fakes to
his right, spins again, and—" He jumped from the
free throw line and arched the ball perfectly through the
hoop. "Looks like Willis isn't going to give his opponent
any chance at all to get on the scoreboard. Now he
moves slowly up the court, his opponent wary now,

impressed by Willis's skill. Willis makes like he's going to charge the basket, holds up, pumps once and—" The boy let go of the ball just at the top of his jump, and at that very moment there was a low whistling noise and the boy's throat was cut open by a crude arrow almost a yard long. Willis's body seemed to fold in slow motion and collapse to the ground. The muscular boy who'd been standing only a couple of feet away just stared open-mouthed in horror. In a few seconds, Willis's corpse began to smoke and steam, and then the flesh boiled away from the bones, and the bones themselves turned to a fine gray powder, sifting across the playground on the mild summer breeze. Only the arrow itself lay where the boy had been murdered.

"*Move!*" cried the blond boy. Already, other arrows were pattering on the pavement.

They bent low and ran toward the street, out of the playground. Just east of it there was a five-story brick tenement. They ducked into the foyer and hurried up the stairs to the second floor. Cope tried doors and found an unlocked apartment overlooking the street. The blond boy shut and locked the door behind them, and they passed the filthy kitchen to huddle in the empty living room, sitting on the floor to avoid the windows. Cope flicked the light switch, but the electricity had been turned off long ago. There was a slightly sickening, greasy smell in the rooms, and the layer of dust on the floor and the window sills was an inch thick. They could hear water dripping from the kitchen, tinking rhythmically into the porcelain sink. Cope touched the wall, and discovered that every surface in the apartment was gritty with old dirt. Still, it seemed like a safe enough place to sit until they could agree on a plan of action.

"We'll wait until nightfall," said the blond boy confidently. "It'll be dark soon."

"Wait a minute," said the hawk-nosed boy. "I'd just like to know who you are, making all our plans for us.

You've got some experience in this, something you'd like to tell us?"

The blond boy looked around the circle. He shrugged. "I was a military man all my life. I was a general. This sort of situation just calls for common sense."

"What's your name?" asked the boy with the shopping bag.

"George. You can just call me George."

"George what?" demanded the bearded boy.

The blond boy winced. "Custer. George Armstrong Custer."

Rusty Cope laughed out loud. "Common sense!" he said. It was one of the best jokes he'd heard since he first woke up in Hell.

"Listen," said Custer, "I had that one big military defeat. That one time when I suppose I didn't exercise proper caution. Okay, I grant you that. But the major part of my career was *exemplary*. And I learned from the experience. I've been approached by the Pentagram again and again. They think I'd make a fine commanding officer, and they're right."

"So you're one of the Pentagram's tame little soldiers?" asked the short, heavy boy.

"No," said Custer. "I also learned my lesson about getting involved with politics. I've always politely refused them. If I really was in the pocket of the Pentagram, do you think I'd be stuck in some absurd situation like this, with the rest of you?"

"That doesn't necessarily follow," said the bearded boy. "You could have done something to piss them off. We might all be here so that you can reenact your most famous moment. We could be tied up with you for some kind of punishment or something. Who the hell knows what the Pentagram is ever up to?"

"He's right about that," said Cope. "Anyone else with credentials?"

The boy with the shopping bag spoke up. "I was a

general also. I was a king in what you would call ancient Greece."

"And who might you be?" asked Custer.

"Pyrrhus," said the boy.

"As in 'Pyrrhic victory'?"

"Wonderful," said the short, heavy boy. "Another one. I guess we're doomed. We might just as well go back outside and get it over with. Take an arrow, see the Undertaker again, and hope to wake up in a better place than this."

"Like General Custer," said Pyrrhus, "I'm well-known for a couple of disastrous battles. But I was well-respected as a hero and a warrior for many years. I defeated the Romans and Carthaginians."

The boy who'd played basketball with Willis raised a hand. "My name is Bo Staefler. I was a soldier for a little while, until I almost got ashore at Normandy. I don't have much experience, but I'd still rather look out for myself than take orders from these two clowns."

"Just a minute—" said Custer angrily.

"No authority, Custer," said Cope quietly. "You have no authority at all here." Custer subsided, but he was clearly furious.

"I am Abd el-Kader," said the young man with the hawk nose.

The other Muslim's mouth opened. "The same Abd el-Kader who fought the French when they began to carve up Algeria?" he asked.

"And who sadly lost," said Abd el-Kader with a shake of his head.

"My name is Ali Hussayn," said the boy with the long hair. "I gladly place myself at your service."

"Another thing," objected Custer. "How the hell do we know you're really who you say you are? Abdul whatever-it-was?"

Abd el-Kader looked at Custer mildly. "When you prove you are Custer, then I will follow suit, if Allah wills."

Custer glanced around at the others. "I was only pointing out that any of us could claim to be almost anyone. In my place, seeing what a wretched reputation I seem to have among you, why would anyone falsely announce himself to be me?"

"Given your reputation," said Cope, "I don't see why *you* claim to be you. You'd have been better off claiming to be Sherman or Sheridan."

"Sheridan!" exclaimed Custer, and he spat in disgust.

"Well," said Staefler thoughtfully, "I don't know anything about this Pyrrhus, and I don't know anything about the Arab—"

"Berber," corrected Abd el-Kader.

"Right," said Staefler. "I don't know anything about you. But I do know too much about Custer, so unless any of the rest of you can impress me with your leadership abilities, I think I may just make my own plans. I wish you all the best of luck."

"What are we afraid of?" asked Ali Hussayn. "One man, killed by an arrow? Do you think there's an army out there? Did you see any sign of an army?"

"No, there was no sign of an army," said Pyrrhus, "but that doesn't mean that all the tenements on this block aren't filled with lunatics, waiting for us to go back into the street. Until we figure out what we've gotten into, I think the best policy is caution."

"All right," said Custer, "you wait here until morning. Wait here until next week or next year, if you want; but I'm leaving now." He pulled out his pistol. "Our best chance is for the two rifles to go out first and cover the street, and the rest of you to follow me." He turned to Pyrrhus, who had one of the .22s. "Sir," he said, "do you concur?" It didn't sound as if Custer truly cared very much what the Greek thought.

"In this case, you are right," said Pyrrhus. He pointed to Staefler, who had the other rifle. "You—"

"My name is Staefler."

"Staefler, will you come with me?"

"Well, I sure don't want to spend the rest of my life in this lousy place."

Pyrrhus and Staefler moved quietly out of the apartment and down the stairs. Custer went right behind him, followed by Rusty Cope, Ali Hussayn, and Abd el-Kader. They paused at the entrance to the foyer. Pyrrhus glanced at Staefler, who nodded, then looked back at Custer. The American general took a deep breath, let it out, and muttered, "Now."

The two boys with the rifles ran out in opposite directions, firing a few shots high and low. Custer was on their heels, but he did not shoot; the only bullets he had were in the gun, and he was saving them for a more definite target. No one fired back. No arrows sliced the evening air. Custer led all of them eastward down the street, in the direction they'd been heading when they paused at the playground. They ran a block, then half of another, before they stopped, out of breath, a little more confident that they had escaped.

"I wonder if we get to find out who shot those arrows at us," said Staefler.

"This is Hell, remember," said Cope. "Nothing inconsequential happens here. This isn't over yet."

"Not while we have to walk all the way across town to find the other bus terminal," said Abd el-Kader.

"Let's get going," said Custer. "Let's walk a couple of miles before we stop for the night."

"Mighty General," said Staefler, "what will you give us to eat?"

Pyrrhus gave a sardonic laugh. "Mr. Custer is making all the plans. He'll think of something."

They finally stopped in a block of upper middle-class brownstones just east of 6,212,446th Avenue. Staefler and Pyrrhus searched one of the buildings and made sure the area was safe. Then the entire group went upstairs and curled up uncomfortably to sleep. Custer divided the boys into watches, one boy with a rifle in the window facing the street on the third floor, one boy with a rifle below him on the first floor.

In the morning, stiff, still tired, and hungry, they talked about what they were going to do. "I think we must find other people soon," said Ali Hussayn. "They'll have food, at least. They can tell us how to find it in New Springfield."

"What if they're the ones who attacked us?" asked Cope.

Ali Hussayn smiled and shrugged. "Then we can always surrender."

"The hell with that," said Custer fiercely. "We'll go on toward the bus station. It's the only goal we've got."

"I like the idea of finding the bus station, too," said Cope, "but I've been doing a little figuring. I estimate that we cover an average of thirty to forty blocks an hour. Call it forty, just to be optimistic. At that rate, it will take a little more than 155,311 hours—at eight hours a day, that's 19,414 days, or better than 53 years—to get just to the place where the west side changes to the east side. Now, if the east side bus terminal is as far from there as the west side terminal was, we can expect to spend the next 106 years getting to it. And when we do, assuming we all live so long, we have no assurances at all that there will be buses going in and out. That's all I wanted to say."

"We don't want to sit here," said Abd el-Kader, "and looking for the bus station seems foolish. What other course is there?"

"We could surrender," said Ali Hussayn seriously.

"To whom?" asked Abd el-Kader.

"We'll find somebody," said Cope. "You can bet on it."

"What if they execute us immediately?" asked Staefler.

Cope looked at him and spread his hands. "Then it's back to Go and collect $200."

"What does that mean?" asked Pyrrhus.

"Take too long to explain," said Cope. There was

silence in the room while everyone waited for someone
else to make a suggestion.

"Well," said Ali Hussayn after a while, "it's written in
the noble Qur'ân, 'When the disciples said: O Jesus,
son of Mary! Is thy Lord able to send down for us a
table spread with food from heaven? He said: Observe
your duty to Allah, if ye are true believers.' So we will
say our morning prayers, put our faith in Allah, and
accept from Him whatsoever it pleases Him to send us."

Custer chewed his lip for a moment, then said in a
soft voice, "How dare you profane the name of Jesus
Christ in the same breath with your heathen god?"

Ali Hussayn stood up, his face dark with fury, his
brows narrowed. "At a time that I will choose, you son
of a dog, you and I will have an accounting."

Custer laughed scornfully. " 'An accounting!' What,
do we stand ten paces apart and have our camels spit at
each other?"

Ali Hussayn growled something in Arabic, but Abd
el-Kader stood up and restrained him. The hawk-nosed
boy said, "Soothe your temper, O my cousin, and turn
your thoughts to prayer."

"Yes, you're right. Allah forgive me."

"Let's go," said Custer. "Staefler and the Greek first,
like last night."

"Wait," said Cope. "Let the two men pray. We've
got all the time in the world."

"You know," said Staefler after a quiet moment, "I've
been calculating, too. In most cities, there are about
twenty blocks to the mile. At that rate, the east side
terminal is six hundred twenty thousand miles away.
That's not possible. That's three times the distance from
the Earth to the Moon."

"It's possible here," said Pyrrhus. "This is Hell. Hell
was specially designed to include everything, particularly the impossible."

"Just think," Ali Hussayn said, "if that's what Hell is,
how more marvelous still it must be in Heaven."

"Haven't you been here long enough?" asked Custer. "Haven't you learned yet to stop thinking about Heaven?"

"I will never stop thinking about Heaven," said Ali Hussayn.

"It's no use to you," said Custer, who then sank back into silence.

The two Muslims finished their devotions, and the group got itself ready to begin the day's journey. "Staefler," ordered Custer, "you go ahead as scout. Pyrrhus, guard our rear. The rest of you stay together, so you don't get lost or left behind."

"Stay together in a bunch?" cried Staefler. "I don't believe you said that. We'll make a fine target like that. We'll walk along in single file, spread out, that's what we'll do."

"This isn't one of your twentieth-century jungle wars," said Custer contemptuously.

"It might just as well be one," said Rusty Cope. "The street is like a narrow trail through unmapped territory. There could be snipers hiding in every window. We don't know who the enemy is, or even why he's shooting at us."

"All right," said Custer, "in the order I said, but Indian file rather than as a group. I'll make a concession to modern theory." He said "modern" as if it was the most disgusting adjective he could think of.

They marched along uneventfully for a few hours, until some of them began to complain of fatigue. Just as Custer was about to call a halt, there was a strained shout from Pyrrhus in the rear, and a sound like thunder that made Cope turn quickly in dismay. As he turned, a great black horse raced past him on the left, and another horse clattered by on the right. If he had taken a single step in the direction he'd turned, he would have been run down and killed. On each horse was a wailing, shrieking warrior, both men dressed like barbarians, swinging long, curved swords above their heads. They rode down to the end of the block, wheeled their mounts, and galloped back toward the group. "Fire! Get them!" shouted Custer. "Save the horses, if you can!" He began firing his pistol at the apparitions.

Pyrrhus ran up and joined Staefler, who was kneeling in the street. They volleyed again and again, but the leather-clad riders never slowed. Then a louder sound shattered the morning: automatic weapons, shooting in a cross fire from both sides of the street. The horses brayed, stumbled, and fell; they lay kicking and thrashing on the pavement. One rider was dead; the other cried out and leaped for his fallen sword, rose up, and gave another tremendous bellow. He took a single step, but then a hail of rattling machine gun bullets brought him to a bloody, gurgling end. A few seconds after he joined his comrade, the two corpses began to smoke. Cope looked away, sickened. He realized that the machine gun fire had stopped after it cut down the second warrior. No one was threatening Cope or the rest of the lost group. When he looked back, both barbarians had vanished. Only their clothes and accoutrements remained.

"Don't shoot," called a deep voice. Cope looked up and saw a tall, well-built young man with Oriental features and long black hair. He had appeared silently from one of the apartment buildings.

"Who are you?" called Pyrrhus.

"I am Chu Jen," he answered.

"We have to thank you for taking care of those guys on the horses," said Staefler.

Chu Jen shook his head. "I had nothing to do with that. It was the soldiers. I've been hiding in that building for two days."

"The Pentagram's men shot those barbarians?" asked Cope.

"Yes," said Chu Jen. "They're trying to clean up all the Insurgents, but it's a hopeless task."

"Insurgents?" said Ali Hussayn. "Don't you mean the Dissidents?"

"No, not that bunch. The Insurgents are insane. They

wander around the city here, slaughtering all the natives. They're natives, too, and they say they're leading a popular revolution against the Administration, but all they seem to do is kill their own relatives and burn villages." Chu Jen shook his head sadly.

"Were you traveling with the Pentagram's army?" asked Cope.

"No," said Chu Jen. "They're insane, too."

"You're welcome to come with us," said Pyrrhus. "You know a lot more about this place than we do."

"Thank you," said Chu Jen. "I've been stranded here for two weeks. I just want to find a way out."

"If there *is* a way out," said Staefler.

"I will take this sword," said Chu Jen, stepping into the middle of the street and stooping to pick up the magnificent weapon of the first barbarian.

"I'd like one, too," said Abd el-Kader. "I've used one before." He took the second man's blade.

"Won't have to reload this," said Chu Jen. Custer grimaced and threw his now-empty pistol aside. The two riflemen had also used up most of their ammunition.

"There's food here," announced Staefler. The great horses had boiled away into nothing, but the bags tied to the saddles remained. There were provisions, including dried meat, to last the two men three or four days. It would make one good meal for the seven survivors.

"Must be the barbarians don't like us for some reason," said Staefler, chewing some of the tasteless meat. "Arrows last night, swords today."

"The barbarians will kill anyone who isn't one of them," said Chu Jen.

"Well," said Pyrrhus, in better spirits now that they'd found a little food, "I'm glad our allies have the modern weapons. We'd have a hard time if it were the other way around."

"If you can be sure the Pentagram is our ally here," said Cope dubiously.

After the meal, they waited while Abd el-Kader and

Ali Hussayn made their ablutions and prayed once more. Then they continued on eastward. There was no sign that violence had taken place on that street a few hours earlier. It was as if the whole affair hadn't happened. Their protectors had melted away into the vast city. It made Cope uncomfortable to think that there were probably well-armed military units all around them, keeping track of their movements, perhaps planning ambush at any point.

Staefler was taking point now, and Ali Hussayn had the other rifle in the rear. Cope shared the afternoon's walk with Pyrrhus. Pyrrhus was a serious, thoughtful man, but he had a good sense of humor, too. "You know," he told Cope, "I did a lot of conquering in the old days. Conquered all of Macedon, took most of it without losing a man. But that 'Pyrrhic victory' thing is something I'll never live down, not if we go on through all eternity."

"That's the way it is," said Cope. "I think people like me, who never were anybody and never did anything, have it a lot easier in Hell. You big-shot big names always have people after you, fawning over you for favors or trying to stick a knife in your back."

Pyrrhus winced. "I've encountered both types here. I've had my back stuck again and again. Remember, I've been in Hell a few thousand years longer than you."

"It doesn't make any difference, after a while. Having seniority in Hell is no great advantage."

"I suppose not."

"Say, listen," said Cope. "I've been thinking about something ever since we ran into those barbarians on horseback. You saw the way the corpses sort of dried up and blew away?"

Pyrrhus shuddered. "Yes. They don't always do that in other parts of Hell."

"Well, they do it here. Even the horses. Did you notice that?"

"Yes. What do you mean?"

"How could those men have had meat? Where did it come from? Why didn't the animals go where the horses went?"

Pyrrhus stopped in his tracks and stared, his eyes squinted in concentration. "I don't have the foggiest notion," he said at last.

"I want to ask somebody that, if we ever find somebody to ask," said Cope. They walked on, each lost in his own thoughts.

When the seven got to 6,212,118th Avenue, they saw that it fronted a great municipal park, shady and cool with maple and oak trees, with a low granite wall running up and down the avenue as far as they could see. Some distance to the north was an arched entrance to the park.

"Either we find a way around," said Custer, "or we have to go in."

Staefler tapped his forehead and said, "West Point training. It never fails him."

"I'm just saying that I don't like the idea of going in," said Custer. "We'll be very vulnerable in there."

"Any more vulnerable than walking down the street between two rows of buildings providing shelter to snipers?" asked Ali Hussayn.

"All right," said Custer, coming to a decision. "I want you—" he pointed to Ali Hussayn; Custer seemed to have some trouble calling the Muslims by name—"to take one of the rifles and walk ahead. Chu Jen, take the other rifle and watch our backs. And this time I want two rangers out to the flanks, as well." He pointed to Abd el-Kader and Cope. Custer followed along on a well-marked path in Ali Hussayn's footsteps, and the others trailed behind, spacing themselves about ten yards apart. It was more pleasant in the park than in the hot, dusty street. The air smelled fresher, there were little animal rustlings and croaks from the treetops—whether of grotesque birds or Hellish flying, flapping monsters it was impossible to tell—and the ground felt good to walk on after the miles of cracked asphalt. Cope found himself taking deep breaths every few seconds, breathing in the revivifying scent of rich loam and healthy greenery. It was as near to truly enjoyable as Hell could come. If nothing else, it made Cope suspicious. He wondered when and how the worm in the apple would show itself.

After a while, they came upon a meadow cleared among the thick stands of trees. Cope could see two or three dozen ramshackle huts thrown together in the middle of the clearing. He could hear the lowing of cattle and the soft neighing of horses. He caught the fussy cackle of chickens, too. Custer called a halt while they were still in the protection of the trees. Cope leaned against a peeling sycamore and waited for the command decision to be made. He could hear tattered bits of human conversation, the crying of a baby, the laughter of children.

"A village," announced Custer. "But are they hostile or friendly?"

"Do they have machine guns or battle-axes?" asked Cope.

"I don't see any signs of weapons at all," said Staefler.

"Pay no attention to the way it looks," said Custer. "I know what I'm talking about here. I've seen Sioux villages that looked even more peaceful than that."

"And they probably *were* at peace," said Cope under his breath. "At least until you rode down to slaughter them."

Before Custer could decide whether to go around the settlement or attempt to communicate with the peasants, a group of five men on horseback rode out of the trees on the far side of the meadow. A few of the village women cried out in fear, and ran to gather up their children. The horsemen grinned. Their leader began arguing with an old man on the ground, waving his arm arrogantly and shaking his great broadsword. It was too far to hear what he was saying.

Two of the barbarians dismounted and came up on either side of the old villager. The poor man looked terrified. One of the horsemen grabbed the old man's long, gray hair and jerked his head back. The second barbarian hefted his sword and cut the peasant's throat with a single quick stroke. Bright drops of blood fell to the grass and began smoking. The old man's body dissolved quickly, and gray powder like ash dusted the ground and drifted away. One of the dismounted horsemen looked up at his commander, who laughed and shrugged.

From the south, out of the trees to the right of Cope's position, a squad of uniformed men charged on foot. Six of them were armed with bow and arrows, the other five with various types of swords, spears, and clubs. They looked odd, wearing modern green army fatigues, yet carrying obsolete weapons. Cope recalled what Chu Jen had said earlier, about not having to reload a sword. The archers fired volleys of arrows, and quickly picked off two of the men still on horseback. The leader of the barbarians turned his mount and charged with a fierce battle cry, as did the two on foot. When they got too close, the archers dropped their bows and drew their own swords. For several minutes the clearing rang with the desperate sound of steel on steel, and the labored breathing and cursing of the soldiers.

Cope saw Ali Hussayn raise his rifle and aim. "Who are you trying to shoot?" asked Cope.

"One of the barbarians," said the Muslim.

"Your sympathy is with the guys in the uniforms?"

"They must be the people who helped us out this morning."

"You don't know that, not for sure. We don't know who any of these people are."

Ali Hussayn hesitated. "But you saw what those savages did to the old man."

"And we don't know why. We don't know who he was or what he'd done."

Ali Hussayn muttered something under his breath. He put down the rifle and watched the action with Cope and the others. There was nothing else to do.

In a few more minutes, it was all over. The men in the fatigues outnumbered their opponents, and it didn't take them long to dispose of them. The corpses—all five barbarians and two of the army men—fumed and turned to powder, and then were gone. The uniformed survivors paused to go about the battlefield and collect arrows and swords left behind by the dead men.

"We'll establish contact," said Custer. "Chu Jen, come with me and bring your rifle. Carry it loosely, point the barrel at the ground. We don't want to do anything to upset these men. You, fellow, stay behind to protect the others." Again he wouldn't say Ali Hussayn's name. "Mr. Staefler, you come along as well. You were in the American army in the twentieth century. Maybe these soldiers will understand you better."

The little party started across the clearing toward the men in fatigues. In the stillness, Cope could hear the village's women already mourning the old man.

When Chu Jen, Custer, and Staefler had covered half the distance across the clearing, the officers of the uniformed men began shouting orders. The swordsmen knelt on the grass, while behind them the bowmen fixed arrows to their strings. "They're going to shoot!" yelled Abd el-Kader. Custer paid no attention. He must have thought that the army men had been caught by surprise, and were only taking normal precautions.

"Ali Hussayn," murmured Pyrrhus, "get ready to cover them. Get out in the meadow as far as you can and lie down. Don't make yourself a target the way that fool Custer is doing."

The Muslim nodded and ran out into the high grass. Meanwhile, the officer shouted out to Custer to halt.

Custer raised a hand, and Chu Jen and Staefler stopped beside him. "Who the hell are you?" called Custer.

"We know who *we* are," said the officer. "You'd better explain yourselves. Friends of these villagers?"

"We don't know these villagers from Adam's off-ox," said Custer. "We've only been in this city a day and we're lost, and we want to get the hell out of here."

"Reinforcements, apparently," mused the officer. "The Insurgents always need reinforcements and, to tell the truth, my company is right at full strength. I guess that makes you expendable." He turned to give an order, but before he could say a word, Chu Jen put a bullet through the man's head.

The bowmen launched their arrows. Custer turned and ran back toward the woods, but Chu Jen drew his sword. "I want one of those bows," he said. He threw the rifle to Staefler. "Cover me, if you can." He charged the kneeling swordsmen, determined to hack his way through them and wrest a weapon away from one of the bowmen. Staefler knelt and began peppering the uniformed swordsmen with the .22.

Ali Hussayn came forward and threw himself to the ground beside Staefler. "Custer is busy regrouping himself back in the trees," he said, panting for breath.

"Well, he said that he'd learned his lesson at Little Big Horn," said Staefler. "He's going to play it safe from now on."

"I have another word for it," said Ali Hussayn. Staefler laughed.

Chu Jen was handling himself well. Three of the enemy swordsmen attacked him; he took care of one of them almost immediately, and then he refused to let the other two get him from different sides. He parried the second man's thrust and made a quick, slashing backhand stroke that opened the belly of the third man. In another moment he was through the line. When two more swordsmen moved toward him, they were shot by Staefler and Ali Hussayn.

"You know," said Staefler, "I kind of enjoy this. I never got to fire my rifle at all at Normandy. I never even made it out of the water." As he said those words, he realized that he was out of ammunition. "Goddamn it," he muttered, as an arrow pierced his chest.

"*Ya salaam!*" cried Ali Hussayn. Between shots, he saw Staefler's body dissolve and disappear.

Back in the trees, Custer was torn by conflicting motives. "I don't want another massacre," he said. "And I hate the idea of calling a retreat. But I can't abandon two of my men to the enemy." He looked around. "You have a sword," he said.

Abd el-Kader just nodded.

"I want you to go out there with your friend. He has to stay there to support the Chinese boy."

Abd el-Kader only nodded again. He felt it was beneath him to point out how useless a sword was long-distance against bows and arrows. He only walked calmly across the meadow to Ali Hussayn's position. As he walked he recited from the Qur'an: "Nor does anyone know in what land he is to die. Verily, with God alone is full knowledge, and He is acquainted with all things." Ali Hussayn was surprised to see him, but Abd el-Kader only knelt beside him and continued to pray.

The arrival of Abd el-Kader caused renewed activity by the enemy bowmen. Flight after flight of arrows whirred and whistled through the air, thwacking into the moist ground. Ali Hussayn picked off one of the bowmen, then another, but there were still four more. "It seems hopeless," he said. There was no answer. He turned, but Abd el-Kader, the noble Algerian rebel leader, was not there. There was only his sword, his clothing, and the flecks of white that were his remains.

Ali Hussayn was distraught. He snatched up the sword, screamed "*Allah akbar!*" in a shrill, trilling voice, and charged toward the men in fatigues.

"He's crazy," said Cope.

Custer looked around himself wildly. "You, Pyrrhus,"

he said in a hoarse voice, "we can't let that rifle fall into their hands. We need it."

"You want me to go get it?" asked Pyrrhus.

"Don't spend any time out there," said Custer. "You can't help the other two now. Just get the rifle and get back here."

Pyrrhus looked at Cope, who sighed and looked away. Then Pyrrhus crept to the edge of the woods and watched the bowmen on the far side of the meadow. He took a deep breath, let it out, and then sprinted toward the rifle Ali Hussayn had left behind. He got almost two-thirds of the way there before he was riddled with arrows.

"Three dead," said Cope. "Is that enough for you?"

"Fall back," called Custer, his eyes wide, the whites showing around the pupils.

"And what about the other two?" asked Cope.

"Nothing we can do for them. I didn't order them to attack like that. We can only trust that they make it back safely."

Cope and Custer moved about twenty yards into the denser woods. They could still see what was happening in the meadow. Supported now by Ali Hussayn, Chu Jen had accomplished his goal. He had cut through the rank of swordsmen, and had killed two of the bowmen. Ali Hussayn protected him as he slung both bows and quivers across his back. Then both men turned and raced back toward the trees.

"They'll never make it," said Custer breathlessly.

One of the uniformed men shouted something and waved his arm back and forth. The archers looked at him, then unnocked their arrows and unstrung their bows.

"They're letting Chu Jen and Ali Hussayn get away," said Cope in wonder.

Custer spat on the ground. "What the hell is that?" he said with a growl. "Gallantry? I don't believe in gallantry anymore."

"That's what it looks like," said Cope. "They're not making any pursuit." Indeed, the uniformed men were already heading slowly back toward the woods, the way they'd come.

"Let's wait," said Custer. "We might be able to get across this goddamn meadow and out of the park."

"Did you notice?" said Rusty Cope. "None of the villagers lifted a finger to help anybody. They didn't help us, they didn't help the barbarians, and they didn't help the Pentagram's men."

"That's natives," said Custer disgustedly. "You die to help them, and they want you to pay because you trampled their flowers."

"I didn't notice that we helped them all that much," said Cope. Custer turned away and didn't reply.

Chu Jen and Ali Hussayn arrived safely, gasping for breath but exhilarated. "In China, I was a bowman," said Chu Jen, the way another man might say, "I was a king." It was the first time he'd looked truly happy. "This is a proper weapon for a man."

"I will keep a sword," said Ali Hussayn. "There is still vengeance to think of."

"I think we'll be all right now," said Chu Jen. "Let's see if we can get across this clearing. I'll lead, and I'd like you to walk beside me." He addressed this to Cope; then he turned to Ali Hussayn. "Would you guard the rear?" he asked.

"It is as you wish," said the Muslim.

"Let's go, then," said Chu Jen. Somehow, the leadership seemed to have shifted from one man to the other. There were no comments, not even from Custer himself.

The air smelled sweet in the meadow. There were Hellish flowers blooming in the grass, and lazy insects with tiny fangs and batlike wings hovered over the blossoms. The sounds from the village had returned almost to normal; evidently, the people didn't devote a lot of time to grieving. It was probably something they had to do rather often.

Once on the other side of the clearing, they pushed again into the woods. It wasn't so pleasant as it had been before. Now Cope imagined armed patrols of barbarians or uniformed men moving along beside them, screened by the trees, spying on them. It didn't feel safe any longer. The park had lost its charm. The worm in the apple had turned out to be a venomous serpent.

Chu Jen appeared to be having the same thoughts. "I want to get out of this park as soon as we can. Let's pick up the pace. I'll feel better when we're back out on the street, where I can at least see ahead of us and behind us."

"We should have taken some of those villagers' chickens," said Custer. "Maybe their horses, too." Chu Jen ignored the suggestion.

As they hurried through the trees, Cope thought he heard faint sounds, mechanical sounds, the first engine noises he'd heard since the Hellhound bus had driven away. "Listen," he said.

"What do you hear?" asked Chu Jen.

"Just stop and let me listen." The other three paused and held still for a moment. "I'm sure of it. This way." Cope pointed off to one side.

"Let's be careful, now," said Chu Jen. "We don't need any more unpleasant surprises."

They crept silently through the woods until Cope raised a hand. They waited while he slipped ahead. The noise was very loud now, not far away. Cope hid behind an oak tree and peered into another clearing. This one was not as large as the meadow they'd left behind. It was less than a hundred yards long and forty wide. The only remarkable feature of the clearing was the helicopter that waited in the middle. It was a Huey gunship with Pentagram markings, its rotors chuttering. One man sat in the cockpit, a submachine gun across his lap.

Cope came back to the group. "That's our way out of here," he said. "And the four of us ought to be able to persuade that pilot to fly us to the bus station. It'll be a lot faster and easier than walking through the rest of this goddamn city."

"Who is it waiting for?" asked Ali Hussayn.

"I don't know," said Cope. "My guess is that it dropped those guys who killed Staefler, Pyrrhus, and Abd el-Kader back at the meadow. If not them, then their friends."

"Then when we get where we want to go," said Ali Hussayn in a chilling voice, "I will let my sword speak to that infidel pilot."

"Let's not risk all our lives seeing what kind of mood he's in," said Chu Jen.

"Let me go," said Cope. "If he won't listen to reason, I'll get rid of him."

"Then who'll fly the helicopter?" asked Custer.

"Don't worry about that," said Cope. "Left, right, up, down: how hard can it be?" He turned to Chu Jen. "Let me take that sword."

"I hope you won't need to use it," said the bowman.

Cope jammed the sword through his belt, bent low, and ran across the clearing to the helicopter. The pilot smiled and waved at him. Cope yelled, but the pilot couldn't hear him. He jumped down from the cockpit. He left his weapon on the seat.

"Move away a little," he shouted into Cope's ear. "You can't have much of a conversation under these rotors."

Cope looked at the man and frowned. "I feel like I should know your face. You're either Lou Gehrig or—"

"Charles Lindbergh," said the pilot, smiling easily.

"Lindbergh. And now you're flying for the Pentagram."

The aviator shrugged. "They have a monopoly on the best equipment," he said. "I just want to fly."

"Yeah, but wearing the Pentagram uniform puts you in league with—"

"Oh, I don't get involved with any actual fighting. I'm not one of your bloodthirsty military bandits. I'm actually just here in the role of advisor."

"Advisor," said Cope skeptically.

"That's right. Now, what can I do for you?"

Cope was getting tired of shouting, but there was no other way to communicate. "I'd like it if you could give us a lift out of here. My friends and I are lost in this crummy city."

"I'd like to oblige, but I'm waiting for the platoon to get back. They'll be looking for me here."

"I don't have time to argue," said Cope. He drew his sword and pressed it against Lindbergh's throat. He shoved the man backward, until they were beside the Huey again. Cope climbed into the cockpit. He tucked his sword back into his belt, and grabbed the submachine gun. Then he jumped back to the ground. He waved to the others, and they started running toward the chopper. "We don't want to hurt you," said Cope. "We just want you to take us for a ride. Then you can come back and pick up your men."

"Don't have much choice now, do I?" asked Lindbergh. Nothing seemed to ruffle his good humor.

"Get in," Cope shouted to the others. He climbed back into the cockpit, and Lindbergh got in and sat beside him.

"Where to?" asked the pilot.

"We want to get out of the city altogether. There's a Hellhound bus terminal on the east side."

Lindbergh laughed. "I figure that must be, oh, better than half a million miles from here. What kind of gas mileage you think this bird gets?" He checked his instruments and pulled back on the stick. The rumbling Huey lifted ponderously into the air.

Cope felt his heart sink. "Am I going to have to spend the rest of my life here?"

"In Hell? Of course you are."

"No, I mean in New Springfield."

"Oh, I can get you out. This place is riddled with tunnels, you know. They lead from here to all sorts of other strange parts of Hell. The Pentagram uses them, the Cong sneak in here from Decentral Park, even the Insurgents use them."

"And you go in and out?" asked Cope.

"Every two weeks or so I go back to New Hell for R&R. If you can call it that." Lindbergh made a disgusted face.

"But the tunnels must be millions of miles long, too."

The pilot turned to look at Cope and grinned. "Not here," he said. "The tunnels are only as long as they need to be. Sometimes it's just a few hundred yards from one side of town to the other."

Cope thought that over. "Is that how supplies get in? The meat we found, weapons, horses?"

Lindbergh just nodded. "And I can take you to a subway entrance not far from here. The train will take you right into the heart of New Hell itself."

Cope turned to give the good news to the others. "Kiss the city goodbye," he said.

Lindbergh tapped him on the shoulder. "But there's just one thing," he said.

Cope felt a chill. "What is it?"

Lindbergh gave him that sunny smile. "I'll thank you to not smoke in my vehicle," he said.

Only a few minutes later, Lindbergh pointed to a public park, smaller than the one where the barbarians had attacked the villagers. "See down there?" he said. "I'm going to set us down in the middle of that softball field."

"I thought you were going to show us how to get out of this city," said Cope.

"Don't worry. There's a subway entrance on the avenue at the park's west entrance. You can change trains when you get to 666th Street."

Cope nodded. As it came down, the helicopter's propwash blasted up a dense cloud of dust. Cope, Custer, Ali Hussayn, and Chu Jen jumped to the ground. "Thanks," shouted Cope.

"My pleasure," called Lindberg. "Do you see the subway?"

"I see it," shouted Chu Jen.

"You'll be all right, then. I've got to get back to the platoon." Lindbergh waved and throttled the chopper back into the sky.

"Let's go," said Chu Jen. He led the way across the ball diamond, toward the avenue. They hurried down the granite steps of the subway entrance.

There was a demon sitting in the change booth, but none of the four had any money. "We need tokens," said Custer.

"Too bad," said the demon with a grin.

"Why don't you just let us through?" said Cope.

"What do I look like?" said the outraged demon. "A guardian angel?"

The rumble of an approaching train drowned out Cope's reply. He looked over his shoulder. It was an express to Disunion Square in downtown New Hell. "Let's go!" he cried. He led the way, vaulting over the turnstile and running for the train.

The demon shrieked. "You won't get away with this!" it yelled.

Chu Jen, Custer, and Ali Hussayn raced behind Cope toward the express train. As soon as they boarded, the doors closed and the train slid out of the station. "Next stop, 666th Street," said Cope.

"New Hell isn't my favorite place," said Chu Jen. "But I'd rather be there than this endless city. At least New Hell makes sense *some* of the time."

"Going away is fun," said Cope, "but it's always so nice to come back home." The others just stared at him.

I, Hermes Trismegistus
Richard Groller

The Archives of the Fallen.
The Book of the Dead.
In it are inscribed the names
of the souls who have been felled
by the sure and deadly scythe of the Grim Reaper.
The Roll is called. I am your guide.
Come. He stands within a pit of vipers
and beckons you on.
Come. He is stilled in a graveyard where he
watches the Four Horsemen of the Apocalypse thunder by.
Come. He will lead you to the cauldron of fire
and the Pit.
Come. He will bring you to the inner sanctum and
enshroud you in the crypt.
For He is the Prince of Darkness.
He, this cloaked and cowled son of Satan,
will show you your futurity in the eyes
of your innermost fears.
Come. He leads you now before Baphomet.
Kneel. You must partake of his fiendish rites

before the altar of the Goat of Mendes.
Suffer. For you poor slave have entered the realm
of eternal death and perpetual darkness.
And know, that the principalities of shadows,
Lucifer, Baal, Lucifuge Rofocale, Sathanus,
all the demons and their minions
by whatever name they are known
will be here to torture you
with a constancy as sure as death,
for the rest of your immortal existence.

FAST FOOD

Nancy Asire

"Hell's going to Hell," Attila had said recently, and Napoleon could not have agreed more. From his perch high on the roof of Louis XIV's palace, he looked down the sloping hill toward the Park and to his unseen house beyond it. To his left, across a vast expanse of carefully manicured lawn, lay Caesar's villa, the true seat of Roman power in Hell; to his right, behind well-kept shrubs and trees, Maria-Theresa held court as head of the Austrians.

He frowned. And himself? Now he stood in control of the French power base, a position he had diligently avoided since his arrival in Hell all those years ago. And, he feared, a position from which he could not again easily disassociate himself.

Hell had lately dissolved into chaos: all semblance of control over what went on in the Infernal Regions seemed to have disappeared. Fighting had erupted in the streets, in the Park, in houses and apartments. Supposed allies had turned upon one another; bands of looters and worse had attacked anything that looked worth taking; and, all through the crazy, upside-down days that had followed, no one had seen any visible effort being made by Administration to turn things right again.

But now, a sense of relative calm had fallen over New Hell: the defeated licked their wounds and the victors set about solidifying their positions. And none of the above knew just how long this uneasy peace would last.

Napoleon snorted to himself and turned away from the edge of the roof. His primary concern had been for Caesar and his household, indebted as both he and Wellington were for their continued "retirement" to Julius *and* Augustus. But Caesar had weathered the storm, as had Maria-Theresa and, as far as he knew, the other major power bases around New Hell.

Descending the narrow stairway from the roof, Napoleon stepped out into the upper story hallway of Louis' opulent palace. Sycophants clogged the halls, each oh-so-eager to curry favor with the new power. Napoleon growled at the closest of those barely visible entities and felt somewhat satisfied when the whole lot of them disappeared.

"Damned butt kissers," he muttered under his breath and took to the wide marble stairway that led downstairs.

When he reached the entry hall, the guards who stood on either side of the huge double doors that opened onto the front porch gave him smart salutes. He frowned again, vowing that as soon as things settled down (God! please let it be soon!), he was going back to his house across the Park and install some figurehead in this damned, drafty palace of Louis' before he lost his mind.

And as for Louis himself: the Sun King still languished in his royal apartments on the second floor, given every comfort he had enjoyed when he had ruled, but under the firm guard of men Napoleon trusted. A prisoner, yes . . . but very much a prisoner in a gilded cage.

"Majesty."

The voice caught Napoleon in midstep; he cringed, thinking he had been close to making a clean getaway to the front porch, and turned around.

Duroc, one of his closest friends, who had served as Lord High Steward of the Empire and as a Marshal of France, stood waiting to one side of the entry hall. Napoleon breathed a sigh of relief: Duroc, of all those French around him, he could trust to tell him only what he needed to know, and *when* he needed to know it.

"What is it, Geraud?"

"Please." Duroc gestured to the back of the entryhall, well out of earshot of the guards. "You have a visitor, Napoleon," he said, when privacy was achieved. "A very *important* visitor, who would prefer to remain anonymous. Perhaps you can see her in the library."

"Her?" Napoleon lifted an eyebrow, but Duroc shook his head, turned and led the way from the entry hall back to the grand library. Napoleon followed readily enough, trusting Duroc's sensibilities.

Someone had drawn the library curtains, and only a few candles lit the cavernous room. Duroc motioned Napoleon in, and then took up a position by the doorway, there if needed, but respectfully disengaged from any conversation.

Napoleon looked at his visitor: she was definitely a she, but she was heavily cloaked and a veil hid her face.

"Madame," he said, bowing slightly.

The woman laughed, a deep, throaty laugh. "I've been called many things," she said in a European accented French, "but seldom 'Madame' by the emperor of the French. I'm Gertrude Zelle."

Napoleon straightened. "Mata Hari," he said in a soft voice.

"Well-read as I've heard you are." Amusement still colored her voice. "Would you care to test my identity? I'm sure you've heard I'm missing one nipple—" She reached up toward her breasts.

"Uh . . . no. That won't be necessary." Napoleon tried to see behind the veil but did not succeed. "I take it this isn't a social call," he prompted as her hand fell.

"No, it isn't. As far as anyone knows, you haven't seen me. The only other person who knows I'm coming here is Caesar."

"Which one?"

"Julius."

"Ah. Julius," Napoleon said, and waited.

"Patient, too. Very good. How much do you know about me . . . about what I do here in Hell?"

Napoleon shrugged, keeping his face expressionless. "Caesar tells me you're connected with the Administration . . . with those called the Devil's Children."

"You're better informed than I'd hoped, but slightly out of date. I've broken with Admin and have placed my services at Caesar's command. Since you and Caesar are friends, I've been told that my services are yours also . . . *if* you need them."

Mata Hari . . . spy *extraordinaire*. Damn! What had gone on that she had switched sides? Where was the Devil? And what the hell was going on in Hell?

"You're aware things have changed here in our beloved abode," she continued, her voice again taking on an amused tone. "It's an intelligent consensus that the survival of Rome in Hell is vital if we're to have any kind of order around us. To have a strong Rome, Rome needs strong allies. That means you and your French, *and* your friend, Wellington, with his British connections." She leaned closer, her voice sinking into a whisper. "And whom do *you* serve, Majesty?"

Napoleon's heart lurched. Could this be a trap? A clever, feint-within-feint trap laid by Administration? "Order," he said. "Whoever can give us *that* has my allegiance."

"Therefore your alliance with Rome. So. I'm here not only to offer my services, but to tell you I have . . . certain allies myself—ones I would prefer remain unknown. You're Caesar's friend and he trusts you, so I'll tell you one of them isn't mortal."

"And . . . ?"

"And, if you're as well-informed as you seem to be, you must know that I consort with one of the Fallen Angels." Mata Hari cocked her head. "Still unmoved? Caesar chooses his friends wisely. Let's leave it at this: you have my services, should you ever need them, and the services of *my* . . . friends."

"Madame," Napoleon said, again bowing slightly.

"You should be made aware of several of my contacts, should you need to get in touch with me and Caesar is unavailable. One of them is a little fellow named Zaki. Another, whom you probably won't see much, is Judah Maccabee. . . ."

Napoleon gestured briefly.

"I know . . . you took part in the raid on the Dissident camp that threw both Maccabee and Alexander the Great into Caesar's hands. Maccabee doesn't know that, and I'll see to it that he doesn't find out." A small, white hand reached out toward Napoleon, holding a slip of paper. "Here's a telephone number where a contact of mine can be reached. Use it with discretion."

Napoleon took the paper. "I shall, Madame."

"Thank you for seeing me," Mata Hari said, dipping her head in a small bow. "I'm sure you won't regret it."

"Duroc," Napoleon said. "Escort the lady to the—" He turned to his visitor. "—the back door will do, won't it?"

She laughed her deep, throaty laugh. "The back door will be fine, Majesty. Until another day, then."

And with a rustle of her cloak, she followed Duroc from the library toward the back of Louis' palace.

"You had a meeting with *whom?*" Wellington looked from Napoleon to Marie, then back again, his expression bordering on the amazed.

"Mata Hari."

"That's who I thought you said." The Iron Duke frowned, rose from his chair, and took another one, closer to Napoleon's desk. "Damned Louis . . . these chairs are hard as boards!"

"Huhn." Napoleon leaned back in his own chair, only slightly less uncomfortable than Wellington. "You can tell Himself didn't spend much time in here," he said, gesturing to the ostentatious office, complete with mirrored walls, baroque gilded ceiling, and mirror-like marble floor. "Have you ever seen anything quite so . . . overdone?"

Wellington glanced around. "Actually, with the exception of the chairs, I think it's rather smashing."

"You would. Well, one thing's for damned sure, I'm getting electricity installed. I'll go blind reading by candlelight."

"Are you really serious about moving back to your house?" Wellington asked.

"I'd be there right now if I didn't have to put on some kind of show to assure everyone I'm in command."

"What do you think about living here, my Lady?"

"It's terrible," Marie commented from her chair beside Napoleon. "Stifling and cold."

"Neither one of you has any taste," Wellington sniffed. He shifted his weight, crossed one leg on the other, and flicked an invisible speck of dust from his white trousers. "I'd cheerfully take up residence."

"You're the wrong nationality," Napoleon said.

"Details." Wellington leaned forward in his chair, frowned, stood and moved it closer to the desk. "So what the devil did Mata Hari come to see you for?" He sat down again. "Did she dance?"

"God, Wellington. She does other things besides dance."

"True. But little that can be viewed in mixed company."

"I suppose. But this is what's really important. It seems she's defected from Administration. She's placed herself at Caesar's service . . . and ours, since we're Caesars friends."

"My, my." The Iron Duke sat up straighter. "She's a superlative spy, so I hear. And, having worked for Administration, I should think she'd be *full* of helpful information."

Marie grinned widely and brushed a strand of blond hair back from her eyes. "Caesar must agree with you. Napoleon cleared this with him right before you walked in."

"And right now, we can use all the help we can get," Napoleon said. "Are things starting to settle down yet?"

"Yes. At least *our* side of the Park is halfway normal. We've got Huns and Mongols everywhere, to say nothing of the DGSE men guarding Hadrian. And the Tulsan has taken his role of hero seriously. He even got the couple from California to join him in a block watch."

"I can see it," Napoleon said, spreading his hands. "A sign saying: WE CALL THE POLICE IF THERE'S AN INVASION."

Wellington snorted a laugh. "So, what are we going to do now?"

"Keep our heads down. That's Caesar's plan and it's the best one I've heard yet. I'm not too happy about our position . . . we're being asked to ally ourselves with Rome."

"I thought we already were." Wellington glanced around the office, spotted a decanter of wine on the sideboard, and went after it. "Allied with Rome, I mean."

"Ah . . . but not *visibly* allied. That's the crux of it. And when I say 'we,' I don't mean just you and me. I mean the French and British."

"Oh?" Wellington lifted his glass and passed it twice under his long nose. "Lovely bouquet, don't you think? Have overtures been made to Queen Victoria?"

"I don't know. I'm not sure it's got to that stage yet. I do know Caesar would be in favor of it."

"I should think so. You're in command of the French now. What will you do?"

Napoleon exchanged a quick look with Marie, then stood, walked around his desk and joined Wellington at the sideboard. "Right now, Rameses isn't sure *where* I stand. He knows we've got Hadrian, but that knowledge will only make him more hesitant to do anything about it. I think he's afraid of what will happen now that I've booted Louis off his throne."

"I see." Wellington rubbed his chin. "And I'm supposed to talk Queen Victoria into this alliance?"

"I suppose so."

"Huhn. I'd feel better about things if I spoke to Caesar first."

"So would I, but I don't think that's going to be anytime soon."

"It had *better* be soon, or I'll kill Hadrian. I *swear* I'll kill him!"

"Is he still being unreasonable?" Marie asked.

"Do birds fly?" Wellington's face reddened. "God! He's still the same, overbearing obnoxious toad as before! If you talk to Caesar again, Napoleon, tell him I've had it with Hadrian. *Had it!* He's eating me out of house and home, *and* depleting my liquor like he's tapped into some inexhaustible source. And his meals . . . Can you imagine someone eating enchiladas topped with Cool Whip? Ugh!"

Napoleon grimaced. "I suppose if it makes him happy—"

"It makes *me* sick! And if I ever have to spend more than a few hours with the DGSE men again, I'll go stark, raving mad!"

"I thought you were getting along better with them," Napoleon said, pouring himself and Marie a half glass of wine.

"Huhn. I will admit they're much easier to work with. They even speak more English now than before."

"Well, then, I suppose—"

The telephone rang. Napoleon walked to the desk and picked it up.

"*Trouble, Napoleon!*" It was Attila's voice. "*Hadrian's gone!*"

"What do you mean, 'gone'?" Napoleon asked of Attila in Wellington's living room. Marie stood by his side, her face registering the concern she felt over this disappearance. Meanwhile, the Iron Duke was assessing the damage left behind by the ex-Commander of Hell's armies and the four DGSE men who had guarded him. Though neater than the last time Napoleon had seen it, Wellington's living room was a far cry from the spotless showpiece it had once been.

"Gone," Attila replied. "Vanished without a trace!"

"Hadrian can't just vanish without leaving *some* trace behind!" Wellington growled over his shoulder, picking up one of his cushions from the floor and brushing stale popcorn from it.

"Ah, this is Hell, Wellington. Or have you forgotten?"

Wellington shot Attila a venomous look, fluffed the cushion and set it back on the couch. "Hardly. Where are the DGSE men?"

"Damned good question." Attila turned back to Napoleon. "I stopped by to see how things were going, found the front door wide open, and—" He gestured to the empty living room and equally empty dining room. "Hey! Who knows? Maybe Mithridates— "

"I doubt that," Napoleon said, walking back to the entry hall and inspecting the door. "No one's seen him for ages. Huhn. I can't find any sign of forced entry."

"I've checked the house," Attila volunteered. "All the windows and the back door were secure."

"Damn! Where the hell could he have gone?"

"And, more importantly," Marie added, "how did he manage to get away?"

"Pompous bastard." Wellington had arranged all his pillows on the couch, and was now picking up candy wrappers, cigarette butts and beer cans from the floor. "I hope the bugger *never* comes back!"

"Did anyone in the neighborhood see anything?" Napoleon asked.

Attila shook his head. "No. I've checked with everyone. Everyone, that is, except the Tulsan."

"How long ago did all this happen?"

"Not more than an hour ago. The DGSE men were having lunch. Their food was still warm."

Napoleon looked around the living room again, frowned and began pacing. "Let's think this through. Four DGSE men (with weapons, we assume), and one potted ex-Commander of Hell's armies. Vanished." He glanced up as Wellington passed him, armed now with a large plastic trash bag, inscribed with block letters on its side: DO YOUR PART—KEEP HELL CLEAN. "Any ideas, Wellington?"

"Not a one," came the muffled reply. Wellington was scooping up a mountain of trash and stuffing it into the garbage bag with religious zeal.

"Some help *you* are." He turned to Attila. "I think we should pay a visit to the Tulsan."

"Good luck. He's got his doors locked and the curtains drawn."

Napoleon lifted an eyebrow. "This from our neighborhood hero? Even more reason to roust him out, *n'est-ce pas?*"

"Whatever you say." Attila grinned. "Just don't make any of your famous plans without telling me where I fit in first."

Hendron's house sat between Wellington's and Attila's, a dwelling no more remarkable than either of its neighboring structures. As Attila had said, the drapes were tightly drawn and after four tries at the doorbell, Napoleon's patience came to an end.

"*Eh bien,*" he said, digging in the rear pocket of his

jeans. "This calls for decisive action." He pulled out his billfold, opened it and drew out a credit card.

"Damn," Attila said, looking over Napoleon's shoulder, "I didn't know you had one of *them*."

"The Ma Hell Calling Card?" Napoleon pocketed his billfold, then slipped the thin plastic card into the edge of Hendron's front door, just to one side of the lock. "They've only sent me forty of the things, unsolicited in the mail. I finally gave up and agreed to accept it." He jiggled the card gently back and forth. "Are you armed, Attila?"

The King of the Huns nodded. "When have you known me *not* to be?"

"Just checking. Now, if I can get this goddamned thing to— Aha!"

The lock gave way and the door opened a fraction. Motioning Marie and Attila back, Napoleon moved to the far side of the door and slowly eased it open.

"Hendron!" he called. "We know you're in there. We can hear you breathing."

Silence.

Glancing at Attila, Napoleon stepped into the Tulsan's entry hall. Marie followed just behind, Attila bringing up the rear, a .45 pistol in his hand.

"*Mon dieu!*" Napoleon said, glancing into the living room. "I'm glad Wellington stayed behind to clean up his house. He would have died of culture shock."

Hendron's living room was decorated in the time-honored style of Early Junque. And orange—orange was everywhere. Sacrificial Aztec Orange. The curtains, the yellow and orange wall paper, the orange and tan shag carpet. The brown, vinyl couch with orange throw pillows. A large, economy size lava lamp sat on the coffee table, lazily blooping globs of (what else?) orange goo up its plastic sides.

"Hendron?" Napoleon called. "It's me . . . Napoleon. All we want to do is talk with you! Dammit, man! Come out!"

"Ya'll *sure* thet's all ya wanta do?" came the faint sound of the Tulsan's voice.

"*Certainment!* Now come out, will you?"

"Well . . . all rot."

Attila spun around, his leveled gun gleaming in the afternoon light, as rustling came from the hall closet to the left. Something large and heavy hit the floor, followed by a muffled curse, more rustling, and then the closet door eased open.

"What the devil's gotten into you?" Napoleon asked as Tommy Hendron emerged into the entry hall.

"Goddamned bowlin' ball," Hendron muttered, turning to glare at the offending object over which he had tripped. He looked back to Napoleon, his eyes suspicious. "Now how in hail didja git in here? I had thet door locked."

"I'm a man of many talents," Napoleon said. "Just a few questions, please. Have you seen Hadrian?"

The Tulsan's face went blank. "Why?"

"He's gone missing, and we need to find him before someone . . . *anyone* . . . else does."

"Thet's *all* ya wanta know? Ya ain't gettin' me into somethin', now, are ya?"

Napoleon put on his best innocent expression. "Me? What have *I* gotten you into lately that you haven't come out of smelling like a rose?"

"Well . . ." Hendron sighed. "I seen him . . . him and them French guys guardin' him. They went thetaway." He pointed across the street.

"Into the Park?" Marie asked. "You're sure?"

"Yes'm. But they didn't go willingly. There was Cong with 'em."

"Oh, gods!" Attila shoved his gun into his wide leather belt. "What were the Cong doing at Wellington's house?"

"I didn't ask," Hendron said. "After I seen over ten of them gooks crowd their way into the house, I made myself scarce."

"Were they armed?" Napoleon asked.

"You betcha, yer Emperorship. Armed to the teeth."

"*Merde!*"

"They've kidnapped Hadrian, haven't they?" Marie asked, touching Napoleon's arm.

"Sounds like it. But why? And whose side are *they* on now?"

"Would you look at this, Napoleon?" Wellington said, his long, narrow face pale. He waved a crumpled piece of paper under Napoleon's nose. "I nearly threw it out with the trash!"

Napoleon took the paper and glanced around Wellington's living room. "Glad to see you've been putting yourself to *some* use," he commented. "In a few more days, you'll have this place back to its original surgically clean condition." He ignored Wellington's glare and read the note.

"*WE VIET CONG OF PEOPLE'S PARK.*" The words were crudely written in a soft, No. 1 pencil. "*IF YOU WANT FAT MAN AND FOUR FRIENDS BACK, DELIVER RIBS.*"

"Ribs?" Attila exclaimed, having read the note too. "What are they—?"

"Oh, shit." Napoleon crumpled up the paper in one hand. "It's the barbeque I promised them. Remember? Hendron got them to shell the mercenaries attacking me by promising them a barbeque. I've never gotten around to it."

"As if you've had time," Marie said.

"Blackmail!" Wellington's expression grew pained. "The bloody bastards are trying to blackmail you!"

"Not trying," Napoleon said. "They *are* blackmailing me. We've got no choice. We'll have to give them what they want or spend God only knows how long going after everything that moves in the Park. And I doubt the Cong are above shooting Hadrian and the DGSE men and letting Reassignments take care of things."

"Where are *you* going, Hendron?" Attila asked, stepping between the Tulsan and the door. "This involves you, too. Stay put."

"But . . ." Hendron nervously fingered the large Western belt buckle half hidden under his protruding belly. "I ain't gonna have anythin' to do with them slant-eyed bastards again. They like t' scared the shit outta me the last time."

"Well, you're dealing with *this* slant-eyed bastard now," Attila said, "and I'm telling you: stay put!"

"No need to git yer dander up. I ain't goin' nowheres."

Napoleon had started pacing again. "All right. Here's what we've got to do. Wellington. How much cash do you have on hand?"

Wellington looked up from his trash bag. "Hardly enough to buy ribs for all the Cong in Decentral Park."

"I'm not asking you to do that. I'm thinking of pooling our resources."

"Oh. Probably about fifty silver-backs."

"Huhn. I've got another fifty or so. Attila?"

"Broke. Lost a big bet last night."

"And you, Hendron?"

"Oh . . . 'spect I've got 'bout twenty."

"A hundred and twenty. Not enough. Damn! We've got to find some cash. And with things turned upside-down like they are, I'll bet the banks are—"

"Louis!" Wellington put the last twist on his trash bag tie. "Check Crazy Louis. He has *bags* of money buried in his back yard. You told me that yourself, Attila."

"Wellington's right. I saw him out there one night, busily burying his treasures by the hedge."

Napoleon grinned. "Well, now. Isn't that interesting. Since this is turning out to be 'Visit Your Neighbor Day,' let's go call on Louis."

Louis XVI, his white wig slightly askew on his head, glanced from Attila's stoney face to Napoleon. He nervously wiped his forehead.

"Napoleon, *mon ami* . . . fellow Frenchman. Have pity. Don't take my money. It's all I have."

"You want the Cong shelling your house again?" Napoleon asked. "Everyone *else* is contributing to the Rib Fund. Why not you?"

"But . . . my money! I've saved it for years! And now that Judgment Day's coming, I—"

"Judgment Day?" This from Marie who stood just inside Louis' front door. "What are you talking about?"

The French King waved a hand. "Word's going around that Hell's coming to an end. We're all to be judged at last."

"Oh?" Napoleon frowned. "What's that got to do with your money? Haven't you heard, Louis? You can't take it with you."

"At least not to Heaven," Wellington amended. "I think it's set out in a clause somewhere."

"But . . ."

"You know, Napoleon," Attila said, unsheathing his long, gold chased dagger. "I've always wondered what Louis would look like without his nose."

Louis clapped both hands over his face. "No! Please! Don't touch me! I'll tell you where my money's buried. I'll even get one of my sycophants to dig it up for you!"

Attila stepped closer, the knife glittering in his hand. "I still think I'd like to try his nose," he said conversationally. "Or maybe an ear."

"*Sacre nom de dieu!*" Louis now had one hand on his nose and the other covering the ear nearest Attila. "Please! Be patient! Henri! Henri, I *need* you!"

The filmy shape of a half-visible sycophant floated into view.

"Bring me a bag of my money!" Louis said, his voice nasal behind his hand. "Hurry! *Vite! Vite!*"

The sycophant vanished. Napoleon traded an amused look with Marie, Wellington, and Hendron, while Attila sighed softly, and put his knife away.

*　　*　　*

Napoleon backed his car out of his driveway, and headed down the street in the direction of the grocery store. Wellington sat cramped in the small back seat, guardian of the hoard of money they had managed to scrape together; Louis' funds had augmented the total to where Napoleon figured he had enough not only to buy a trunkful of ribs, but the best Kansas City barbeque sauce to top them.

If, with conditions in Hell the way they were, the grocery store was still in operation. Or still standing.

"Napoleon." Marie turned toward him from her place at his side. "I wonder what Louis was talking about?"

He glanced her way. "About what?"

"Judgment Day." Her face had gone serious; her eyes sought his. "That Hell might be coming to an end."

"Huhn." He turned a corner, and looked at the other cars on the road: in spite of everything, traffic was near to normal. "Sounds to me like the crazies who used to run around saying the world was coming to an end . . . the ones with the signs, the long robes and ashes on the forehead."

"I don't know," Wellington interposed, leaning forward. "There might be something to it."

"Look what's happening," Marie said. "Right here in New Hell. Everyone who could weathered the last storm. Might this only be a harbinger of worse to come?"

Napoleon grinned. "Possibly. But one thing's for sure . . . if it's true, then a lot of people are going to start cleaning up their acts."

"Hell coming to an end," Wellington murmured. "It boggles the mind."

Wellington sounded so pensive, Napoleon glanced in the rearview mirror to look at his friend's face. "Boggles is hardly the word," he said. "But, if Hell ends, then what's the use of Heaven?"

Marie cocked her head and gave him a long look.

"How can something be a reward if there isn't its opposite to fear?" Napoleon drew to a stop at a red light. "Think of it another way. If man on earth proved—and I mean proved *without a doubt*—there was no God, then there wouldn't be a need for religion. And, if man proved there *was* a God, there *still* wouldn't be a need for religion. Heaven needs Hell, and Hell needs Heaven."

"*I*, for one, wouldn't mind being judged," Wellington said. "I've tried my best here in Hell."

"And it's no easy thing to do good here," Marie added. "Napoleon . . . what if it *is* true?"

The light turned green in record time. "There's not much we can do about it, is there?"

"But what if . . ." Marie reached out and touched his arm. "What could lie on the other side of Hell? Something even worse?"

"Or . . ." Wellington's voice sounded hollow. "Nothing at all."

The grocery store was not more than three blocks ahead; Napoleon could already see the line of cars waiting to get into the parking lot that was never big enough.

"We all get what we deserve," he said, "in one way or another. *That's* the frightening thing about it."

"Well, I certainly don't deserve to be among the damned!" Wellington exclaimed.

"Few of us here in New Hell think we do. And that's our chief torment: trying to figure out what we did that doomed us." He pulled into line, behind a '59 Chevy station wagon. "Damn . . . we're a morbid lot! I'll bet Attila and Hendron have found something less gloomy to discuss."

"Oh, I don't know," Wellington said, leaning back in his seat, prepared for the long wait for a parking place. "*They've* got the Cong to worry about."

Attila led the way through the overgrown edge of Decentral Park, trying to make as little noise as possible. He finally gave up any thought of stealth: Tommy Hendron, walking just behind him, sounded like a bull elephant in the brush.

"Thet's fur enough," the Tulsan said, stopping by a particularly tangled group of shrubs. "I ain't goin' one step more into this here Park. I already died once, an' I don't wanta do it again."

Attila sighed and lowered the stick to which he had attached a white flag. Hendron was probably right; there *was* no need to penetrate deeper into Viet Cong territory.

"All right. Talk to them, Hendron. They'll recognize your voice."

"Me? Why not you? You all look alike."

"We don't all *talk* alike. Now, talk, Hendron . . . talk!"

"Shee-it. No need to git testy." The Tulsan licked his lips and took a deep breath. "Hey ya'll! Cong in the Park! We're here to parley! Come on out, now! We'll negotiate!"

Nothing happened; the Park was still, with only a fitful wind running through the leaves.

"Damn." Hendron looked at Attila. "We *could* be in the wrong part of th' Park. We better—"

Attila held up a hand. Something had rustled in the brush, off to his right.

"You come in peace?" asked a voice from ahead.

"Damned rot!" Hendron called out. "We ain't got a weapon on us!"

Attila turned quickly to his left as a short, black-clad man stepped out of the bushes directly opposite from where the voice had spoken, all the while knowing he and Hendron stood in the sights of more automatic weapons than he was comfortable thinking about.

"Talk," the Viet Cong said. "You come to buy back fat man and friends?"

"Not us," Attila replied. "We're here to tell you you'll get your barbeque. My friends are buying the food now."

The Viet Cong stared at Attila so long he wondered if he had spoken too quickly to be understood.

"Ribs?" the Cong asked.

"Ribs," Attila replied. "*Lots* of ribs. When we have the ribs, we'll exchange them for your hostages."

"When?"

Attila glanced around. "In three hours."

"Where?"

"You tell *us* that. We won't give you the ribs until we see you haven't hurt anyone."

The Viet Cong's expressionless face cracked into a small smile. "You bring ribs," he said, "we give you fat man and friends quick. Double quick. He eat too much for us to keep long."

Hendron cleared his throat. "Where ya'll want us to bring them ribs?"

The Cong gestured back through the Park toward the street. "Across from redcoat's house. In three hours. We be there. You be there, too . . . *with* ribs."

Attila nodded. "Done."

The Viet Cong turned away and quickly vanished into the undergrowth. Attila still felt himself and Hendron encircled.

"Damn," the Tulsan whispered, turning around and starting back toward the street. "Let's hope there wasn't a run on ribs at the grocery today."

Attila blinked. His very prayer. Maybe ESP *did* work after all.

The grocery store was packed wall-to-wall with customers. Napoleon's heart sank as he, Marie and Wellington hurried back toward the meat department. If all these people were stocking up on food, unsure what tomorrow might bring, a massive purchase of ribs might be out of the question. Marie rang the bell to summon the butcher, while Wellington began pacing up and down by the poultry section.

"Ah, General," said a cultured voice from just behind

Napoleon's shoulder. "Or should I say, Emperor. I'm surprised to see *you* here."

Napoleon turned and looked up into the mild blue eyes of T.E. Lawrence. Lawrence was in his confusion mode today: clad in a white burnoose, he wore his RAF uniform, complete with officer's boots.

"Likewise," Napoleon replied, knowing every word he said would be repeated to someone somewhere by the myriad of spies that followed anyone of importance in New Hell.

"I've made a smashing discovery," Lawrence said. Reaching out and taking Napoleon's elbow, he led the way two aisles down to the ground coffee machine. "Delicate blend," he said, pointing to one of the coffee grinders. The machine was going and Napoleon found it difficult to hear. "Have you talked with J.C.?"

J.C.? Ah . . . Julius. Napoleon nodded slightly.

"I just got back from a very interesting trip. You might mention to our friend that his two Admin contacts are still out of hand. We're working on it."

Napoleon had caught most of what Lawrence had said and wished he had not. He had enough problems of his own without getting embroiled in more of Caesar's.

"I'll do that," he murmured.

"Marvelous." Lawrence glanced around, touched his forehead in a mock salute. "Cherrio, old chap. I'll be seeing you."

Napoleon stared at Lawrence's retreating back and cursed the coincidence that had brought them together here at the local Unsafeway in front of God only knows who. But the damage (if any) was done, and he had ribs to think about.

Marie was talking with the butcher by the time Napoleon made it back to the meat section. The fellow's expression bordered on the skeptical, but Marie smiled her most charming smile, and the butcher nodded.

"Trouble?" Napoleon asked Wellington, who had

moved from the poultry section to the hot dogs and balogna.

"Not any more," Wellington replied. "The butcher said he didn't have that many ribs, but it looks like Marie has convinced him otherwise."

"Huhn." He considered telling Wellington about meeting Lawrence, but decided that was information he could sit on for now. "I wonder if Attila and Hendron have set up the exchange yet."

"Let's hope so." Wellington shifted the bag of money from hand to hand. "I really think we should have deposited this at the bank first, Napoleon. I'm damned nervous carrying it around."

"Shit, Wellington . . . it's in a Baker's Dozen Doughnuts bag. Nobody's going to notice. And besides, I don't know if I still have check cashing privileges here. You know how they are . . . one week you can write fifty checks, the next week they've lost your card."

"Ah . . . success!" Wellington pointed.

Napoleon turned around: the butcher appeared from the back of the store, wheeling out a cart stuffed to the top with packages of ribs. Marie smiled her sweet smile again, touched the butcher lightly on his arm, and murmured her thanks.

"Let's find the barbeque sauce and get out of here," Napoleon said, taking the cart from her. He led the way down a crowded aisle, dodging fellow shoppers on the way. "You're marvelous, Marie, you know that?"

"Sometimes." Her expression was mischievous. "Now why can't I sweet-talk *you* into things?"

"Like what?"

"Let's teach Wellington fluent French," she said, her smile widening into a grin, "and have *him* live in Louis' palace since he likes it so much."

Attila paced up and down in font of Wellington's house, glancing every now and then down the street in the direction Napoleon had gone. Tommy Hendron sat on the doorstep, his arms balanced on his knees, staring morosely into the Park.

"They better hurry up," Hendron said. "We only got an hour 'fore them gooks come to trade."

"I don't think they stopped off to see a movie," Attila growled. "They'll be here soon as they can."

He resumed his pacing and looked over at Napoleon's house. Two French soldiers stood on either side of the front door, professional, armed, and looking like they meant business. Attila had seen other Frenchmen around the house—some tall Moderns, some from the *Grande Armée*. Now that Napoleon ruled in Louis' place, his protection was of high priority. Attila grinned: Napoleon detested being smothered in attention, and the French undercover agents who had followed him to the grocery store would be in for a dressing down if they had made their presence known.

"Hey!" That was Hendron. "Here they come!"

Attila looked down the street and saw Napoleon's dark blue Honda Prelude. The car was one luxury Napoleon afforded himself: he liked responsiveness behind the wheel, and—above all—speed when he needed it.

"You got 'em?" Hendron asked, jumping up from the doorstep and trotting over to Wellington's drive.

Napoleon exited the car, pocketed his keys and nodded. He looked at Attila. "Have you set up the exchange?"

"Yes. Less than one hour from now."

"Where?"

"Right across the street."

"*C'est bon!*" Napoleon turned around and reached into the back seat. "Help me with these ribs, will you? We've got more in the trunk."

"How're them gooks gonna want these ribs done?" Hendron asked, stepping forward to take one of the heavy brown paper bags.

"Barbequed in the best Western tradition," Napoleon replied. "You've got the grills going?"

"In the garage," Attila said.

"*Next to my car?*" Wellington started up the drive-way. "No! Never! We'll spatter grease all over the—"

"For God's sake, Wellington," Napoleon said, shov-ing a bag of ribs into the Iron Duke's arms. "We don't have time to worry about that now." Marie handed him another bag. "Let's get cooking!"

Wellington's garage was full of smoke and the mouth-watering smell of cooking ribs. Napoleon had appropri-ated every paper plate anyone on the block could provide which, in Hendron's case, was plenty. The Tulsan must own stock in a paper company somewhere; Napoleon had never seen as many paper plates as Hendron had dragged out of his kitchen.

Between Wellington and Marie, the barbequing was proceeding at a good clip. Attila was in charge of bast-ing the ribs with sauce, while Hendron and Napoleon loaded up the plates and set them aside on tables Wellington had provided from his basement.

"Damn, Wellington!" Napoleon had exclaimed at the sight of the ten card tables. "What were you expecting to do—throw a bridge party?"

Wellington had sniffed something under his breath and Napoleon knew he had scored a direct hit. Bridge. It figured.

Things were proceeding right on schedule. Napoleon set his latest plate of ribs on one of the tables and turned to go back for more.

"*Mon empereur!*"

The French words brought him up short, as did the voice. He turned to face Duroc.

"Geraud! What are *you* doing here?"

"You've got four DGSE men over at the palace," Duroc said, looking around the garage with a mystified expression on his face. "They say their names are Anbec, Mirabeau—"

"Barré and LeFlore!" Napoleon finished. "Dammit! Did they have Hadrian with them?"

"No." Duroc nodded a greeting to Wellington and Marie who had joined them. "Anbec said to tell you that the Cong still have him."

Napoleon's heart sank. "Oh, shit. How did the DGSE get away?"

"LeFlore said they made their break when the Cong were occupied with keeping Hadrian pliant. They ran off into the brush and somehow made it to the palace."

An escape from deep in Decentral Park, through Cong-held territory and God knows what kind of opposition?

"Hey, yer Emperorship!" Hendron said. "Look there!"

Napoleon turned around: across the street, on the very edge of the brush and undergrowth, stood a black-clad Viet Cong, waving a white flat on the end of a stick.

"Now what?" Attila wondered.

"I don't know, but we'd better find out." Napoleon started down the driveway, Duroc and Attila on his one side, Wellington and Marie on the other. He stopped a few paces from the Viet Cong.

"Where ribs?"

"We're cooking them," Napoleon replied, hooking a thumb over his shoulder in the direction of Wellington's garage.

"Deal off," the Viet Cong said.

"What do you mean, the deal's off?" Wellington exploded. "We've gone through hell to get these damned ribs for you! And now you say the deal's off?"

Napoleon glared Wellington into silence. "Why is the deal off?" he asked, trying to sound reasonable.

"You got four friends back."

"What about—" Attila looked into the brush. "—the fat man?"

"You got him back, too."

Napoleon traded a glance with Duroc. "Not that *we* know of. Did he escape with the four Frenchmen?"

"No. We let him go. He too big trouble for us to keep."

"Sounds like Hadrian," Wellington growled. "*Nobody* wants him."

"Dammit, Wellington!" Napoleon snapped. "This is no time for a personal vendetta."

"You still owe us ribs," the Cong said. "And you deliver."

Napoleon took a deep breath. "Or?'"

"We shell houses here. We shell palace on other side Park."

"Now, lookie here," Hendron said, taking a step forward. "Ya cain't change demands in the middle of a stream!"

Attila drew Hendron back. "I'm afraid they can. They've got the fire power to back it up, too."

Napoleon frowned. If he said no, the fragile peace established around Decentral Park would disappear. Granted, he now had Louis' cannon (in poor condition), and could likely get more artillery, but not before the Viet Cong could do serious damage.

"All right," he said. "We'll be finished with the ribs soon. You and your comrades can meet us here—"

"No good. Plan change. You bring us ribs in *center* of Park, or we shoot. Bring by nightfall."

"But—"

"That all I say. Bring ribs."

The Viet Cong turned away and trotted off into the concealing vegetation.

"Damn!" Napoleon's shoulders slumped. "You know what they're after, don't you?"

Attila was still staring off in the direction the Viet Cong had taken. "You," he said, "or some other hostage. Whoever takes those ribs into the Park won't come out real soon."

"I don't think we should deal with terrorists," Wellington said sanctimoniously.

"What do you think you've been doing for the last

hour?" Napoleon shot back. "Cooking ribs for a Girl Scout troop?"

Marie touched Napoleon's hand. "You're not going to—"

"No." Napoleon rubbed his chin. "I'm not. And I think I have a solution that will make everyone happy." He turned to Duroc. "Geraud. I'm going to need your help for this one."

Afternoon was waning when Napoleon walked from the drive to the edge of Louis' property. His car and Wellington's white Eldorado were pulled up along the side of the road; Wellington paced up and down between the two vehicles, scowling and muttering under his breath. Marie waited quietly beside the dark blue Prelude with Attila; Hendron had perched on the Cadillac's bumper and sat staring into the Park.

Grand Marshal Duroc walked to Napoleon's side. "We've done what we can, Napoleon," he said, gesturing behind him. "I hope it's enough."

Napoleon looked at the ten old cannon that Duroc had ordered lined up at the edge of the street. All of them were 48 pounders and had considerable range, but Louis had used them mostly for show. "Now the only question is, Duroc—will they work?"

"You checked them out after you returned from the fight in the valley," Duroc said. "I trust you."

"Huhn." So he had been an artillery officer, one of the best in the business. Napoleon frowned: he had seldom had to work with such out-of-date weapons, but they were all he could find on short notice. "Well," he said, "let's get on with it."

He walked over to the first cannon, greeting the soldiers manning it with a smile and a handshake.

"Primed and loaded, *mon empereur*," one of the men said. "Trajectory set to your specifications."

Napoleon nodded. "Fire when ready," he ordered, and stepped back.

The cannoneer saluted and walked to his place at the

rear of the cannon. Napoleon turned toward the cars. "Here we go!" he called, and the first cannon roared.

The projectile flew into the park, burst apart, and fell in the form of a white flag tied to the end of a stone.

"I hope the Cong understand your message," Wellington said, coming to Napoleon's side.

Napoleon glanced up at the Iron Duke. "They'd better, or it's going to get damned noisy around here." He watched the flag disappear into the trees far out in the Park. Dead center. "Numbers two, four, six, eight . . . fire!" he yelled. The cannons thundered. Marie covered her ears with her hands and Hendron winced. Attila stood watching the Park with rapt fascination. "Three, five, seven and nine! Fire!"

The other four cannon shot into the Park. Napoleon lifted his head, tracking the projectiles' descent. Not a sound came from the Park. The acrid smoke made his eyes water. When he felt sure there would be no reprisal, he called out, "Ten!"

The last cannon boomed into the fading light. Napoleon sighed and turned to Wellington.

"Let's hope this works," he said.

"The Cong certainly can't complain." The Iron Duke took out a lace handkerchief and fanned at a cloud of smoke. "Barbequed ribs, delivered by cannon shot to the center of Decentral Park. One thing though. What was in the last cannon?"

Napoleon held out his hand to Marie who had joined him, and grinned. "Paper napkins. I wouldn't want the Viet Cong to think we were barbarians."

Night had fallen over Decentral Park, the villas, the palaces and the houses around it. Napoleon sat on Louis' front steps, Marie at his side. Wellington, Attila and Hendron had stayed for dinner, along with the soldiers who had manned the cannon, and then left for the other side of the Park. Now, after having spoken

with Caesar on the telephone, Napoleon had taken
Marie outside for a breath of moderately fresh air.

"So Caesar's not angry about losing Hadrian?" Marie
asked.

"Oh, he's upset, but not at us. Now that he's got
Mata Hari and her friends at his service, he said he'll
be putting them to good use." He shook his head. "I
still can't believe the DGSE men fell for the old 'my
car's out of gas can I use your phone' routine. They
should know better than that."

"They're suitably embarrassed," Marie said, leaning
her head on Napoleon's shoulder.

"And equally glad to be free of their assignment." He
hugged Marie and laughed quietly. "They—"

A loud thud came from the bottom of the steps.
Napoleon stood, called for the guards to hold position
and, motioning Marie to remain on the steps, cau-
tiously descended to the driveway. He bent over a
large rock, stirred it with his toe, then picked it up. A
piece of paper had been tied to the stone; he carefully
unknotted the string.

"What is it?" Marie asked.

"I don't know." He trotted up the steps, led the way
to one of the lights at the doorway, and unfolded the
paper.

*"YOU MAN OF HONOR. YOU SMART MAN ALSO.
WE KEEP OUR BARGAIN. NO SHELL YOU."*

"Well," Napoleon said, lowering the note. "I suppose
when you treat the Park to a barbeque, the least you
can expect is a thank you note."

THE SIBYLLINE AFFAIR
C.J. Cherryh

Noon in Hell. The convoy wended its way back from the field, slow grinding of gears and treads—damn Tiberius, who refused it passage over his manicured lawn. The only route back was the series of lanes that ran toward city streets—the streets of New Hell, specifically by Decentral Park and down narrow, concrete Park Avenue, the genteel high rent district—high rent, by Hell's definitions, meaning a lot of things. And genteel meaning that you tried to keep the noise to a minimum.

Slipping an armored unit down Park Avenue past the villa was delicate, to say the least. "Just be fast, be quiet," the Old Man had said—Caius Iulius Caesar, the original, *The* Old Man, who was trying to save the collective asses of the Roman establishments in Hell. His men, veterans even as Hell counted time, *tried* not to muck up.

But there were cars behind them honking, there was a large gap in traffic in front of them, and the aged concrete pavement was showing an embarrassing tendency to scar and crumble under the metal treads—when an ex-Assyrian half-track, near the front of the column, went *chunk!* and grindddd! and spun a little skewed.

"Oh, shit," the driver said. Latinically.

* * *

Noon in Tiberius' palace—drafty halls full of priapic statues and tintinnabula, erotic and sadistic frescoes, and lamps of highly improbable design.

The lamps and the wall-paintings in the library— likewise, ithyphallic lamps that illumined rows upon rows of pigeonholes for scrolls; of codices, sleazy paperbacks and sex magazines in forty languages; and untold numbers of religious texts, all of which reflected the interests of the Emperor.

Who was at the moment swathed in a black toga, seated in a curule chair at a table the legs of which were fauns, and reading his house budget, trying to decipher the requisitions of the Guard and to decide whether (as his sycophants whispered) there was pilferage of wine from the kitchens.

Certainly there was. Heads would roll. The question was how many. He *liked* the present cook. He adored stuffed trout.

Perhaps a boiling in wine. Saute the cook. He chuckled.

And looked up as a figure oddly shadowed paused by the restricted case, the glass case in the center of the room in which the Holy Books resided.

No one was permitted in the library when the Emperor was using it. But a second blink showed no one.

He got up, shoved his chair back and walked down the middle of the room to peer into the shadows beyond the lamplight. Despite age, despite syphilis, he was still a soldier. He had proved that—had proved it in the field, lately, himself leading the Praetorians when Antonius proved unreliable—

But he at least counted on the presence of the guards at the door, who stood there, the fools, as if there was nothing at all.

And the case! The case was empty!

"Robbery!" he shrieked, startling the baboon from its explorations of the back shelves. It screamed, and scampered to cling to a statue in the shadows. "Robbery! Treason! *Antoni! Antoni! Quonam es, Antoni? Perfidia nos ambit!*"

Lunch in Augustus' villa, next to the park, across the tennis courts from Tiberius: a light and airy place of tasteful, chaste marbles and heroic bronzes, electric lights (Julius' idea) and modern plumbing (Kleopatra's) —and in the upstairs office, a 20th century desk papered from edge to edge, not mentioning the careful stacks of papers that spread outward across the carpeted floor; remnants of an anchovy and pepperoni pizza distributed throughout; and a desperately harried First Citizen, Caius Iulius Caesar Octavianus Augustus, awash in reports and damage control.

"I don't *care* what your problems are, centurion, I want that half-track off the street! It's provocative!"

A thin voice of protest from the other end. "First Citizen, I'm getting orders from field command and from intelligence and from your office, and with all respect, First Citizen, I'm just a stand-in. A half-track howitzer—?"

"Is blocking traffic in front of the villa, it's opposite the Cong, who are *damned* touchy, and it's broken down, centurion, which makes it *your* problem, so I suggest you get somebody up the street with a mechanic—"

"We can't, First Citizen. That's what I'm telling you. We're running thin here, and the General's standing order—"

"Well, *tow it in!* I want it off this street, hear me? I want it off in the next half hour."

"Please, First Citizen. My standing orders—"

"A half hour!"

Augustus slammed the phone down. It jingled and he regarded it with mistrust, posed a hand over it.

Pro di, he hated electrical gadgets.

It stayed quiet. The divine Augustus scowled at it

and searched through the stacks of papers for the letter from Her Majesty of England.

R-r-ring.

He pounced, snatched the receiver up and held it a safe distance from his ear. "Hello, hello! Speak up! Who are you?"

And held it further away.

"*Scaevola!*" he shouted, and punched buttons. Regulus assured him, absolutely assured him, first the red button, then the unlighted buttons, then the house number. "Scaevola!"

Click. Buzz.

"*Scaevola!*"

A sycophant popped into the room—a ghostly shimmer, a flunky scenting usefulness. "Scaevola'sssss downstairsssss," it said.

Augustus slammed the receiver down. "That was the New Hell street department. *Find* Scaevola. Tell him they're blaming us for a water main. Tell him move that damned gun, *pro di*, I've had calls from the police, from the *Pentagram*, for the gods' sake . . . Where's Julius?"

"Juliussss." The mote dimmed, brightened again. "Find Juliussss. . . ."

"FFffffoooollll," another one said, popping in, and suddenly a whole crowd of them, petty officials in life, paper-pushers. "Ffffinndddd Juliussss. . . ."

Which the others echoed, diving out again.

Augustus rested his head on his hands.

The mop-up from the Assyrian mess was still proceeding. Tiberius was ranting about expense and damages to his precious statue, threatening to take them to the Extreme Court, the bills were rolling in, some of them *Hell's* kind of bills, which Julius attempted to handle—

Napoleon was dealing with the Cong, Hadrian thank *gods* had just turned up wandering Park Avenue, and some of Attila's lads had him in tow before Rameses laid hands on him, Machiavelli was off pursuing essential diplomatic contacts in the Victorian Quarter, and in the luck that attended such moments in Hell, a returning Roman convoy had stalled on Park Avenue, blocking both lanes as a half-track howitzer decided to die in a narrow thoroughfare just outside the villa. The street department wanted to route the convoy *and* city traffic off over the curb, through the villa's rose garden and back around through the villa's parking lot and the driveway. The Helltours bus line was complaining about schedules.

It was *his* rose garden, *pro di,* which had survived Cong bombardments and Assyrian attacks. It was the indignity of the thing. Roman dignity. Which counted for more than a rose garden. Give up a point in Hell, hint at culpability—that was to invite more such challenges on the diplomatic front, the legal front—gods *knew* how many lawsuits it might encourage from the recent skirmishes.

Meanwhile a city water main, broken under the convoy, was inundating the end of Decentral Park, which was Cong territory, and Uncle Julius had the whole motorpool tied up on a mysterious no-budge order because Uncle Julius was doing some very secret and very dangerous things involving Assyrian serial numbers and Pentagram registrations on captured vehicles being cycled through the East Armory garage, and it was not that mechanics were scarce at the moment, it was the fact that Julius was so tight-fisted with parts and so scarce himself that a quartermaster at the New Hell East Armory had to scrounge for a vehicle adequate to handle the damn thing, while the park flooded and the Cong rethought the recent truce.

Perfectly wonderful day.

Lunch, in the garden room, glass table, yellow wire chairs, potted palms on yellow and white tile: petite blond woman in an elegant crepe de chine blouse and black pleated skirt—Kleopatra of Egypt.

It was French today. It was an absolute fury. Klea

pushed the bits of quiche about her plate and tried to disguise the fact she was not eating—which fact her fellow Pharaoh observed—dark-haired, athletic woman in a 2480's mauve jumpsuit, with the most amazing bracelet, or ring, or both, that flexed with her hand and glittered with lights—Hatshepsut took no chances lately, and (Scaevola had sworn, privately, to his intimates) lately *slept* with enough weaponry to take out a legion, not mentioning what she wore at her hip.

"He won't *do* anything," Klea said, and her chin trembled. "Julius won't. Augustus certainly won't."

Which meant that Klea had made another assault on the powers of the Caesars—the *do anything* meaning *with Tiberius about Caesarion*.

Hatshepsut rested her own chin on her hand, avoiding a lethal contact, and shook her head.

Hell had bounced them out of Augustus' domain, all of them who had no birthright in Roman territories— had sent Machiavelli and Dante to the Italian quarter and dispatched them in an eyeblink to Egyptian domains: but it had not sent Caesarion, not Klea's son with Roman Julius.

Caesarion it had sent to Tiberius' palace.

"That damned lecher," Klea mourned; meaning Tiberius; and Hatshepsut, whose own proclivities were legend in the household, patted Klea's hand.

"We are no strangers to politics," Pharaoh said to her latter-day sister. "Julius will help. Julius *will* help."

"Julius blew up the damned statue!" The little Pharaoh glared, her eyes aglisten. "We should just march over there—"

"T-t-tt-tt. Against some things we have no power. The natural forces of this place are what they are, and armies are no good against nature: if Hell *assigns* us here and there—if Hell disposes Rome in two seats and not one—*I* would not go against that force and waste my energies fighting Hell itself—as long as diplomacy serves better. That force sent Antonius there—but *this* time he applied diplomacy, and lo, he commands the Praetorians."

"Damn him! He won't even return my phone calls."

"He was your husband. He *dares* not talk to you." Hatshepsut poured more wine—herself, outmaneuvering a hovering sycophant. It chittered at her, tugging at her shoulder. "Damned things. —Dear Klea, *if* you want to stage an assault on Tiberius by force of arms—I've no doubt we could get in there. But if you want to *keep* your son—that's another consideration. How else am I here in Caesar's household—or Machiavelli—"

"Don't mention that conniver!"

"I don't doubt he is, and does, and is presently: let's leave Niccolo aside. He's a perfect example of having your way with Administration—as am I a perfect example of persistence. Hell drops me into Egyptian domains—and I persistently return. How? By taxi, my dear, just as we did, because I *want* to be here, I *enjoy* it here, I learn, and I find the company congenial. If you want your son back, you have first to gain *his* cooperation."

"He won't, he can't—Julius, damn him, prefers that Roman boy—" Klea dabbed at her eyes with a forefinger. "Not, not, understand, that I dislike Brutus. Who could?"

Hatshepsut sighed wistfully. "Indeed." Thinking of dark eyes and a young lad—forever seventeen, touchingly naive in certain things—and off-limits by Julius' specific orders. "But Caesarion's fond of Brutus. His jealousy would diminish with time. . . ."

"Not under the same roof as Julius! Not—competing for Julius' affections. Caesarion's too proud. And Julius—damn him—" Another breath. Another dab at her eyelashes.

"—is too much like Caesarion," Hatshepsut said, pursing her lips. "Yes. Both proud. And Brutus the innocent—affectionate to both of them—"

"Salt in the wound," Klea said. "I *hate* it! I hate Brutus being here—"

Not entirely, Hatshepsut thought. Somehow the Roman boy had wound himself into Klea's loneliness—become a son-surrogate, tangled himself with her as well—

—and saved her life, one memorable day.

Hatshepsut looked up then. Looked at the door and saw a teenager in faded jeans, a tee-shirt that said *Dodgers*. A teenager whose handsome face was for a moment just frozen in pain—

But he was looking at her looking at him, the eyes met, and Marcus Brutus tore away from that glance and plunged away down the hall.

"Oh, my gods," Klea whispered, from across the table.

Hatshepsut got up. For once the Pharaoh of the Two Lands, armed with the might of the star-traveling future, stood powerless.

It was certainly a sight out front. Sargon of Akkad stood by the window at the landing, hands on hips, watching while a swarm of legionaries attempted to get a piece of broken tread free from the half-track, while cars wended their way past the entire convoy, some pieces of which had been too wide to pass the half-track without taking out the curb on the far side, the resultant train of which went halfway down to the corner—so cars from either direction passed the obstruction by turns, rolling waves of water up and over the curbs, while the New Hell police stood shin-deep in the flood trying to direct traffic.

The worst was, the broken main was starting to undermine the street. Supposedly they had sent for a construction crane to move the half-track. Motorpool had a crew out there. They had sent for equipment. They had put a call in to Julius and Mouse, and no one had been able to reach him by radio or phone—itself a cause of anxiety.

Footsteps sounded on the steps, rubber soles of ten-

nis shoes ascending in haste. Sargon turned about with
a cheerful face for the boy, who with a boy's enthusiasm
for commotions, had doubtless come to see—

Bang! right into Sargon's shoulder, a shove, a blur of
tee-shirt and blue jeans and a youthful figure hurrying
up the stairs with a vengeance.

Sargon stared in amazement. Brutus? Indubitably.
And *not* like him to bash the king of Akkad on the stairs
and rush past like that.

Temper or pain, one or the other. Teenage years
were full of it, and a man remembered well enough to
know the fragility of a young boy. But such behavior
was not like this boy, and Sargon hitched up his kilt and
went downstairs to deal sternly with whatever had per-
turbed the lad.

In the next instant, around the corner at the bottom
of the stairs, Sargon came to an abrupt halt, staring, as
a gray-haired old woman with a basket came wandering
down the lower hall, in spite of security, in spite of
guards, in spite of every precaution against invasion.

A man felt the fool reaching for a sword against an old
lady—even one who advanced, tapping her stick, as if
she were both blind and slightly daft.

"Who are you?" Sargon demanded. The hair stood up
on his nape. Not a reaction to the rasp of a drawn
sword. Deaf, daft, and blind, then—or one of Hell's
more sinister entities, which feared no bronze blade
and no iron either. The soft scuff of the granny's sandals, the tap of the stick in the terrazzo hall, maintained
a sinister rhythm as if she meant to walk right through
him—indeed, as if she might *do* that; and while the
Lion of Akkad had no wish to run, he had no wish to be
touched by some Power, either, so he flinched aside
and pressed his shoulders against the marble of the
corner. She had the smell of mildew and dry rot.

"Stop there!" he yelled, and finding the anomaly of
the basket the out-of-place thing, the perhaps signifi-

cant thing in this apparition—"What do you have in that basket?"

The granny turned, slowly—she was veiled in cloth that might have begun as gray; or maybe it was black. The movements of her head were slow and deliberate as a snake's; and the small, jerky movements of her yellow-nailed hand as it peeled back gray gauze or cobweb, unveiling the contents of the basket, sent a chill down Sargon's back that very little in Hell had ever put there.

Scrolls. Scrolls new and bright, tied in red leather. "Bookssss," she hissed. Maybe it was the lack of teeth.

It was a riddle-game, then. Akkad and Sumer understood the like. Sargon stood with his sword between himself and this—thing—and asked the next evident question, because to stop—to break the spell—seemed more dangerous than to go on.

"Why do you bring them here?" Two questions in one. Was it allowed?

"To sssssssell them. Nine sssssssscrollssssss . . ."

Magical numbers. A transaction by exchange, a magical act in which some onus might pass from one to the other, a clearing of debt . . . for the former possessor.

"What is your price?" Sargon asked—always the thing to ask—when contemplating Hell's bargains.

"Sssssssix thoussssssssand talentssssss."

Six thousand talents. His stomach heaved. "Not quite the sum of money a man has on him, grandmother." *Be polite to the old witch, it always does to be polite. Where in* hell's *Niccolo?* —Because Niccolo, among other things, saw things more pragmatically, was half a modern, was a walking encyclopaedic reference on the odder residents of Hell. "All or each?"

"All or nothing. That'sssssssss alwaysssss the bargain."

"Always?"

"Alwayssssss. Will you pay?"

"Not myself, woman. I'm a guest here. I'll trust it's Augustus you've come to see. . . ."

"Pay now."

It was the sad fact that the King of Akkad, exile from the Eastern quarter, had not two coppers on his person, that he had whatever the sycophants might bring instantly, such was Augustus' hospitality—but he did not think that Augustus' hospitality of the sycophants' abilities extended to sixty millions of dollars destined to be handed out to a lunatic old woman.

"Wait," he said. "Just wait right here." And: "*Guard!*" hoping someone would hear, that a sycophant might prove brave enough to dare this hallway and get word to Augustus.

A legionary came running, spatter of sandals and a rattle of a rifle from up the further stairs.

But the old woman was just—not there, leaving a very shamefaced, a very foolish-looking king of Akkad standing there with a sword in his hand and not a thing in hell to show for cause.

So he said, frowning, on the edge of his dignity: "I thought I might have seen something. A shadow. Check it out. There might be an intruder. Reassignments dumped one on us, Inanna knows what *might* be."

The legionary saluted. And called for help.

The Lion of Akkad still felt the fool, after a quarter hour and nothing.

"Exactly what are we looking for?" the centurion asked, finally, as meticulously respectful as a Republican Roman could be to a king he surely suspected had imbibed a bit much at lunch.

And Sargon might have passed the encounter off, or lied and magnified it, for his honor's sake; but he was too old in Hell and too experienced to deceive his own side, so he folded his arms, looked the sane, plain-as-dirt centurion in the eye and said: "An old grandmother with a basket full of scrolls. Appeared out of nowhere and went out the same route."

Whereupon a stalwart centurion frowned, started to

write a note, and frowned again from under a black brow. "Old lady with a basket of scrolls. How many?"

"Nine."

The brow arched and descended. The Roman mouth made harder lines at the corners.

The stylus stayed absolutely still.

"What did she do, exactly?"

"Offered to sell them."

The tablets snapped shut. Whack. The Roman stared at him in dismay, as if now both of them were crazy. And said: "I think this is a problem."

Brutus slipped into the upstairs salon, very quietly, moving quite determinedly, because otherwise he was shaking and the lump in his throat swelled up so large he felt the tears coming, if he let them.

And if one kept moving, and set one's mind on what one had to do, then one could act like a man instead of a boy, and perhaps one could think, here, in the quiet and the privacy.

They would look for him in his room. Hatshepsut and Klea. They had never meant for him to hear, they had never meant for anyone to hear, and now he knew how Klea felt, and imagined how they must feel—

Imagining how they felt was easy for Brutus the bastard, for Marcus Junius Brutus who carried one father's name and knew that the whispers the relatives made, and the looks his father and his mother gave him, were all wishes he had never been born, some thoughts angry, some guilty, some simply hurting through the years.

People said that this place was Hell. They said it was a place to be punished for all the wrongs one had done. He had never understood this. He had thought it a wonderful place, having arrived seventeen, forever seventeen, to find his true father wanted him—Julius Caesar wanted him, and acknowledged him, and treated him with the love he always dreamed of having—

He had found a brother, Caesarion—

Then he had learned the truth, that he was Julius' assassin—that he had, after a much longer life than he remembered, killed Julius. . . .

That Augustus had killed him—*and* Caesarion—

And his father forgave Augustus; but Caesarion could not forgive either of them.

Now he learned something else—that he had been deaf to whispers, blind to pain.

Now he knew that people were not mistaken. This *was* a place for punishment. And he was seventeen, robbed of everything he had learned in his life, but everyone else remembered their lives, *they* remembered, they had all their griefs and all their loyalties, and he was there in the middle of things, that was all, not understanding, not knowing anything the way a grown man might know,—like why he had killed someone he loved, or what had changed him, or whether he was going to change again, in the centuries and the ages people lived in this place, and become their enemy —when he loved them more than he had ever loved anyone, even his mother, even his father, especially his relatives or the boyhood friends who whispered about him, he's a bastard, you know, he's really Caesar's . . .

Klea was in pain. And because she was Klea, and good, she tried to love him anyway, no matter how he fouled up Caesarion, who was his brother, whom he loved so much, whom he wanted most of all to rescue from where Hell's computers kept putting him—

That turned out to be his fault too. He was not sure how much else was.

He *was* growing. A while ago, before he had learned about Julius, about himself growing up to be a murderer —he could not have understood anything that was going on. Now he did know, and the fact that he *could* change—

I'm supposed to do it again, he thought, knotting his hands together until the knuckles popped. *It was Julius'*

*enemy that sent me here, to him. And every time he
holds me and calls me son—he knows that. Caesarion
knows it. Klea does. All these people. Augustus was
always afraid of me. And Augustus is very smart about
people. Smarter than most anyone. Didn't he—the first
time he saw me—know I was an enemy?*

*O gods, could I kill myself and would the computer
send me anywhere but here? The dead come back. You
die and you come back to the place you're Assigned.
The way Niccolo has. And Marcus Antonius.*

*Antonius helped kill me too. He was Caesarion's foster-
father. They say I was a suicide. But Augustus and
Antonius gave me no choice.*

*Would they give me good advice now? Or would my
father?*

Would even Klea, if I went to her?

*Is it me they see, the way I am? Or somebody I might
become?*

Footsteps came and went in the halls, some distant
and some that passed the door. Sometimes they came
quietly as far as the door and stopped—at such times
Caesarion listened for the rattle of the lock. He was a
little crazy, perhaps, sometimes he thought that. Sometimes they brought him food and water, and sometimes
they forgot. Sometimes they beat him. Sometimes they
only said they would.

Thank gods Tiberius never came. The old man forgot
a lot of things, like where he had put his prisoners, or
what they were in for, or what they were guilty of.
Sometimes he just forgot them altogether, until he
expected them to be back on duty, and then the guards
began to figure out that they had better let whoever-it-
was go before the old man got pissed.

So he was not particularly surprised when the door
opened and a Praetorian came in, and he was not
particularly surprised when it turned out to be Antonius who, the last he knew, had been down here with

Tiberius' guards walking all over him. He only let go a little breath and figured it was still trouble, it was just a different kind shaping up, and he mouthed, lip-synching with Antonius: "The emperor wants you upstairs—"

Which pissed his foster-father and stopped him in mid-sentence, right at the part he wanted to hear—

Like: *The old man's crazy today and he's forgotten and you're free.*

Or: *The old man's remembered your case. I'm sorry.*

Antonius was his foster-father. When he was sober he was all right. Antonius would not beat on him.

There was nothing else Antonius would do, either. Which was no damn help at all.

"Well, which is it?" Caesarion asked, sitting easier against the wall—no pretty sight, he could figure that, chains and bruises and all. And the stink.

"I've got you out," Antonius said. "For gods' sake, don't—"

"—foul it up," Caesarion lip-synched that too, impatient, with aches in his bones and a sudden case of the shivers threatening; so the way to go was to clench the jaw, fix mama's number-two bedmate with a cold eye, and plunk a chained wrist down on his knee with the solidity of an ultimatum. "Just get a key, will you, pop, and skip the lectures, I'm as old in this place as you are. You got a cigarette?"

"No," Antonius said shortly, and squatted there all clean and tidy and sober, just the usual little wine-smell about him. "I can leave you here, son."

"How'd you get back? Kiss ass?"

Antonius was focussed today. Antonius was getting further pissed and it was time to shut up, so Caesarion did, just looked elsewhere while Antonius got the chains unlocked.

Getting up was a problem. Antonius had to help him with that. Antonius had to help him upstairs, to Tiberius's elaborate, bordello-style baths, where he sat chest-deep in warm water, with a plate of cheese and a pitcher of wine by him.

"You listen to me," Antonius had said, then spilled it to him in brief, exactly what he had expected: Tiberius had gotten confused and recalled that Antonius was commander of the Praetorians, forgetting that Antonius had been deposed in favor of Harmodias. Which situation the Praetorians had remedied with bloody efficiency, since Tiberius had promised them a bonus, diced Harmodias up for dogmeat and re-installed Antonius with cheers and the absolute fervor of the thoroughly buyable.

It could go the other way at any given hour. In this place anything could happen at any given hour. Tiberius thought some damn baboon was his heir Caligula, and kept getting his advice from him.

Which might give the old goat some stability in crisis, who knew?

Getting caught with his half-brother Brutus inside the statue of Tiberius' dead brother—that mechanical travesty that decorated the atrium of this house of horrors; worse—having Tiberius tumble to the fact that someone *knew* the mechanical secrets of his favorite oracle—could be fatal.

Caesarion attempted to shave—at least the little beard that he ever raised, or *would* raise, since Augustus had murdered him some thousands of years ago—dear *pious*, god-loving Augustus; murdered him and pushed Antonius and Kleopatra to suicide— Not a sycophant in sight—but there never were for him. Not when he wanted them. He scraped his chin with hands that trembled and finally gave it up as good enough, because he was sick and exhausted, and he had cut himself twice.

Did Brutus get home? he had asked Antonius; strange that he should ask. He owed Brutus nothing—owed him damned well nothing, considering who they both were and what trouble Brutus had gotten him into.

Evidently Julius owed him nothing, either, since Julius had nothing to do with getting him out of that hellhole downstairs; and Antonius said Brutus had gotten home—that there were *diplomatic contacts* underway. . .

Big deal, he had said to Antonius then. *Big deal. I don't know why you put up with him.* . . . He had said worse things to his foster-father on occasion. It hurt, watching Antonius ruin himself. It had hurt in life. But Antonius was Antonius.

Julius screwed him over the same as he did everyone and Antonius came whimpering back for more. *He* did not. He was not so taken in.

Only now, he wished, he wished—sick and exhausted, while the blood made little clouds in the water from a razor nick—that some miracle could come for him, Julius with a dozen legions come to burn the palace down and get him out.

Only trouble was, he had no use to Julius. So screw that.

Screw all of it. He was going downtown, he was getting out of here—live on the streets. He had done it before. He could take care of himself.

His head nodded forward. He made a grab after the rim and dropped the razor, that made a dangerous companion in the bath. He felt after it gingerly, and damned the sycophants that refused his small calamity. *Brutus* had one, dammit, small though it was, *Brutus* merited one—

He heard steps and a tapping on the marble, a sinister, slow tapping, that in *this* place could mean almost anything. He twisted his head around, not risking other portions of his anatomy, and seeing the gray, shrouded figure in the dim baths—searched the bottom more desperately.

Closer, closer—it looked like an old woman, some grandame with a basket on her arm, wrapped in cerements, grim, gray and totally out of place in this place of priapic statuary and erotic red-toned frescoes. It was

Tiberius' kind of joke. It might *be* Tiberius, except for its gauntness.

It came to the edge of the bath, moving as if it was blind. Caesarion felt the razor under his hand and carefully gathered it up as he stared up at the old woman.

"Who are you?"

A thin, gray hand like a mummy's moved to uncover the contents of the basket and Caesarion, fearing snakes, scrambled up the marble steps, splashing water as he slipped and landed on his rump, brandishing the razor.

"I have booksssss," the old woman said, a voice like the wind in leaves. "Sssssix booksssss."

"So? So what am I supposed to do? I don't run this place."

"Sssssix thoussssssand talentsssssss."

"Six thousand—? What do you think I *am?* Get out of here!"

As sycophants sputtered into existence and out again, as one shrieked: "*No*, no, no no! Treason! Treason!"

Not a sign of the old woman, with soldiers and security searching the villa top to bottom. "Not on the grounds," Horatius Cocles reported, "as far as anything we've got can pick up,"—and Augustus, with the phone ringing, looked despairingly in Sargon's direction.

"I had no idea," Sargon said, looking truly chagrined.

Augustus snatched up the phone, expecting more complaints from the street department—there was a construction crane moving up on the obstacle outside, the East Armory crew was demanding it move off—

Julius had called to say, *don't let city equipment touch that piece!*

That was not exactly the way Julius had put it, but Augustus got the gist of it in no uncertain terms—that was *not* one of the pieces Julius wanted any official scrutiny on, if he had been there at the outset he *would* have ordered the armory to move on the emergency a damn sight faster, and it was highly important that the Armory solve its own problem before someone created a record of the serial number.

Right.

Of course.

Get over here! Augustus had said, unwilling to give Julius the full details, and when Julius gave him the coded query Is this really necessary?—Absolutely, Augustus had said, just that, which was the Situation Critical code.

Which meant that Julius was on his way as fast as he could, *not* because of the half-track and the convoy which *had* to be moved before the flooding totally undermined the street and found them a new route to the nether hells—*not* an impossibility in the odd tricks of hellish geology—but because an old woman was wandering around with a basketful of books for which sixty million dollars was a pittance—

"Hello, hello!" Augustus said, hoping for Julius, hoping for divine interventions and a celestial rescue with Jupiter and all while he was at it.

"*Tu quoque sicarius!*" the voice on the other end spat.

"*Salve tu honestissime Tiberi,*" he said, and winced at the shrieking and sputtering which proved he was right and Julius was wrong, it *was* a good idea to hold a phone receiver well away from one's ear. "*Audi mi, Tiberi, non! Non illas habe— Audi! Non habemus, per divos ipsos iuro!*"

More shrieking, the gist of which was Julian plots.

And downstairs a jeep, the brakes of which had a familiar—thank gods!—squeal. Augustus held the phone, signaled to Sargon, who went to the study window and looked out, confirming the arrival.

Thank gods, thank gods.

"Listen, Tiberius, —listen, dammit! Julius is in. Jul— Caius Julius, dammit! We haven't *got* them, we didn't send her, we don't know where she is—"

Just appeared there, was the gist of what came back.

"Well, she appeared here," Augustus said, "with—
Appeared here, yes! With nine! We weren't buying!"

Six, came back from the other side.

"Listen." Augustus was sweating. He mopped at his face with the sleeve of his toga, while the other buttons of his phone lit alarmingly. "Listen, dammit, I've got a half-track stuck in a street over here—"

Gibbering from the other end.

"I know you don't care, divine son, but we're down to six, we've got an incident out front that can fry our asses with Administration, and we *daren't* lose those scrolls! She's popping back and forth, that's what she seems to be doing, and she's not damn careful who she targets—for the gods' sake, get the word out—*buy!*"

More gibbering. Possibly it was the baboon. It was hard to tell.

"*Tiberi*, doesn't it occur to you that this visitation is ominous for all of us, in the present emergency? Which is of *your* making, dammit-to-Dis!" Augustus sucked air. No, no, not wise. "Listen, we'll be on the lookout."

Click.

As a racket sounded on the stairs, heavy boots, coming up from the front entry.

Julius.

"Look," Antonius said, "I'm sorry, son, I'm really sorry."

"Sure," Caesarion said, cradling sore ribs, as his foster-father let him down to sit on a bench—in the dank basement of Tiberius' palace, short of the cell where he was sure he was bound a second time—if he was going to be that lucky. He looked at Antonius with the eye that was not swollen. "What do I get this time, —papa?"

"Locked up. I'm *trying*, boy."

"You're damn trying." Old joke, thin the first time. Caesarion held onto his ribs and wished they could get where they were headed, if it was only there. Where his foster-father, being guard commander, had to lock him up and gods knew what else, if the old goat took it into his head. Antonius would, too. Antonius would save his own skin. He always had. But he was dead sober at the moment, a point on his side, and trying to be decent, as far as gestures went in this place. Lately Caesarion had figured that out, the way he had figured out a lot of things that had confused him all his life and all his much longer death—some folk *tried* to be decent, even if they screwed up everything they did.

Even if right now Antonius was risking landing both of them in the same cell, and even if Antonius would do about anything Tiberius told him to, so long as papa Julius was not at hand to give Antonius the backbone that made him, sometimes, more man than anyone expected.

For Julius. For Julius, over and over, like Julius was a drug he wanted more than booze—like Julius took parts of people and kept them and only lent them back when he needed something out of you—

Like Julius tried to get his hands on him, tried to drag him under the same roof with Augustus, never mind Augustus had murdered him and the kindest man he ever knew, never mind Augustus had murdered Antonius—Antonius came back.

Gods, at the moment he thought about the villa over the hill and thought about a clean room and a clean bed and a brother so naive he made his gut hurt—but a brother who wanted to share with him everything his feckless innocence got from Julius—

And get him out of this hellhole, away from madmen and baboon oracles and Guards who kicked hell out of you for no reason at all.

"What'd I do?" he had asked them. And they had asked him where the books were and where the old woman was and asked him if he had planned it all, or took his orders from Julius.

"What'd I do?" he asked Antonius now, sitting there,

leaning on one hand because changing position hurt. "What books?"

"The Sibylline books," Antonius said. "They're missing from the library. Three of them."

Caesarion shook his head, unenlightened.

"Any Roman schoolboy—" Antonius said.

"I'm not a _Roman_ schoolboy," Caesarion said between his teeth. "I'm Pharaoh. What about these books?"

"The books of prophecy. There were nine. The Sibyl brought them to the king of Rome—asked an enormous price—"

"Sixty million bucks."

"Is that what she asked you?"

"Say it was. What books are worth that?"

"If you had the nine, you'd know the whole future. The three have rested in the library, in that sealed case— They're gone now. The Sibyl took them. She offered the full nine to Augustus. Then the six to you. Next time—if we don't stop her—"

"Zip."

"You've got it. We'll lose the only edge we have in Hell. She burns three after every turn-down. _That's_ why the emperor called me back to duty—and you—"

"I was minding my own business!"

"She picked you. For some reason she picked you. If—"

A sycophant popped into being right between their faces.

"_The divine Tiberiussss_—" it said, exuding an oily smell, "_wantsssssss_—"

The Sibyl, they said. That was the word Brutus' sycophant had brought back to him, small, shivering light almost too faint today to hear—but it had come when he called it, it had found out the things he wanted to know, things that raised the hair on Brutus' nape; and he had not forgotten, because it had been, for a sycophant, uncommony zealous, to thank it—

It had brightened, then, bobbed in the air and embellished its story with Sargon coming up to Augustus' office and Augustus going berserk, between the mess in the street and the terrible thing that stalked the halls.

"Is she still here?" Brutus had asked, with a little shiver despite his private troubles.

"Don't know," it had confessed, dimming slightly. *"That'sssss a Power—sssscarey . . . Dangerousssss . . ."*

Brutus was not sure that the Sibyl would attack anyone. But to think that the agent of the Fates was prowling the halls—

That it might at any moment pop into his room or anywhere it liked—

He had more reason than most to fear it, he thought, he, who did not want to be what he would become. The Sibyl of the Books—

With all the terrible things that had happened, already his doing—he knew that they were his doing. None of it would have happened, except for him, except that Mithridates had planned harm to Julius—

The old woman knew, that was her terrible power. She was the one entity that might tell him the things he was afraid to know—

So he had put on a clean shirt and a clean pair of decent slacks and washed his face and combed his hair and gone out hunting what everyone else was hunting—with different purposes.

He watched Julius come in—he watched Mouse as he talked with the duty officer down in the lower hall, and he slipped around the other way, because, he thought with what religious faith he still cherished, if the Fates were going to set him to do harm they would give him a chance to turn away, and if the harm he was supposed to do was to Julius—that was no little thing: it was not an inconsequential thing; it was not a question the Sibyl would turn away, if she was disposed to help Rome and not to hurt them—

It was possible, he thought, that the answer was in the books—if they did not lose the chance.

That was what he was looking for, when, at the far end of the salon hallway, he ran into Klea and Hatshepsut, also looking—

—and froze.

"Boy," Klea said in English, ever so gently—as if he was a rabbit that would start and run. He wished he could. But he was Julius' son, so he straightened his shoulders and stood there. "Boy, how much did you hear?"

"It's all right," he said, gently himself, because there was a lump in his throat and he had no wish to carry on a war with Klea. "It's all right. I understand what you mean. I don't blame you at all."

"I don't hate you!"

"Of course not," he agreed, agreeing to anything, everything, because discussing it was no use, nothing was any use, because he could not say himself what he might be, or do, or who he might hurt. "Of course not, majesty. I know that."

"I want to talk to you," Klea said.

"I don't think there's time," he said, temporizing. Close in with Klea was the last place he wanted to be today, now, with so much at risk. "I'm looking for the Sibyl. I thought—" He wanted to reassure Klea, he wanted to take that pain from her face. "I thought if there *was* anything wrong with me, she might warn me. Maybe—if we found her—she could tell us . . . what I am."

Klea looked terribly upset. Hatshepsut frowned, and said: "*I* can tell you that, boy. —Come here."

"I haven't time. I—"

Hatshepsut reached out, grabbed him by the wrist, and jerked him a little down the hall and around a corner, to tell him something, he was sure—and to rescue him, somehow, he was sure of that, because Hatshepsut had always been kind to him, Hatshepsut had always—confused him in certain ways, and he did not know how to say no to a woman of her disposition.

"You heard the whole thing, didn't you?" Hatshepsut asked him. "The sycophants tried to warn me. I know from when."

He nodded, with that lump back in his throat, that started out with one reason and quickly developed another reason for being, because Pharoah reached up and touched his cheek in a way that might be motherly, except she did not smell like his mother, the feelings she roused in him were altogether something else.

"You're looking for an oracle," she said. "*I'm* one, do you want a prophecy?"

"I—" He was not thinking very well. He was not thinking at all well when Pharoah bent her head—she was quite tall—and kissed him in a way not at all like his mother. He knew Pharoah's reputation. He had heard the men talking—he thought with a flash of panic that his father would find out—he thought ten thousand things all in two seconds, before Pharoah clenched her arms around him and hissed:

"This is my prophecy:

A prophetess whelped twins,
The wolf's children,
Two thrones in foursquare Rome.
Two powers in Hell."

He was smothered. He had his eyes shut. He felt her holding him, felt her give a heavy breath and touch his face again and then he could look at her, shaken the way the earth could shake with the god's presence—

"There," she said, patting his cheek again, as if he was a child; and *she* was breathing hard, her eyes very dark and very large. "You have your oracle."

He drew a breath and moved away, and got to the corner before he looked back.

She *was* oracular—he had heard that too—

She was also Klea's best friend.

And she wanted him. He figured that out without any trouble.

Klea was waiting in the hall. Hatshepsut walked out behind him. He looked at Klea, shaking all over, and Hatshepsut said:

"Klea, you can trust him. He won't hurt Caesarion. He'd never do that. —Would you, boy?"

"No," he said, finding breath enough. He thought that his face was red. He was sure it was. He was not ready to deal with grown women, especially two of them, *especially* Hatshepsut, and especially his father's wife and his brother's mother, whose look in his direction *was* motherly, and whose hand as she straightened his hair and patted his cheek *was* exactly like his mother's, and made him realize all over again that home was a long time ago and he would never see it again.

Just these people. For all time to come. These people who—in Hell's years—he would have to deal with somehow, the way his brother did, who had lived thousands of years—when he had arrived, Hell's own joke, virtually yesterday—

A boy had to become a man—in some sense or another. He had to find his way. And the part about the twin sons of the wolf—

Romulus and Remus—

Foursquare Rome—That was Romulus' line, the *pomoerium*, the sacred bounds across which no weapon could come—

The two thrones—

Romulus had kept an empty throne beside him—for the brother he had killed. . . .

"Get that fucking crane out of here!" Julius yelled, waving an arm at the advancing monster that made miniature waves as it came. "You trying to break the rest of the street?" He waded out into the small sea and shouted in the ear of one of Hell's finest. "Block that thing off! It's going to collapse the whole damn main!"

The cop shouted back: "Move your damn gun!" Or something like, in broken English.

As something came screaming out of the Park and exploded, throwing water everywhere.

"It's the Cong!" the cop yelled, and: "Return fire!" Julius yelled at Mouse, who had the jeep parked on the inundated edge of the lawn.

Guns swiveled. Fire hammered out, and fire came back, sparse as it was.

There was one benefit. A shell got the crane. It ground to a ponderous halt, frozen dead, with a broken tread.

Civilian traffic was suddenly making U-turns in either direction, sending up waves that splashed over the edge of the curb.

Julius ran for the jeep, while the batteries on the roof of the villa cut loose.

But Mouse, at the wheel, in charge of the field phone and their communications with the convoy, the Armory, and the villa itself, met him with: "It's Augustus. *Tiberius* is coming."

The ceiling shook, the windows vibrated with every round that went off from the roof. Pizza crumbs did a dance among Augustus' papers and he grabbed in vain as a sliding stack left the desk and spread across the floor.

A last paper landed at sandaled, dusty feet, a frayed, cobwebby hem.

Augustus looked up from his snatch after the papers, hauled himself upright by the corner of his desk and stared into the eyes of a Power of Hell.

"I have bookssss," she said, uncovering the basket.

"Will you take a check?" Augustus gulped, and heard, amid the sounds of artillery and the thump of shells in his rose garden—the hammering of fire from a new direction—over the back lawn.

*　　*　　*

"*Dear* neighbor," Tiberius said, advancing—a remarkable sight, Brutus thought as he stood by his father and the First Citizen on the back steps of the villa—the old man in his armor, the straps of which had to be let out considerably. Tiberius walked with out-held hand, from the jeep to the steps, smiling—in itself an appalling and terrible sight.

But Brutus was more taken with the ones following—with Antonius, resplendent in the armor of Tiberius' guard; and most of all with the boy in jeans and the torn black tee-shirt . . . whose right eye was black and mostly swollen shut, who walked by Antonius' side as if he were in pain—

Brutus wanted to run down the steps and haul his brother up to safety, up the steps where Julius and the rest could protect him—

But he had learned enough of the ways of First Citizens and generals and people who called themselves gods—to know that Tiberius was crazy and dangerous, even if Tiberius had just helped them beat the Cong; and that an irresponsible boy might dash down the steps, but Julius' sons had to be men and do no more than stare at each other, one from the top of the steps, one from the foot, while the powers of Rome shook hands and congratulated each other on a victory.

Brother, Brutus framed with his lips, looking over the heads of his elders—in English, which Caesarion preferred to Latin. Caesarion said nothing, but he might have understood: there was a flicker in the good eye, a visible intake of breath.

"Son," Augustus was saying, embracing that terrible old man in the too-small armor, while Julius stood there, arms folded, frowning and watching them, and Mouse, rifle in hand, watched everyone in sight.

"You've got them," Tiberius said, his jaws clamping down on the words as if they were painful. "You've got them, haven't you?"

"I don't say whether we have or we haven't—" Augustus said.

"You have them, you have them, you have them! Thief!"

"Ours by purchase," Augustus said. "Residing safely in the house—*deep* within the house. Theft can't be in question. They were sold by their owner."

Tiberius frowned thunderously, then took on a sly, crafty look. "Oh, I thought," he said. "I did think—first she came to you, then to us, then to you again—and of course you'd buy. You wouldn't let them be destroyed . . ."

"I certainly wouldn't," Augustus said.

"But you could sell them!"

"Not for love nor money."

"Not for money—" Tiberius made a small, throaty laugh, and reeled back and flung Caesarion forward a step. "But for a son of great Julius? I'll release him to Egypt, I won't even mention my Germans—or my statue! A god releases the son of a god—all for a few scrolls— scrolls I've *guarded*—"

"Hoarded," Julius muttered.

"—*guarded* for thousands of years—" Spittle flew. Caesarion stood still while the old man came and held him by the shoulder. Brutus' heart was in his throat. And Caesarion looked just at him, just at him, as if there was no one else involved.

"Give them to me," Tiberius was saying. "And I'll release this boy from my guardianship, my *legal* guardianship— I'll even throw in Antonius. For free. —Isn't that generous?"

"No," Julius said, short and hard.

Caesarion's expression hardly changed. Brutus was not sure his own did: he stood there looking down at Caesarion, knowing that there was too much at stake, that the deal was not the winning throw Tiberius thought it was that—a fact which a thing like Tiberius surely could not even remember,—Roman honor would not let Julius ransom a son at such a cost.

"You'll be sorry!" Tiberius howled. "*He'll* be sorry! You'll see."

"Don't—" Julius said between his teeth, "don't lay a hand on him."

And Julius turned and came up the steps, walked past with an expression killing-cold.

Brutus knew he ought to follow. He ought to observe his father's dignity and turn and leave—but he hesitated for a look at his brother, who, Egyptian as Klea, just looked hard and lost, and averted his eyes with a shake of his head and went away with Tiberius.

"We'll just tell Administration we had advance word of a Cong attack and set the whole thing up to get artillery into position," Julius was saying matter-of-factly, to Mouse as he walked inside. "Find out who ordered that crane—find out his record; we'll have his hide if we can, watch him if we can't." Julius was old in Hell. Julius was thinking clearly and taking care of his own.

Klea was not going to understand—when some sycophant got the word to her. Brutus stopped in the hall and looked back at Augustus, who was giving rapid orders of his own.

For honor's sake. He was man enough to understand. Being Roman, he could reason that way. But it had no power at all to dispel the cold in his gut, or to make him forget Caesarion's battered, sullen face—looking up at him as if Caesarion also was storing away memories.

Without a hope in hell of Julius.

And now none, he was sure, of him.

MOVING DAY
Janet Morris

The tractor-trailer truck parked in front of Mata Hari's apartment building bore the dread red logo of a clawed hand squeezing the world and the legend GOING DOWN? DAMZIONE BROS. MOVES YOU TO HELL AND GONE!

Beneath that, in smaller letters, was stenciled: *A Division of Demonic Industries/Dial 6-666-SOUL/ We Move The Underworld*.

Mata Hari shuddered and shouldered her way by a bearded bag lady munching from a bag of kibble and between two cars crawling in creeper gear past the semi, which took up so much of the narrow tenement street that traffic was backed up around the corner and horns were beginning to blow.

On Mata Hari's doorstep were boxes and crates, trolleys and dollies, and four men in teamsters' caps with little felt horns sticking up from their crowns. They all wore t-shirts that said PACKERS DO IT TILL IT BREAKS.

She walked up to them and said, "Excuse me, I need to get by you. I live upstairs."

One of them picked up his clipboard and said, "You Gertrud Margarete Zelle?"

"Something like that," Mata Hari replied, suspicion rustling uncomfortably at the base of her spine. "Why?"

The mover who'd spoken tipped up the bill of his cap and squinted at her. His face was grimy and unshaven and, beneath the white dirt and the pimply stubble, so black that it seemed nearly purple. The whites of his eyes were red and yellow and his teeth were the color of aged ivory.

"What you mean, 'why'? You the shipper, ain'cha?"

"Shipper? I certainly am not. What do *you* mean, shipper?" Her composure, she knew, was beginning to slip.

The black muttered a curse and turned to the three other packers sitting on the steps. "Schliemann, go upstairs and get Carnarvon, wouldya? Shipper's gonna give us some trouble otherwise."

Before Mata Hari could again protest that she wasn't anybody's "shipper," the German whom the black had called Schliemann rose to his feet. Manic eyes bored into hers from under weary brows as he said, "Madam Zelle, if you will only take me with you, I will be your slave for—"

"Shaddup, Heinrich," growled the black team boss. "Get your kraut butt in gear."

Schliemann bowed his capped head and disappeared into the tenement.

Mata Hari stepped back to crane her neck. She could just see the front window of her second floor apartment. There were men moving around inside. She hugged herself. What trick of Authority was this? What punishment from Admin? Or was it nothing but another of the bureaucratic foul-ups for which New Hell was justly infamous? She mustn't panic. Having shifted her loyalties from Authority, from the Pentagram, from His Infernal Majesty's Secret Service, to the Roman West and its Julian power base, she was vulnerable as never before. But that didn't mean that this move was a sign

she'd been found out. It meant only that there were
men here packing her belongings.

She shivered and let her gaze roam to the ruddy,
scuddy sky full of hellfire and threatening storm.
Asmodeus, king of the demons, had been returned to
her. Her lover was again among the denizens of New
Hell, and with him came such power as no other mortal
here enjoyed. And such danger as none of these putrified
souls could even imagine. For all she knew, this sudden
appearance of moving men could be Asmodeus's doing:
the Order in new Nell was coming apart at the seams;
souls were at risk as never before in eternity. Perhaps
Asmodeus was trying to protect her from something
. . . or from someone.

There were rumors of Judgment. There were whispers of the approach of the Last Trump. There were
prophets and doom-criers in the streets in unprece-
dented numbers. Those who credited the prophets maintained that this was a time to gird oneself for the final
battle—to look eternity in the face and hope that Hell
was the holding facility some thought it to be. On the
other side of Judgment lay manumission, or oblitera-
tion, such folk believed.

But then, folk will believe anything that comforts
them, if they're uncomfortable enough. For every Heaven
of every culture, there was a Hell, and all of those Hells
were here—along with every presiding Judge for every
period of humankind's trudge through darkness. At the
end of Hell, rumor had it, enlightenment might await
the faithful among those mortal sinners who'd tarried
here waiting for God's second glance.

But Gertrude Zelle was the consort of a Fallen Angel, of an immortal Presence whose very name, Asmodeus,
struck fear even into the highest towers of the Hall of
Injustice. For her, Judgment Day could hold no promise but the promise of anguish: at the end of all things
Hellish, when heaven and earth and hell became one,

Asmodeus would go where a Fallen Angel who had thrown in his lot with the Devil must go. And she?

She was but a damned mortal soul. Not even the king of the demons could make her more than that.

So perhaps this trailer truck complete with moving men was not the doing of her beloved demon, whose face was swathed in shadows and whose soul had come straight from God; whose eyes glowed red with hellfire and whose embrace offered such comfort to Mata Hari as no human arms could ever match.

To a woman who had made treachery a way of life, who had proved Machiavelli's dictum that a person's security could be assured by that person only; to history's master spy, no man could ever offer a love that could be trusted—or trusted even to be false.

Only Asmodeus—who had run the Devil's Insecurity Service, the Fallen Angels 13th Battalion, the Infernal Bureau of Investigation, and the most sensitive secret service of all, the Devil's Children—had the power and the glory, and most of all, the *permanence* that Mata Hari sought from a lover.

He was a lover she could not disappoint, because he expected nothing from a damned soul. He was a lover she could not outwit, because his wisdom was more than mortal. He was a lover she could not outflank, or betray, or outthink or overpower, because he was not . . . human.

And she had taken comfort in that, used his strength and his office as her own—until the purge that had set New Hell reeling. Until Asmodeus had crossed the very Devil himself, and been tried and convicted and sentenced and punished like a mere mortal sinner. She had contrived, with the help of one Judah Maccabee, a certain Machiavelli, an Israeli named Zaki, and a Brit called Lawrence, to bring the Angel back among the "living."

From the moment he'd come back to them, Asmodeus was changed. She could feel it. He was . . . sentimental, for a demon lover. He was . . . compassionate, for an avenging angel. He was . . . different.

And because of that change, everything in Mata Hari's life had become different. He and she had defected to the Roman West, oh so covertly. The repercussions of that treachery against Satan Himself were yet to come.

Asmodeus came and went now on secret missions. Where before he'd seemed to tell her everything she needed to know, now she knew little of what was in his heart.

And yet when he held her, it was with a new urgency that put an almost unbearably sharp edge on their lovemaking, and even on their platonic time together. The assumption she'd drawn from his behavior had been one she dared not examine too closely: Asmodeus and she had something to lose now.

They could lose everything. They could lose each other—this had been shown to them by Satan. They could lose their love, which was more to risk than just their souls.

In Hell, you could lose your way, your home, your memory, your body, your life (repeatedly), your sense of purpose and your self respect, if you were human. Thus Mata Hari never chanced a human lover. She loved the King of the Demons, who should have been eternal.

But Asmodeus, when he came to her, which was infrequently now, was full of veiled innuendo, as if the prophets crying doom in the streets were right. As if Hell itself could come to an end. As if the Host would sweep down upon the damned and mete out final dispensation and final punishment.

Someone called her name. She realized she'd been standing there with balled fists; her palms ached from the fierceness with which her nails had bitten into them. She spread her fingers and focussed her eyes on the doorstep.

Heinrich Schliemann was carrying a huge cardboard

box down the stairs. It was marked fragile. Beside him, the man who'd called her name held a riding crop with an elephant-hair fly switch on the end. He slapped his knee with it and the elephant hair tangled around Schliemann's legs. Man and box went sprawling with an awful crash.

Mata Hari winced. The sound of shattering crystal was unmistakable.

Without an apology or even a glance, down the steps toward her came the man in khaki and desert boots. "Madam Zelle, I presume. Lord Carnarvon—the fifth Earl of Carnarvon, actually . . . George Edward Stanhope Molyneux Herbert—head of this expedition."

"Expedition?" Mata Hari repeated.

From the steps where he'd fallen, Heinrich Schliemann snorted, "Let Carnarvon head this expedition, lady, and you'll end up on an express trip to the Undertaker, struck down by a curse like he was when he bashed into Tutankhamon's tomb like some bull in a china shop."

Carnarvon ignored Schliemann's comment by speaking over it as if Schliemann weren't present: "Expedition to the Valley of the Queens, yes. Of course, you'll be thinking of it as a mere move of your domicile. But for us, who are honored to be packing and moving you, the very idea of resettling you in the lost tomb of Nefertiti is . . ."

"*What?*" Mata Hari gasped. "Where did you get your orders? Your Authorization? Who sent for you? Who made the call, I say, and when? I need to see some documentation, or I'm going to sick the Children's—"

"Madam, I assure you, everything's in order," said Carnarvon, pulling on his moustaches.

Schliemann made a derisive noise, this time an impolite and consumately Teutonic expression of disbelief.

Carnarvon, for the first time, acknowledged Schliemann, saying with a flick of his fly-swatter, "A man who died of a *cold* after Troy, who had to *sell* the finest of his finds to defray expenses, who made unsubstantiable claims as to what was Helen's and what was not—such a man shouldn't even begin to critique a professional's organizational abilities."

Schliemann, still where he'd fallen on the steps, hung his head in shame.

Carnarvon turned back to Mata Hari. "All's in readiness, Madam Hari. A jolly good show of it, too. Let's see . . . I've got the packing estimate, the box estimate, the shipping estimate, the unpacking estimate, the mileage estimate . . ." As he spoke, he was pulling flimsies from his breast pocket. "Of course," he said as he handed the wad of them to her, "you'll realize that estimates are almost always fifty per cent under, but your credit's good with us." He showed broad lordly teeth. "You come, shall we say, highly recommended."

"Asmodeus," she breathed when she saw the name of the contractor on the top of the document. Relief flooded her. But then she saw that, on the bottom, Asmodeus's signature wasn't his own, but was "signed in his absence" by someone whose name she didn't recognize.

"Nefertiti's tomb?"

"That's right, Madam. It's never been opened, even in Hell. So you see, if you'll allow me, I'll personally handle this expedition . . . the native bearers, the camels, the . . ."

Schliemann had gotten his wind back. His pantleg was rolled up and he was dabbing at a scraped knee. "Mata Hari might prefer it if I were the one to guide her party, you know, Carnarvon. At least *I* didn't die of a curse from being an overanxious fool. Having bollixed up one tomb opening doesn't give you primacy over an opportunity such as this—Tutankhamon's course still follows him, even in Hell. I tell you, Madam Hari—"

"I'm not going anywhere, gentlemen, until I make certain that this moving order is correct, and all the particulars are as I'd like them. And as for Nefertiti's tomb, I've never heard of it. I have no title to it, no deed, no lease. I don't even know where it is."

"No one does, my dear, that's the fun," said Carnarvon with another broad and patronizing smile.

"But I thought you said the Valley of Queens . . ."

"—Which is a very big valley indeed. And still uncharted, unplumbed. Of course, she might have her tomb—her real tomb, you understand, not one of these decoy jobs—in the Valley of Kings, as well. She was one very canny lady. Or on the other hand, it could be Nileside at—"

"Enough!" Mata Hari bore down on the Englishman. "If you'll excuse me, I'm going upstairs to make a few phone calls. Don't leave without me."

"We can't wait forever, my dear. Do hurry. You won't want to pay storage fees for overnighting this truckful in New Hell, when you're covered once we're under way. And penalties for lateness. And then of course there's the per box—"

Mata Hari wasn't listening. The black man who'd called Carnarvon downstairs suddenly barred her path and handed her his clipboard. On it was an EVICTION AND RELOCATION NOTICE, duly executed by the Infernal Housing Administration.

Down at the bottom of it was the notice that, "Any failure to comply is punishable by law. Extreme prejudice may be invoked. The Unwelfare System reserves the right to withold all benefits to any and all offenders eternally."

She snatched the clipboard from the black whose breast pocket name-tag said *I. Amin* and charged by him, up the stairs into her topsy-turvy apartment. The Unwelfare System! Somehow, someone in Authority had put her on the Unwelfare Rolls! She was furious. More, she was frightened. Asmodeus would never have done that to her.

Asmodeus couldn't have done it—not invoke Law and Bureaucracy: both of them knew law and bureaucracy too well ever to attempt to use either as a shield or an advantage. And . . . Unwelfare?

Under her anger, she was frightened. Someone was shipping her and her belongings off to a tomb in the nether hells. It wasn't the sort of thing one took lightly. It wasn't the sort of fate to which one went meekly.

She found her phone, amidst pyramids of boxes and strange men wrapping everything she owned, including toilet paper, in more paper. But her phone had been disconnected.

She slammed it down again and ran out.

On the street, the traffic jam had gotten worse. As she dodged Schliemann with his dolly, she heard Carnarvon demand to know where she was going.

She didn't answer. She wasn't sure. She had to find somebody in Authority to help her wipe this "expedition" from the Resettlement computer, or she'd be up the Nile without a paddle.

And she had to find Asmodeus, or make sure he could find her.

Fast.

Mithridates wasn't anywhere in the Pentagram, hadn't been for days unnumbered, if truth be told. Rameses was running the Pentagram from behind the scenes, as well as Supremely Commanding the armies since Hadrian was officially still listed as Missing. And would stay Missing as long as Rameses could contrive it.

In the wake of the purge, which had unseated fully a third of New Hell's bureaucrats and caused a round of musical chairs worthy of Poe's *Dance of the Red Death*, everyone was proceeding with caution in Administration.

New faces were everywhere. New underlings and new superiors meant no one could trust anyone with whom he was working. New bureau chiefs brought in different styles and different corruptions. In Reassignments, for example, clerks were busy learning Italian since Il Duce took command.

Things were too disorderly for the man who'd bested, he still maintained, the Hittites at Kadesh. In his lifetime, if you had a problem like this, you married your way out of it. Or you sent Nubians or Ethiops to the unsettled provinces, whereupon the local governors and vassal princes sent speedy dispatches with wondrous presents, begging that the king recall his troops, who were "eating up the land" and "trampling the vineyards" and "ravishing the daughters of Naharin" . . .

Rameses sighed. Those were the days of his life that he cherished in memory, but those were not the days of his afterlife. Here in New Hell, inefficiency was the rule and incompetency the primary basis for promotion.

So when Mata Hari came storming in through his office door, without so much as a warning from his secretary, he shouldn't have been surprised, he told himself. Not really. MacArthur was out to lunch, and wouldn't be back until tea time.

But he was surprised. He was chagrined and nonplussed when the woman strode up to his desk in her jackboots and her spurs, pounded her fist, and demanded to know by whose authorization she was being moved, lock, stock, and personal possessions to some as-yet unfound tomb on the Nile.

"I'm on the Unwelfare Roll, you ninny. Don't look at me with your mouth open, drooling like the inbred fool you are! When Asmodeus hears about this, someone's going to pay with the marrow of his bones! I want you to stop this eviction right now, summarily, or—"

The part about 'marrow of his bones' made Rameses blood run cold enough that he hardly heard the rest of the woman's threats. Asmodeus's consort, mad as a wet hen.

"The Nile, did you say?" he asked the woman carefully. "Eviction, did you say? Unwelfare, Madam? Surely you don't mean Unwelfare?" Asmodeus' consort on Unwelfare. The Fallen Angel who was chief of all Fallen Angels, the Presence who'd given humankind the template from which all demons had been drawn . . . you didn't mess around with the lover of such a one.

It was like asking Sekhmet to guarantee a fruitful harvest. Like petitioning Set for Peace. Like . . . Suicide. That's what it was.

Mata Hari's eyes seemed to gleam as red as her demon lover's. They bored into him, waiting for a more cogent response.

Rameses took off his glasses and stabbed at his desktop terminal. "The Nile, you said; yes I heard. Let me check."

The Nile. He couldn't get there from here, no matter how or what he tried, no matter what strings he pulled or butts he kicked. And he had tried. He was the loneliest man in New Hell, enmeshed in Persian plots and Roman plots and Assyrian plots that made the machinations of the Karnak priests seem like games of Monopoly. And in this afterlife, he had no brilliant Hittite grandaughter of Suppiluliumas to help him with astute pillow talk, no princesses from Naharin to soothe his soul, no Mittanian spies or Alashiyan advisors. Not even a priesthood did he have to count upon.

And this twentieth-century slut, this whore among generals, this warrior woman from the most decrepit age since the sunset of Rome, had a free trip to the holy river and *she was complaining*?

Up came the Admin database, in a shower of Mata Hari's abuse.

Rameses stared at it and then at the woman, his silver eyeglass stem finding its way between his teeth. "Madam, I regret to inform you that your employment among the Devil's Children has been retroactively terminated, your lease has expired, you have indeed been placed on the Unwelfare Roll. Simultaneously, your hardship case was forwarded to the Resettlement Division of Reassignments, since the Infernal Housing Authority has already rented your former apartment and can't find you commensurate housing in New Hell itself. Given your, ah, abruptly reduced status and your job profile, it seems that someone in Resettlement has chosen this expeditionary Foray as your next form of gainful employment."

"Tell me something I don't know, Baldy." Mata Hari's booted foot was tapping on Rameses' marble floor.

"Everything's perfectly in order here, Madam. There's nothing I can do for you."

"It's not. It can't be. Asmodeus didn't sign that document. It was signed in his absence. I saw it. The signature's illegible. Somebody in Authority has got to be responsible for this. I want to know who. Asmodeus will want to know who. *And I want it stopped*. I want my apartment back. I want my job back, my status, my—"

"Surely you realize that your apartment already belongs to someone else. Obviously, your termination interview has been delayed, and the terminating Authority will contact you, wherever you are, sometime soon. Meanwhile, why don't you accept the new post of head of the Expeditionary Foray into the Valley of Queens with some grace? I wish I could get up from this desk, walk out of here, and join you. The Nile, even Hell's Nile, is beautiful this time of year—any time of year. . . ." Rameses' eyes clouded with remembrance.

"With Carnarvon and Schliemann? You think this is fun? You think it's a damned *promotion?* Then *you* go."

Horemheb had been fond of the axiom that a low voice in a woman was a beautiful thing. Obviously, no one had ever told that to this Mata Hari woman. Rameses took the stem of his eyeglasses out of his mouth and opened his lips to respond with comparable volume.

Before he could, the woman said, "How can I be unemployed, evicted, and on Unwelfare if, by your own admission, I have this new appointment as Head of the Expeditionary Foray to Fill-In-The-Blank? Tell me that!"

Rameses had a moment to reconsider entering into a shouting match with a Modern female who rubbed her eyes upon wakening because she didn't have balls to scratch. And another moment to consider the ramifications of what Zelle had said. He hadn't been the most successful Middle Kingdom monarch for nothing. Opportunism was Rameses' true religion.

So he took a deep breath and answered patiently, "As soon as you accept the appointment—that is, take up your position and sign the forms awaiting you with the trucks—you'll be gainfully employed once more. Unwelfare will have to be notified, of course. . . ."

"Of course. How many millenia is it going to take before you fools get anything right? Before my name comes off those damned computers? Unwelfare, my ass! I'll get a job hooking for Sappho before I'll go to some damned muddy river of polytheistic barbar—"

"I do want to solve this for you, Miss Hari, but it's not my purview, you well know. This is a matter for clerks of the realm. However," he held up a hand that stifled any reply she might have made—and to give himself another moment to couch his words in just the proper style. "If you really would not be comfortable heading the Foray, perhaps we could work something out, off the record, for now . . . Please pull up a chair and let's get this onto a new, nonadversarial footing."

The Nile. Palm trees. Dates worthy of the name. Eucalpytus and Sirius rising. Hathor and Nut in the night sky. The alluvial plains. He was so weak at the thought of Her, his beloved river, he was sure that the callous Modern would see. And realize her advantage. And make bargaining hard.

But now that he'd seen the possibility, nothing could stop Rameses from trying to make it a reality. All he would leave behind here was a Roman mess and a bunch of angry Assyrians and the Devil's eventual retribution. He could set up a pro tem administrator—unofficially, of course. He might even work it so no one knew he was gone for years upon years.

And he'd be home. If someone had to open the tomb of Nefertiti, then that someone should be Rameses, a

lord of the Nineteenth Dynasty, a person capable of
treating the relics of his heritage with proper respect.

It remained only to cut some sort of deal with this
woman, who was obviously being railroaded, trifled
with, used and abused by powers hostile to Asmodeus
and the Devil's Children and therefore to the Order of
Hell itself. . . . Yes, Rameses could find a way to twist
the truth to serve his needs. When he got finished with
forming this story into the requisite shape, he would
have sacrificed the comforts of New Hell and his own
safety in a profound show of patriotism, to save the
demon's woman and foil a treacherous plot against
Authority.

After all, people like Mata Hari knew too much. You
couldn't allow them to get stuck in the Nether Hells.
Whereas people like himself . . . what he knew was not
so much a matter of secrets, but of administrative style.

Yes, he would go in her stead, if he had to go in drag.
And there he would be content to stay for thousands upon
thusands of years—one man in Hell who had turned it
into the afterlife of his anticipation and preparation.

Perhaps he could even find his own tomb, or its
simulacrum, with all the wonders stored there for his
own afterlife, centuries ago.

"Now, Madam Hari, let us talk the turkey about how
we can scratch each other's hands and make this matter
right. What I shall propose to you will entail some
extraordinary measures, the greatest of secrecy—which
I know you can provide—and rewards proportionate to
the effort involved."

"Lay it out, Pharaoh," said Mata Hari. "But if I don't
like it, I'm going over to Reassignments and tear their
databases out and feed 'em to them."

"I don't think that will be necessary," said Rameses
II with a faint, pharaonic smile.

Perhaps she should have gone to Caesar, to Julius
and that lot, Mata Hari thought dreamily, two hours

later, as she surveyed her new abode. There was only one Caesar, to her mind, and that was Julius; although the Augustans would argue the point.

Should she have trusted Rameses? More to the point, *had* she trusted Rameses? He'd admitted some frightening things, not the least of which was that Hadrian the Boy-lover was on the loose somewhere, and might soon show up to reclaim his Supreme Command of Hell's armies.

She sat now in the marble floored office of Rameses, a central point in the web of intrigues that had caused the purge in which Asmodeus, and she herself, had been caught.

She tapped at the Ramesseid computer dreamily, letting the data flow into her. Some was encoded, but she was a cipher maven. She'd find out all there was to find out about who had done what to whom, and why, and for whom, before this night was done.

She'd have to. Rameses had left in her stead on the Expeditionary Foray to Nefertiti's tomb, with all her belongings and Carnarvon and Schliemann and the rest.

And she? She was Supreme Commander of Hell, pro tem. Very pro tem. And Secretary of Offense, as well. She was, until someone queried it and queered it, everything Rameses had been, without knowing even what he had been.

He'd warned her, in his way. "Beware the snakes in my basket," he'd said with a smile. "Keep your flute handy. Should Mithridates raise his head and hiss at you, do not say I have not warned you. And as for the Assyrians and the Hittites and the other mercenaries . . . the accounts are all in my computer. Surely, with your skill, you'll find out what you need to know. Now I must hurry, before the moment is lost."

And he'd gone, a balding man with a new spring to his step, out the door before his secretary returned from lunch.

MacArthur was in for quite a surprise. So were many

others in Hell, including the Roman Julians. So was, when she found him, her beloved Asmodeus.

Heads were already rolling with the tap of her computer keyboard—of Rameses' oh-so-powerful Offensive Computers keyboard—over in Reassignments/Resettlement; in Unwelfare; at the Infernal Housing Administration. More heads would roll when she uncovered the guilty party who'd tried to railroad her into a deeper hell.

She kept scanning for a likely instigator. In the back of her mind, she was certain that the culprit was an American. All of her worst problems in life had come, one way or another, through the Americans.

And, to support that suspicion, a certain fact had emerged; her apartment, from which she'd been unceremoniously booted, was now the abode of two Americans called Welch and Nichols, just back from disciplinary posting to (wouldn't you know it?) the Nether Hells.

She wrote on her list of Things To Do, *Visit W. and N.* Then she went back to hunting through the database for the whereabouts of one Asmodeus, Fallen Angel.

Nichols' sycophants were hard at work trying to make the second-floor walk up look like home. Maadi AKs and bullets molds and Unique canisters were floating around in the "hands" of beings who looked (to the extent that they looked any way at all) like heat devils rising off a stretch of Bechtel blacktop in Riyadh.

Nichols was sprawled in a half-collapsed box that had once held, "Handguns, power strips, effects bags, EO (explosive ordnance), toiletries," according to the notation sprawled on the cardboard under his elbow. Under his arse was wadded paper—enough to have packed the small arms that the sycophants were now distributing on window ledges and shelves around the room.

So far, all they'd managed to unpack were downlinks and hardware, but then, that was all he and Welch really cared about. They'd been living out of gear bags so long they weren't sure what was in half these boxes, anyway. At least, Nichols wasn't.

He was sure about what he had in his hand, though— Old Number 7, straight up in a Dixie cup, with the rest of the bottle clamped between his legs.

There wasn't any reason to stay sober right now, that Nichols could see. Although he was having trouble getting drunk, which usually meant that his subconscious didn't believe he was on R&R. Well, there was always the Oasis bar, a couple blocks away. Nice convenient location Welch's Children had found for them. Almost enough to make up for what they'd been through on this last assignment. But not quite.

Nichols shifted sufficiently to ease the jab of the Desert Eagle against his hip. Maybe he'd go to the Pentagram range and get himself some therapy. You could get live pop-ups downrange, if you got there at the right time—crazies from the last insurrection, captured Dissidents, souls still awaiting punishment due who hadn't been processed from the Purge or whatever.

It wasn't quite as bad as shooting fish in a barrel. But Nichols was itching to shoot something. At least at the Pentagram range, the pop-ups shot back.

The boss—Welch—was out somewhere, "networking" them back into the system, so he'd said. Looking for Tanya Burke, more likely. Nichols pulled his thoughts away from the woman who was part of their ops team: the team had had real problems, last time out. The kind of problems you don't forget.

The kind you couldn't forgive. The Nether Hells were like that, though. Nichols was content to let his rage cycle, lubed by the mash he was drinking. To forget the mess they'd made of their last assignment, to believe Welch's analysis that "We were sent there to screw up; we screwed up. So what? It's Hell, isn't it?"

Sometimes Nichols couldn't understand his Harvard-educated superior worth a damn. But until this last sortie, he'd always followed Welch unquestioningly. That was what Nichols liked: you had your orders; you did your job.

Welch seemed always to give good orders, and that was the other thing Nichols needed: to know that the man asking you to do something had no agenda you couldn't share, wasn't fucking with you for the hell of it, or to prove a point, or for no sane reason. Welch was a sane, respectable officer. As good as officers got in Hell—one of the best, in fact, not only in the Devil's Children, but in all of Hell's proliferate agencies.

Until the trip to the Nether Hells, Nichols had believed that implicitly. But the Devil had come down on Welch with both clawed feet, and Welch had stood there and calmly taken responsibility for intent as well as result. And that had scared the crap out of Nichols. Nichols didn't have any axe to grind, any hidden agenda, any special interests except performance of the mission— any mission—to the best of his ability. He wasn't looking to flout the Devil or confront Authority or change the pecking order or do any damn thing at all but the best he could, as hard as he could, as often as he could, for whatever perks he could get out of it.

All of a sudden, down there in the Nether Hells, Satan himself had gotten real displeased with the job they were doing and the way Welch was running the operation. Nichols had never expected to see the Devil at all. Nichols was just a grunt in Authority's service, and he liked it that way. A face-to-face with an angry Satan just wasn't what Nichols risked his life for.

Split loyalties weren't something he was comfortable with, either. You had a bad officer, you fragged him. He'd learned that in life. Some guy went out of his way to bust your butt, you whacked him because otherwise, he was messing with your ability to do your job. You did it because the job was what mattered. You did it without exception and with no hesitation and you never, ever made exceptions to that rule, because that rule kept you doing your job the best you could.

That rule had worked in life. It worked in afterlife. Treachery was something that Nichols didn't tolerate; he obliterated it at its source. If he couldn't manage that, he put as much distance between the betrayer and himself as possible, and that worked just as good: out of sight, out of mind, out of his experience—since in Hell you couldn't get anybody permanently dead, you made do with breaking contact when you had to.

He'd have broken contact with Welch, gone AWOL, or at least put in for a transfer, if things were just a little clearer. He was uncomfortable being here. He was confused. His loyalties didn't split easily. He liked a nice clear chain of command and a nice clean designated target. If Welch had betrayed the Devil, Authority, the Children, even, then Nichols shouldn't be part of that betrayal.

But the damn parameters of the betrayal weren't clear. Hell was a place for torment, as Welch had explained to him, so kindly, so gently, when Nichols tried to voice the torturous doubts that had him nearly paralyzed.

Nichols was the fastest, deadliest thing on two feet when he was clear about what needed to be done. When he was confused, he entered a motionless state, like a spy-plane in a holding pattern. He just circled over himself, scanning the terrain below for trouble.

Welch said the Devil was just making sure they got their own bit of misery, that's what the sortie into the deeper hells had been about. That there wasn't really any target, no hairy proto-man to bring back to New Hell, no real mission—that the whole thing had been a set-up and Nichols should realize that Satan was "messing with our heads, man."

He hated it when Welch got colloquial with him, because Welch wasn't a colloquial kind of guy. But it showed him that his superior was reaching for ways to ease his distress, which was part of what Nichols liked about Welch.

What he didn't like was the negative points he was picking up from association with Welch, lately. Nichols never wanted to be in the presence of the Devil again. As long as he had afterlife to live, he wanted to live it as an anonymous cog in hell's machine, just a nice, well-oiled part of the system.

When they'd gotten back here and found they had this apartment, he'd tried to talk to Welch about it. Welch said, "Let's just pick it up from here, Nick, okay? Shit happens, like they say."

Nichols had wanted to know, "But how come *that* shit happened?"

Welch had shrugged almost irritably, and his well-formed head had seemed to retreat into those tense shoulders. "Look, I'm going to go get a decent shave and a haircut, buy some clean clothes, today's paper. You get this stuff unpacked. Then maybe we'll go see Machiavelli. If anybody's got those sorts of answers, he does."

And that had been that, so far as Welch was concerned. To Nichols, it was the final straw. Could the Devil himself have been fooled into acting as a pawn in Machiavelli's game of vendetta against Welch? Or was Welch still working some weird, purposeless subversion, and enmeshing Nichols once more in something Nichols didn't want any part of?

The Devil had come to them in the Nether Hells and accused Welch of the worst thing possible—of disobeying orders, of having done something "good."

That "good" something, whatever it had been, had gotten them the disciplinary posting to the Nether Hells in the first place. Nichols didn't see how you could do something "good" in Hell; he didn't understand the ethical debates and the moral hair-splitting and the rest of the jabberwocky that men like Welch and women like Tanya talked about.

And Nichols knew damn well that Welch had gone looking for Tanya, not any haircut or evening paper. It occurred to him that if he shot Welch when the officer returned, he'd feel better.

Welch wouldn't be on his case so bad, with his confusing smile and his multi-purpose feints against whatever he was fighting. You shouldn't be doing personal stuff; you should be following your damned orders.

Because that's what they were—damned orders. You had to be damned to get here. You were damned forever here. It shouldn't matter what you did, as long as you did something: followed orders.

Nichols took another swig of his Jack Daniels and sighed. If it didn't matter, then there was no use shooting Welch, because whatever Welch was doing, that didn't matter either.

Nichols got up off the carton onto which he'd flopped hours ago and stepped right into a sycophant's "body." He pawed at the warm flicker in front of him. For an instant he couldn't breath; his face was in its ectoplasmic self and that self was sweet like a wheatfield.

He staggered back, spilling his drink. The thing twittered apologetically and he cursed it, blinking back tears. There wasn't a wheatfield in the whole of Hell, not that he'd ever seen. The smell was so evocative of everything he'd fought for in life, and lost in afterlife because he *had* fought for it, that he nearly wept aloud.

He brushed a scarred and hairy forearm impatiently over his eyes and growled, "Get outta my way, stupid thing." He charged forward and three or four of the flickers scattered before him.

He didn't know where he was going until he was standing in front of the computer console on its black roller stand. He flicked it on and watched it do its self-check.

By the time that was done, a chair was butting softly against his calves. He sat in it without a thank you or a backward look. His sycophants didn't need strokes; they knew him. They should know enough to stay out of his face.

The bottle of Old Number 7 floated to rest beside the computer, and a dispenser of Dixie cups followed. He didn't say thanks.

He was punching up an access code he didn't often use, because what he accessed when he did so made him almost as uncomfortable as Welch had.

But not quite.

He typed HELLFIRE.COM and sat back to wait.

Pretty soon, he'd have answers to more questions than he wanted to ask, like was there any other officer looking for the kind of man Nichols was? What kind of trouble was Welch in, as far as Authority was concerned? Was there a good operation, with plenty of action, going down anytime soon that he could hook into? And could he get live pop-ups down at the Pentagram range?

"I thought I'd find you here," said Mata Hari to Asmodeus, whose Bell 501 was parked on the chopper pad on the roof of the Oasis Bar.

The bar's back room was a place of subterranean assignation. She hadn't known what she'd be walking into, whom he'd be with—not for certain. But she'd guessed, after she'd cracked the Ramesseid encoding.

She hated the Oasis. She hated the One Weapon, One Clip No Shit rule; she hated the clientele, from the Ombudsman to the Beirut marines to the Hittite and Assyrian mercenaries, the diminutive Old Dead with their whetstones and their skirts.

But most of all, she hated interrupting Asmodeus in a meeting here, when she was full of questions and those questions had most pointedly to do with one of those he was meeting with.

Asmodeus rose to his full height; his flicker-dark face turned toward her, bowed slightly. "Gertie, you know Judah Maccabee, Zaki, Tanya Burke, and Dick Welch."

She said, "Of course," and nodded generally, not

letting on that she'd come here, at least in part, because of the American called Welch.

She detested Americans. Their zeal for "becoming" overrode their respect for "being" and made them disastrous cohorts in Hell, where "being" was the best you could do and "becoming" was a figment, a temptation, a farce.

"May I speak with you outside, Asmodeus?" she said when he'd asked her to join them and she'd shaken her head.

She made him go all the way to the roof and into his chopper before she'd tell him what she wanted. There, nestled among the revetments of the Oasis and caught between New Hell's skyline and the docks, she explained about her apartment, about the Foray to the Nether Hells, about Rameses and Carnarvon and Schliemann and Unwelfare and Resettlement.

When she'd finished she said, "What I want to know is, did you have anything to do with it?"

He was watching her, and his gaze made her insides ache. The fire in him heated her groin, and she had to grab her own knee and squeeze it to keep her hand from going to his.

"I wanted you somewhere safer."

No apology. No cogent explanation. Just a statement of intent. She slapped him. Across the face. Backhanded. It happened so fast that she didn't recognize the impulse until her body had followed through on it.

He caught her wrist and held it. Squeezed it. She thought it would splinter in his grip.

"You should have gone," he said.

"It wasn't your signature."

"Protection. For us both."

"I thought so when I couldn't track the decision tree on it, but by then it was too late. You could have consulted me."

"I could not."

"You can now. Why?"

"It doesn't matter. The opportunity is gone, wasted on an Egyptian."

"Are you tired of me? There are simpler ways to—"

Finally he let go of her wrist. She cradled it in her lap, rubbing it with the fingers of her other hand. The unfinished sentence hung between them.

"I wanted you somewhere safer," he said again, looking away from her, out across the burning night and the unsettled waters with their reflections of the blood dark hellfire sky shimmering, distorted, to the horizon. "There was nowhere better. Nowhere I couldn't have found you, when it's over."

"When what's over?" She heard the quaver in her own voice. Until now she had been angry. No more. Now she was frightened.

"You've heard the rumors. They're more than that. In the Nether Hells, things will be easier. Something will remain. Time will not stand still."

She couldn't think of anything to say for a long time. A foghorn wailed, somewhere far off.

Eventually she said. "I'm sorry. You should have told me."

"You should have trusted me."

"It's not too late. I can still go—"

"It is too late. You can't. Not now. It would be suicidal. This is no time to line up for the Undertaker's table, no time to risk Reassignments. We've brought too much attention to you. Like the rest of us, you'll have to take your chances."

She wanted to weep. She wanted to throw herself into his arms. Then she wanted to jump from the chopper, slam the door, and run down from the roof, leaving him alone. She did none of those. She said, "Well, then I can have my apartment back," defiantly, because she couldn't admit to being wrong when he hadn't bothered to include her in his plans.

He sighed and it was a sigh that cracked her heart. "Human souls have free will. You have freely willed to make yourself responsible for the entire Department of Offense and the Pentagram's armies, at the worst of times. Stay in the quarters you have chosen, in the position you have secured for yourself. I will spend what time I can with you. We will make what we can of this turn of events."

"We could consult with Caesar, put a Roman in my place. He'd jump at the chance. . . ."

"He might. He might not. That is for him to decide. Right now, I have a meeting to attend."

"And I'm not invited?"

"Come if you like. We're going to mend a rift in our ranks."

"Our ranks?"

"Welch's ADC, Nichols."

"Since when is Welch part of—"

"The Devil's Children will soon have need of a spokesperson, and the good Mr. Welch is the only soul among them qualified to serve in that capacity."

"A spokesperson? For what? To whom?"

Asmodeus turned his head back to her and his red eyes glowed so brightly she could not look upon them. "For the Last Judgment. To God. Is that clear enough?"

"Surely you can't mean . . ." But he did. "Not *now*!"

"Not in the next few moments as your Rolex tells time, no. But the Judges are roaming the hells. Altos, the angel from On High, is here. The Ombudsman has been given greater appropriations. The bounds between good and evil are becoming unclear. . . ."

Some sign of what she felt must have showed on her face. Asmodeus leaned forward and took her chin in his fingers. "Fear doesn't become you. All things end. All things begin. There will be chaos, and confusion, and darkness and light—as always."

"And you wanted me out of harm's way—"

"I still do. It will be a little more difficult, this way. But not impossible."

"I have my own fate." She raised her chin, out of

contact with his fingers. "I have my own fight. I won't be treated like a child."

"You're a human soul whom I have . . . feelings for. How else should I treat you?"

There wasn't a suitable answer for him, or for her, she knew. She said, "I want my goddamn apartment back," and opened the chopper door.

"Then take it," he said. "You have access to whatever you choose of Authority's inner workings now."

She barely heard him. Her eyes were so full of tears that she'd stumbled, jumping down out of the chopper. Or maybe the fall that had turned her ankle had brought the tears. She didn't want to think about it. She got to her feet and stood there, in the bright and awful night, letting the wind off the harbor dry her eyes.

The unimaginable was coming. Coming soon. Before Asmodeus, she wouldn't have cared. But that was Hell for you: the afterlife got you where it hurt, every time.

The pop-ups Nichols was chasing through the Pentagram's fun house were remarkably agile. He'd shot out the tires of their semi first, against a backdrop that looked like the road through the swamps that led to the nether hells.

On foot, they were easier. The fat black had gone down first, and the adrenalin rush had been substantial: the black, and the German who joined him, had been returning Nichols' fire with 7.62X51 NATO, and it was all armor piercing.

Nichols didn't want to end up with a hole in his chest the size of his fist, which was what those explosive-tipped rounds would do, if they recognized him as a hard surface at all instead of sailing through him to shatter the masonry at his back.

He walked to the next bay, following his quarry the easy way. It had taken him a while to get used to the Gallery, the way reality fanned out from each shooter's bay. You walked about five yards, and your field of fire and view fanned to maybe three hundred. Each bay was the point of a wedge of terrain, as if you were at the center of a giant circle.

The guy in the antique Brit uniform was diving behind a bush when Nichols' sniper sight gave him a laser lock-on. The kill came up with a beep on the score above the shooter's benchrest.

The Egyptian was the last high-score target, and the canniest game of the lot. Nichols went through a whole bay with a zero score, missing him twice. He was just about to shift to the next bay rather than take the negative points against his total when a hand came down on his shoulder.

He slapped it away, all pumped up like he was, and wheeled with his rifle at ready.

Welch was so close that the rifle's muzzle was right against his chest.

The big guy beside him wasn't anything that Nichols had ever encountered before at close range, but he knew who he was looking at. Or trying to look at.

The demon in the trenchcoat with the slouch hat pulled down over his sort-of eyes said, "We need to speak with you."

"Yeah, well, I'm in the middle of a game, here."

"No, your game is over," said the demon and raised a finger toward the shot clock above Nichols' head. It zeroed.

"Damn," Nichols said.

"Indubitably," said the demon.

"Put the rifle down, Nichols," said Welch.

"I—" Part of Nichols still wanted to shoot Welch, not the target he'd been chasing through the Fun House bays. The other part knew that something was up, something that might end the confusion that was his real enemy. "It's not you, sir," he said, half to himself.

"I know, Nichols. I know."

Nichols' rifle came down, slowly, wavering. He thumbed on the safety without looking away from the officer to whom he'd given his total loyalty and who had damn well better deserve it. "I just got . . . antsy, is all. Somethin' up?"

"Oh yeah," said Welch.

Asmodeus reached out and took the rifle from Nichols' unresisting fingers. "We need your team reconstituted, on call, working as tightly and as smoothly as it can for the next little while, Sergeant."

Nobody had called him that for a long, long time. Nichols looked at the demon and at Welch and said, "Whatever you say, sirs. I'm at your service."

After all, that was what the Devil's Children was— His Satanic Majesty's Secret Service.

As a member of an elite service organization, a cog in the wheel of Authority, Nichols couldn't expect to understand, and shouldn't be asked to approve, every order that came down to him—only to execute those orders to the best of his ability.

Nichols couldn't figure out how he'd forgotten that. But then, seeing Welch with brass as high as Asmodeus answered lots of questions that Nichols just wasn't verbal enough to ask.

And that was a relief. Hell was bad enough, without having to Question Authority.

He vaguely regretted having to let the Egyptian target go, but there'd be another time. In Hell, there was always another time.